Jane Duncan

My Friends The
Hungry Generation

CORGI BOOKS
A DIVISION OF TRANSWORLD PUBLISHERS LTD
A NATIONAL GENERAL COMPANY

MY FRIENDS THE HUNGRY GENERATION

A CORGI BOOK 0 552 08966 4

Originally published in Great Britain
by Macmillan London Ltd.

PRINTING HISTORY
Macmillan edition published 1968
Corgi edition published 1972

All chapter headings are taken from the ODE:
INTIMATIONS OF IMMORTALITY FROM RECOLLECTIONS
OF EARLY CHILDHOOD by William Wordsworth.

This book is set in Intertype Plantin

Corgi Books are published by Transworld Publishers Ltd.,
Cavendish House, 57–59 Uxbridge Road,
Ealing, London, W.5.
Made and printed in Great Britain by
Hunt Barnard Printing Ltd, Aylesbury, Bucks.

This book is dedicated to all those readers who have written to me saying : 'Please say that there are more books to come,' and also to my niece and nephews, who used to end every meal with the words : 'Is there no more?'

Prologue

'Turn whereso'er I may,
By night or day,
The things which I have seen I now can see no more.'

IT WAS a day in July, the day after what is now known in St
Jago as the Earthquake of 1956. I sat looking through the empty
frame of the window, across the glittering heap of broken glass
which the yard boy had swept together on the lawn, at the
jagged and torn roots of the acacia tree which formed an arc
of distorted skeleton arms between me and the harsh blue of
the tropical sky. The skeleton arms, torn from their element
the earth, looked as if they were praying but the hot pitiless
sky gave back no answer. I felt an affinity with that uprooted
tree, felt that I was torn from my element, withering away, in
a disintegrated world whose shattered splinters I had neither
the will nor the energy to gather together into a new coherence.

'There is the ambulance coming out of the driveway now,'
said my husband's voice from the bed behind me and, through
an angle made by two roots of the dying tree, I saw the white
vehicle, gleaming in the sun, begin to make its slow way across
the parkland towards the burial ground. This is the efficiency
of the great estate of Paradise, I thought bitterly; the efficiency
and the self-sufficiency. When an earthquake kills two of its
people, the Paradise machine has no need to call on the services
of an undertaker. It has its own medical staff to deal with the
corpses, it has its own burial ground and it uses its ambulance
as a hearse. I felt that I was enclosed within this machine that
was Paradise without, yet, being part of it; that I was inside it
yet able to see it from some point outside although it cut me off
from the world to which I belonged. The violence of the earthquake, followed by the efficiency of this machine, made me feel
that I was spiritually nowhere, that I had no identity, that I
was suspended in an alien element that would soon destroy me,
as the alien air would soon destroy the roots of the uptorn tree.

'I should be driving my car with you beside me in that cor-
tège,' said my husband's voice now, 'and not lying in this

damned bed.' I did not answer him. He had a weak heart and the doctor said that, following the shock of the earthquake, he was to spend three days in bed. At any time hitherto, I would have exerted all my energy to make him obey the doctor's orders but, today, I had no energy to exert and no confidence in anything. After all, an earthquake could bring the house down, killing him even while he lay in bed resting his heart, as the earthquake of twenty hours ago had killed Rob and Marion Maclean thirty yards from where we stood in the garden of Paradise Great House.

'I have made up my mind about one thing anyway, as a result of all this,' came the voice from behind me while I looked through the tree roots at the cloud of white dust raised by the cars of the vast funeral procession. 'You are going home to Scotland for a holiday.'

I did not trouble to turn round to look at him as I said: 'You are out of your mind. Lie back and be quiet.'

I got up to leave the room and as I passed his bedside he caught my wrist. 'No, I am not,' he said, 'but you are just about to go out of yours. Even Reachfar rock has a breaking point and this is it. You are going home to Scotland, Janet.' I did not answer him, except by shaking my head, shaking my wrist from his grasp and leaving the room.

The veranda at the front of the house gave me another view of the uprooted tree. From here I could see the prone trunk and the great spray of fallen branches and already withering leaves, but the view of the dust cloud that contained the corpses of Rob and Marion Maclean was much the same. People in death, I thought, were less elegant than trees.

At last, the dust cloud settled and there was a sunlit silence that seemed to flow towards me from the little burial ground among the tall trees about a mile away. Soon, now, Rob and Marion would be a small mound of rotting corruption in the grave dug in that porous volcanic earth, earth so different from my native Scottish rock, the rock of Reachfar that my husband had mentioned. But this did not matter. Nothing mattered to me on this day, suspended as I was in this brilliant void that contained no coherence or feeling.

After half-an-hour, perhaps, I saw the funeral cars come back across the parkland and disperse, saw one of them take the turn that led to the entrance to our garden. Out of it came our friend Sashie de Marnay, who added to rather than diminished my feeling of unreality because, as a rule, he affected very gaily coloured clothes and today he was wearing a sober grey suit, white shirt and black tie. He had been to the funeral, of course, I told myself. People wore soberly coloured clothes at funerals. Today, this seemed to me very absurd, that there should be conventions about death. There was no connection between clothes and death. There were no connections anywhere.

'How is Twice?' Sashie asked from the doorway.

Twice, I thought, is my husband. No. Twice was our nickname for a man called Alexander Alexander, who was my husband, who had a weak heart, who had to be looked after and who wanted to stop me looking after him and go away to Scotland. Clumsily, I tried to string it all together in my mind while I looked at Sashie but it would not go together, connect or become comprehensible. 'In his bedroom,' I said and Sashie went away across the hall while the bright emptiness closed round me again.

The next thing that I remember was Sashie pouring tea from a pot that, a long time ago it seemed, had belonged to me and handing me a cup of a pattern that I vaguely recognised.

'Janet,' he said, 'Twice has asked me to book an air passage for you to Scotland at the end of the week, I shall get you on the same flight as Roddy Maclean if I can.'

'I am not going to Scotland,' I told him dully.

'Let us not argue, Janet. You have no choice. That affair of last evening has been the last straw which was bound to come. If only you would stop *fighting* everything, even earthquakes!' he said exasperatedly.

'I am not fighting anything,' I said.

'That is just the trouble!' he snapped at me, contradicting himself. 'You are going back to Scotland to refuel or reload or re-whatever-it-is that you fight on. If you stay here, you will kill. Twice with worry and that I will not allow.'

'Twice? Worry? What about?'

'You. Are you so far gone in egotism that you imagine that *you* have a monopoly in worry?'

I stared at him, frowning, trying to understand, trying to find something to grip in this staring void that surrounded me and his voice seemed to come from somewhere beyond the rim of the emptiness. 'Twice will never forget that, because of his health, you did not get home to see your father before he died and now he is afraid that Tom and George may die too without

9

your seeing them again.' Something stirred in the emptiness around me and there came the thought that George and Tom were mortal, that one day – one day, not a white ambulance would carry them to a tropical burial ground but a black hearse would make its slow way up the hill to Achcraggan churchyard. 'Twice is too kind and gentle to say these things to you,' Sashie was continuing, 'but I am neither kind nor gentle and I can say them. Janet, if you care for Twice, you will make this trip. I shall cable your family and make all the arrangements.'

Four days later, accompanied by Roddy Maclean, the son of Rob and Marion, I boarded an aeroplane for London.

Chapter I

'To me alone there came a thought of grief.'

RODDY and I were silent companions on the high, cloudbound tedious trip across the Atlantic. I would have preferred to travel alone but that I should travel with Roddy was Sashie's suggestion and it pleased Twice, who, when the plans for my going suddenly became concrete, began to feel the strangeness of this new departure in our lives as strongly as I did. Neither of us, in all the time we had been together, had ever gone on a pleasure trip without the other and that I should be going to Scotland, leaving Twice in St Jago, was a thing that eluded our comprehension, even while we planned the practical details. I am, as Twice well knew, a reasonably efficient traveller and it was no guidance or protection of a physical sort that he was seeking for me in Roddy's company. It was more that, if Roddy and I were together, Roddy would form in Twice's mind some sort of link between himself and me.

Before we left St Jago it had been arranged that I would spend my first night in England at Roddy's London flat and travel north the next night after I had bought myself some warm clothes. We hardly spoke to one another until we reached London, for I felt hollow and light-headed, suspended as I was now, literally, in the void of upper air above the Atlantic, while Roddy had many sad things to think about, things that, as yet, could not be talked about at all.

In London, we took our luggage to his flat, had baths and then went out into the sunlit evening streets to find a place to have a meal. The flat was in a side street on the borders of Fulham and Chelsea and we walked along by the river and eventually up Oakley Street to the King's Road. In Oakley Street, I said: 'I once lived here, a long time ago.'

'So did I,' Roddy told me. 'It seems long ago.'

It was all very dreamlike and nostalgic, misty with the long ago and far away, as a summer evening in London can be and we were silent again until we were seated in the little restaurant when Roddy said: 'Janet, I have an idea. I would like to hire a

11

car and drive you up to Achcraggan.'

'But there is no need for that, Roddy,' I protested. 'Twice and Sashie were just being silly when they wanted me to travel with you like this. I can find my own way from – '

'It is not so much a question of you finding your way as of me finding mine,' he interrupted me, frowning. 'I want to go north anyway, to be quiet, just to sit down and try to think things out.'

When I was a child at Reachfar, my Aunt Kate had been subject, in winter, to very severe head colds which made her feel really ill but she was a very beautiful young woman and the more severe the cold, the more the fever mounted in her cheeks, the more her big eyes swam, the more beautiful she looked, and now, looking at Roddy, I remembered how my grandmother used to say, when Aunt Kate was in bed and out of hearing: 'Poor Kate, she feels real sick but her looks never pity her.' Roddy, like my Aunt Kate, had looks that did not pity him. He was powerfully built, lithe, swaggering strong, not yet thirty and nobody, looking at him, could have imagined the shock that he had sustained less than a week ago when both his parents were killed before his eyes. Also, he was a writer by profession, with the observation and sensitivity of his kind and there was no doubt some hideous tumult of chaotic horror crashing in the brain behind his brilliant dark eyes.

'I can go to the croft,' he said. 'It is watertight if not much else.'

He had recently bought a little house and few acres of land in Inverness-shire.

'The trouble is that I am not going to Achcraggan, Roddy,' I told him. 'I am going to my brother's place in Aberdeenshire and George and Tom are waiting for me there. It is right out of your way.'

'That doesn't matter. What is an extra hundred miles or so?'

'All right,' I agreed and, after a moment, I added: 'You can stay with us at Culdaviot if you like, Roddy. I have never seen my brother's house but I know it is a big old Victorian barracks – he is a schoolmaster – and there is lots of room. That is, if you would like to be – to be with people for a bit,' I trailed away hesitantly.

'Thank you, Janet. I may take you up on that. I don't think I want to be on my own for the moment but I don't want to see the others as yet either.'

By 'the others' he meant his six brothers who were all in Britain at work, university or school and to whom he would, no doubt, have to describe the earthquake and all that followed it sooner or later.

'When we go back to the flat, we'll telephone your brother,' he said, 'and then, tomorrow, while you shop, I shall organise a car for us.'

We spent the following night in a shabby hotel in Durham and, about four-thirty the next afternoon, we drove through the gate in the stone wall into my brother's garden at Culdaviot.

It was all very strange and unreal for me to be arriving with Roddy like this at a place that I had never seen before because, in the five years since I had been home, my brother had moved to a different school and a different house. George, my uncle and Tom, our family friend, were the first to come out to greet us and my heart gave a bound at the sight of them after this long time, so that the tears sprang to my eyes and I felt my mouth twisting as I tried to control myself. In this moment, I discovered how right Twice and Sashie had been. I was more in need of this holiday than I had known.

George and Tom had changed and, yet, they were just as they ever were. Their hair was pure white now, the bone structure of their faces more pronounced but their eyes glowed and smiled with love and laughter as they had always done and their voices shook when they spoke, vibrant with welcome.

'So it is yourself, lass,' they greeted me in the old way, then drew back, looking me over, before Tom said: 'Man, George, she is as stylish as ever, for all she is an old wifie of forty-six but a little on the thin side.'

'She wouldna do to be fat,' George said. 'With her big bones she would be a proper greasy old mare if she was fat.'

'Stop talking about my age in front of everybody,' I said, my voice high-pitched and unnatural, as my brother and his wife, Shona, came out of the house. Shona, I noticed, was heavily pregnant, something which had not been mentioned to me in letters. 'Heavens,' I said, 'are you two having another one? Aren't three enough?'

Everybody began to laugh, the tension wound down a little and I began to introduce Roddy.

'I feel that my coming is a terrible imposition, Mrs Sandison,' he said to Shona, his eyes commenting on her pregnant condition.

13

'Oh, nonsense,' she said, taking him by the arm and leading him into the house.

It suddenly struck me that Shona, since I had last seen her, had blossomed into fullness. Five years ago, she had had only one child, my niece Elizabeth and was expecting her second, my nephew Duncan but, now, she also had little George and was expecting her fourth child and she seemed to have found herself. She was in the truest sense a mother, all mother, and this thing in her went out to the bereaved Roddy, who responded to her at once, going inside this ambience of hers and permitting himself to be led inside her home by the hand, as if he were a little boy.

'Where are the children?' I asked my brother.

He looked vaguely around him. 'Somewhere about. You will see them soon enough. Come in and have a quiet cup of tea first.' We went in through the back door, across a back hall and into a big square kitchen, off which there was a scullery that looked even bigger. Shona switched on an electric kettle and said: 'I don't suppose you have ever seen a household like this before, Roddy. We practically live in this kitchen, except when we sleep. But when you get tired of the gang and the noise, there is plenty of room in the front of the house.'

'Too much damned room,' George said.

'Have you any help, Shona?' I asked.

'Goodness, yes. Fat Mary comes in every day. We manage very well. Sit down, Janet, before you blow away. You are as thin as a rake.'

She was twelve years younger than I was but, in a curious way, I felt myself enfolded in a warmth and wisdom that had no connection with years and age and, obediently, I moved a feathered Red Indian head-dress and two toy motor cars from an easy chair and sat down. Shona herself did not sit but made the tea, served us all and then stood by the big centre table – the big old table from the kitchen of Reachfar, I noticed – that was covered with a white plastic cloth. She stood quietly, looking happily round at us out of her beautiful eyes above the heavy swollen body.

'How is Jean?' I asked Tom and George.

Jean was my stepmother, with whom Tom and George lived at Achcraggan and she was also the reason that I had not gone there but had come here to my brother's house instead. I had never liked Jean since I first met her when I was ten years old but Jean had surpassed me by coming to hate me more and more intensely down the years.

'She has the rheumatics now,' Tom answered, 'and is worse in the temper than ever.'

'But Tom and I just take no notice,' said George.

'She is an old devil, Janet,' my brother said. 'We never go up there now. George and Tom come here whenever they can.' He turned to them. 'And you know that you can come here for good if you want to and not be bothered with her any longer.'

'We know that, lad,' Tom said, 'but George and I are quite fit to keep her in order and we like to be there to see that the garden is kept right, like Himself left it.'

By 'Himself' Tom meant my dead father who had been a gifted gardener, to whom all growing things responded.

A shadow darkened Shona's lovely face and with a little sigh she said: 'I wish one could do something for Jean but one can't. She seems to *want* to be at odds with everybody but she can't be happy.'

'Don't you go worrying your head about her, Shona, lassie,' George said. 'You have better things to do than be worrying about that old thrawn twisted stick.'

'Stand by for boarders,' my brother said suddenly. 'Here comes the Hungry Generation' and, in the same moment, Shona seized a sponge-cake and a plate of biscuits from the table, pushed them into a large cupboard, locked it and put the key in the pocket of her bulging smock. 'We don't starve them,' she explained to Roddy with a smile. 'We only try to stop them killing themselves with greed and gluttony.'

In 1951, when I had last seen my niece, she had been an entrancing three-year-old who was just beginning to read and when the door opened now I was quite unprepared for the leggy coltish eight-year-old dressed in very short navy shorts and a very dirty white shirt. The first things I noticed about her were the long, beautifully-shaped bare legs, the long, light brown pigtails and the large eyes, shaped and darkly lashed like the eyes of her mother but, in colour, the brilliant blue of her father's. The two boys, who stood on either side of her in the doorway, I had never seen before, of course. Duncan, called after my father, was five and seemed to have no connection with Shona at all, for he had bright red-gold curly hair and blue eyes and looked exactly as my brother had looked at that age, but George, aged four and called after Shona's father and, incidentally, after his great-uncle, George Sandison, had been obliging enough to go entirely to Shona's side of the family and was, I was told, very like the grandfather whose name he bore, with his dark grey eyes and straight jet-black hair. My eyes returned to Elizabeth at the centre of the group. This was the true cross-breed of the marriage, this first-born and, in her bearing, there was an air of domination, of being the eldest, of being of the other sex, of being the leader of this new generation. Even at eight years old, she made me think of the proud figure of my grandmother, Catherine Sandison.

Meeting the three of them as people was something of an ordeal, quite apart from the mental adjustment to the fact that my 'little' brother – Jock is ten years my junior and six feet one inch tall – and his young wife had brought this trio into the world while I had never had a child. Elizabeth, Duncan and George in themselves made an impact on me of some force. Their eyes, neither friendly nor hostile but piercingly clear-sighted and intelligent, seemed to show to me a picture of myself as they saw me, very old, very strange, somebody who had been only a name and who had now taken on flesh and was to be approached only with caution. They behaved with cold formality, coming forward in order of age, one by one, to shake hands with me and then with Roddy. Then they turned away with a curious air of suspending judgement and Elizabeth said: 'Mum, we are hungry.'

'Just fancy that,' Shona said and pointed to the table.

The three pairs of eyes scanned the plates with the remaining sandwiches and scones and turned as if on a swivel to look at the door of the locked cupboard before all three fell upon the food on the table, cleared the last crumb in a matter of moments and then, with one accord, quietly went out, closing the door behind them.

'Jock, what a regiment!' I said out of sheer nervous reaction.

'Elizabeth is a beauty,' Roddy said enthusiastically, not seeming to have had the sense of ordeal that had overtaken myself.

Shona smiled. 'Liz is the ringleader,' she said. 'If you have any trouble while I am in hospital, Janet, go for Liz first and don't spare her.'

'Och, there will be no trouble,' George said.

'Janet, come up to your room,' said Shona. 'I think you should lie down for a little.'

'I am all right. What about the tea things?'

16

'Fat Mary will be in soon. She will be here all day while I am away.'

We climbed the stairs. 'When do you go?' I asked.

'Any minute now. I am just at the drop, as George and Tom call it. In here.' In the big square bedroom, she sat down on the window seat. 'I am so very glad to see you home, Janet, but you look really ill. No wonder – that terrible earthquake. Goodness, the relief when that cable came!'

'What cable?'

'About you and Twice. You didn't know about it?' I shook my head. Twice and I had sent no cable. Shona looked down at her hands and her voice trembled a little as she said: 'It was addressed to – wait, I'll get it.'

She went across the landing to another room, came back and handed me the cable form on which I read: 'Reachfar Achcraggan Scotland Alexanders safe Paradise.'

When I looked up at her, she said: 'The Achcraggan postmistress took it to George and then he and Tom telephoned here. Janet, I am sorry. Don't cry.'

'God,' I said, 'I don't know what is the matter with me, I can't help it. Shona, please go away for a minute or two but not downstairs. No. Stay here. Where is the bathroom?'

Behind the locked door, I began to discover what was the matter with me or, rather, what had been the matter with me for, already, the glaring void in which I had lived since the earthquake was losing its terror as it filled with connections, coherences, the inter-relations which are the fabric of life and which seemed to have been destroyed in my mind. The cablegram had been sent by Sir Ian Dulac, the owner of Paradise, which meant that, in the midst of the chaos following the earthquake, he had had enough feeling for the people in his employ to use his considerable influence to get the message through in spite of the island's disrupted communications. I, I thought with shame, had been too anxious about Twice to remember my family and Twice had been asleep under sedation an hour after the earthquake had passed, but Sir Ian had remembered that, even in the face of cataclysm, life goes on and that life is a fabric of inter-relationships, their joys and sorrows, anxieties and fears.

When I returned to the bedroom, Shona spoke with all the ferocity of which she was capable, which was not a great deal. 'These horrible Sandison nerves!' she said.

'Nerves?' I laughed at her. 'It is a well-known and long-established fact that I have no nerves at all.'

She emitted a scornful little snort. 'You and John – ' she always gave my brother his correct name and never called him 'Jock' as George, Tom and I did ' – are as alike as two peas in many ways and one of the ways is these nerves that respond to everything and far too much until they are all tangled up like a radar system except that radar systems don't get tangled up,' she ended in an indignant muddled way. 'I can never say what I mean,' she added and bustled again into defiant indignation as she further added: 'but *I* know what I mean.'

Thinking of how she had referred to Jock as John and in order to change the subject, I said: 'I notice that you are calling your daughter Liz. I thought it was to be Elizabeth and no corruptions or abbreviations?'

'With children,' she said impatiently, 'you can't cope with everything. The boys call her Liz and she refers to herself as Liz and there it is.' She turned away from the subject literally by hitching herself round in her seat. 'Look here, *you* ought to be going to hospital, not me.'

'Nonsense! And stop worrying. I feel quite different already. I suppose the earthquake was more of a shock than one realised and then there was this sudden trip and everything.'

'When we had that second cable saying you were coming, it seemed like a godsend because it meant that you would be here while I was in hospital, but now I am not so sure. The one thing I don't like about having a baby is having to leave the others. Mother and Dad used to come before but the Generation is too much for them now, especially Liz, and I am afraid they are too much for you too.'

'Too much? Don't be silly. Honestly, Shona, I am all right.'

'You are nearly transparent. And there is a lot to do. They eat so much. The days are one long meal.'

'A bit of cooking won't worry me. I shall enjoy it.'

I was wryly amused that the anxiety in Shona's eyes was generated by her fear that I was not physically fit enough to take over the management of her household. She had no conception at all of my frightening sense of inadequacy in the face of those three children of hers, no conception of the ordeal that those three pairs of clear critical eyes were for me. As I reassured her that I would manage the household, she began to

18

smile at me, placidly, contentedly with an ineffable sweetness and a confidence that, like herself, I would know by instinct what was good and right for the children and I did not attempt to explain to her, for she would never understand that, to me, the children were people whose good I had no confidence in myself to know and people, besides, who might find me not to their liking and meet me with hostility.

'Jock will be here since it is the school holidays,' I said, comforting myself.

'He will be in at the hospital a lot. It is then that I worry about them but it is all stupid anyway. They have plenty of sense.' Impatiently, she dismissed her own affairs. 'Tell me, how is Twice *really*, Janet?'

'He is much better than the doctors ever thought he could possibly be,' I told her, but it was easy to go on to tell her of the long anxiety of the last years, an anxiety which I had tried to exclude from my letters but which had seeped through to this sensitive sympathy of hers. When, at last, she was satisfied that she knew about Twice 'really', she said: 'And now this dreadful earthquake. When Mr de Marnay's letter came yesterday, telling about Mr and Mrs Maclean, I just could not believe it. My heart goes out to that Roddy boy down there. What *can* he be feeling?'

The cliché that she used was, in her case, both apt and true for she seemed to have a heart that was out, roving about the world to find all those who were in need of its warmth and comfort. As she talked on in her light gentle voice of George and Tom, her father and mother and her only sister, I felt that I was discovering this woman Shona for the first time, that she was someone I had never met before and again I paused in my mind before the miracle that she and my brother had produced those three freshly-minted new individuals that I had met downstairs.

'I cannot get over the children,' I said. 'I knew they were there of course but they were only names. I hadn't imagined them. One couldn't.'

This made no sense to Shona and little wonder. She saw in her children nothing miraculous and she merely smiled at me in an indulgent way and said: 'They are a very ordinary lot but at least they are healthy.' She rose heavily to her feet. 'Lie down for a bit, Janet. We will give you a call at supper time.'

I lay down on the bed thankfully, not because I felt tired or ill, because I suddenly felt calm and well, but I was grateful that I could spend a little time alone before having to face those three pairs of eyes again. It was suddenly terribly important that I should pass muster with these children, although this was something that I had never thought about before. When I had thought of my brother's progeny, I had thought of them in a loose way as probably a 'very ordinary lot' as Shona had put it but now they had taken on a new significance. They were the new generation of Sandisons and it was frightening that I, the proudest Sandison of all those left alive, should be feeling that I was on trial before the representatives of the future of my line.

Naturally, I had brought little gifts for the children – books and sweets, the latter bought in quantity against the ration coupons issued to holiday-makers in Britain for, eleven years after the end of the war in Europe, certain luxuries were still in limited supply. I rose from the bed and stood looking at the parcel of books and the shoe box full of bags of sweets and slabs of chocolate for a few minutes before I decided that I would make no pathetic attempt to bribe my way. If these children decided against me, a few books or sweets would not alter their decision and, picking up the packages, I stowed them out of sight in the bottom of the large wardrobe.

It was a scared but defiant old aunt who went downstairs at supper time, stiffening her spine as she opened the door to the big kitchen but only the grown-ups were there and a very thin, spry, dark-eyed little woman who was bustling about laying the table for supper.

'Where are the children?' I asked, sighing out my nervously held breath.

'In bed,' Jock said. 'A dram of whisky, Janet?'

'Yes, thank you.'

Nobody seemed to understand how very important these children were to me and, as I took my glass from my brother, I thought that, now, it would be another twelve hours before I would know what was going to develop. While the others sat talking, Shona sitting on the old sofa close to Roddy, I was silent, wondering how George and Tom, Shona and Jock, these people of my family, could be unaware of this tremendous thing in my life, this discovery of – of this hungry critical generation. Suddenly, there were three taps at the door in rapid succession, each tap obviously made by a different hand.

'One might have known it,' my brother said and then added loudly: 'Go away! Get off to bed!'

'Aw, Dad!' came a chorus of three voices behind the door.

'Couldn't they come in?' I asked nervously. 'Just this once, Jock?'

'You will probably rue it,' he told me and then called: 'All right. Five minutes,' and the door swung open.

Fashions in dancing, like fashions in all else, are subject to change and 1956 was the year of a form of dancing known as Rock 'n' Roll and it was also the year when the word 'teenager' was coming from the United States into British usage. Elizabeth, Duncan and George were not as yet teenagers but they had the greedy forward-looking nature of the young, the urge to get on through time and with the business of living and to be able to Rock 'n' Roll before their time was a manifestation of this urge. Dressed in blue-and-white-striped pyjamas and red felt slippers, Elizabeth in front, Duncan behind her with his hands on her waist, George behind Duncan with his hands on his brother's waist, they came prancing into the kitchen, making their own music as they came, in high shrill voices:

> 'We three
> Have a certain solidarit-ee
> And it was not kind,
> Leaving Uncle Twice behind –'

they now swung round to face me and three felt slippers stamped the floor –

> ' – we mind!'

They glared at me before turning pointedly away to Tom and George while I felt so shattered that I wanted to cry.

'George,' said Elizabeth, 'tell about the ferret in Miss Tulloch's shop!'

'As long as your Aunt Janet is here,' said George and I knew that he knew I was discomfited from the joking stress he placed upon the word 'aunt' – it was a little joke intended to comfort – 'I am not going to tell a single one o' these old Reachfar yarns.'

'No, nor me either, forbye and besides,' said Tom. 'Your Aunt Janet knows far more about Reachfar and ferrets and Miss Tulloch's shop than I do.'

'And no ferrets tonight anyhow,' Jock said. 'And you were

21

told that Uncle Twice was not coming this time because he is too busy. Now, get off to bed.'

Suddenly, the three of them disintegrated from a group into three individuals, as suddenly as if an earthquake had destroyed the bonds of their unity, as physical earthquake destroys a telegraph system, communications were broken off between them and they were at war.

'Liz Sandison,' said Duncan. 'Uncle Twice did *not* let you drive his car at Reachfar!'

'No, did *not*!' little George supported his brother.

It was a combination of the war between the sexes and the war between younger and older and in an instant all three were yelling and clawing at one another indiscriminately. My brother, without moving from his chair, reached out an enormous hand, snatched George from the mêlée, gave him a resounding smack on the pyjama seat before clamping him between his knees and reaching out for the other two at the same time. He then turned both over his left arm, smacked the two bottoms with his right hand and stood Liz and Duncan upright and, with all three yelling at the pitch of their lungs, he said quietly: 'All right. Yell it out and settle down' whereupon he picked up his whisky glass with cool unconcern. Elizabeth was the first to stop crying and, sobbing pitifully, she looked at me, her big eyes very wide.

'You remember Reachfar?' she asked with grudging hostility.

'Yes.'

'I did drive the car, didn't I, with Uncle Twice?' She was asking for corroboration but with no faith that I could give it. Tensely, the two boys, bright tears still on their cheeks, were listening. It was borne in on me that this story that Elizabeth had been telling them was part of her kingdom, one of the supports of her throne, something that contributed to her sway over her younger brothers who, I now saw, wanted, although maybe only momentarily, to break away from this older female yoke. A great deal can pass through the mind in a very short time and, while all six wet eyes looked at me, I thought: 'But she *is* some years older than the boys are and they have to accept that she is that much ahead of them in memory. But she has no right to tell them lies –'

'Down the long road where the sea was far away at the bottom, I drove it –', she sobbed, '– I drove it –'

She stood looking round at us all, clinging to her story but herself becoming doubtful of its truth in the face of the general disbelief, but at the phrase: 'Where the sea was far away at the bottom,' my memory clicked and I was standing at the granary gable of Reachfar with my father while Twice, driving his car, with Elizabeth on his lap, one of her hands holding the wheel, the other pressing the horn button, went down the long straight road where the sea was far away at the bottom.

'Twice is just foolish fond of that bairn,' my father's voice was saying.

I held out my hand. 'Come here, Liz,' I said and when she came to me I turned her round in front of me to face all the others and then spoke over her shoulder. 'Yes,' I said. 'Liz used to drive the car down the road towards the sea and back up again. Didn't you, Liz? You sat on Uncle Twice's knee and drove.'

'Yes,' she said with a tremendous gulp.

'But not really *driving*!' said Duncan scornfully.

'No, not *really*!' said George.

Liz stiffened between my hands. 'But more driving than you two!' she said. 'And with Uncle *Twice*!' she pressed home her unique advantage.

'Aye, boys,' said Tom. 'That's right enough. Fair's fair.'

'And now,' said Shona's gentle voice, 'the three of you have got a little past yourselves with all the excitement and you must go off to bed now. You will hear about the ferret another night.' They coalesced into a group again and Liz spoke for them. 'You will tell us?' she asked me.

'Yes, about the ferret and lots of other Reachfar things.'

They nodded, formed into their dancing formation again and pranced towards the door singing:

> 'We three
> Have a certain solidarit-ee
> Good night!
> Put out that light!
> Good *night*!'

'I warned you it wasn't to be risked,' Jock said when the door had closed. 'They are a little over the edge with you people arriving and the baby coming and everything.'

'Which one is the family poet?' Roddy asked.

23

'The jingles are a joint effort and they can be damned irritating. They use them for routine things like saying good night but they also use them for things that are important to them but difficult to express, like their disappointment about Twice not being able to come.'

'Where did they get the phrase "a certain solidarity"?' I asked.

Jock looked rueful. 'From me. That was what started the jingle thing. The minister next door has a boy of seven and a baby girl and when he first came here, those three ganged up on the boy. You know how youngsters do. As a rule, Shona and I don't interfere but Robert is a nervous delicate little chap so I had our lot on the mat and I used the phrase "You three have a certain solidarity", trying to make them understand that they must not use it as a weapon, especially in the way of three against one. I have had plenty of time to regret using that phrase. How long have we been having these jingles now, Shona? About a year?'

Shona was unmoved. 'It is a phase,' she said. 'They'll get over it.'

'I notice,' Roddy said, 'that your child psychology is the old-fashioned sort – what my mother used to call the flat of her hand.'

'They don't get it often,' Jock said, 'but it is the best thing for near-hysteria, like that show tonight. They are very reasonable as a rule,' he went on, as the little dark woman began to put plates of soup round the table, 'and it is very odd that all the things in them that irritate me most, they got from myself, like "a certain solidarity". Come and have some supper.'

As we sat down at the table, Shona turned to Roddy, who was beside her. She had noticed, as I had, that for the first time since he arrived and, indeed, since the earthquake, Roddy had mentioned one of his parents. He had not spoken of either since they died.

'Roddy,' she said, 'I always hoped to meet your mother one day. Janet was always writing to us about her and you and your brothers. She must have been a wonderful person.'

'Yes,' Roddy said. 'I think she was,' and, as if he and Shona were in a private world, he began to talk to her of his parents and his childhood.

Although Roddy talked as if to Shona alone, the rest of us listened and as the picture of life in St Jago became graphic in

24

Roddy's words, Shona's big eyes became childlike with wonder, as if Roddy were an exotic creature from another world, and I saw George and Tom glance at myself now and then, as if some of this exoticism must have rubbed off on to me so that they suspected me of being no longer the person that they once knew. Later, I came to the conclusion that my interpretation of their attitude was not correct but, on that evening, I was tired, I had been more run down in health than I had been aware and I was bitterly hurt by the children's seeming suspicious disapproval of me.

I have never been able to take up a condescending attitude towards children or to consider that their immature opinions do not matter and, these things quite apart, I was stunned into near-shock by the impact they had made on me. I kept looking from Shona to Jock, wondering how these two had brought about this miracle and, at the same time, I was scornful of myself, telling myself in the words of Tom and George that I was 'going on as if no bairns had ever been born before and as if I didn't know what caused them'. And, too, at the end of this long journey undertaken so suddenly and at the end of this long emotional day, I was missing Twice. Sitting within the circle round the fire, I felt that I was not of it and I became more and more depressed until, at last, when we went up to bed, I cried into my pillow until I fell asleep.

When I awoke the next morning, I felt ashamed of myself and, later, I went downstairs timidly, fearful that my family might have come to know in some mysterious way of my childish behaviour of the night before. I myself could hardly believe now that I had sobbed so harshly into my pillow and, while I had cried, it had seemed to be with a deep grief that came from my heart but now, in the summer morning light, what I had felt, all that had been so muddled and indescribable was transmuted into a deep gratitude for this family of mine, all the generations of it, gathered together here in this cumbrous ugly house.

Chapter II

'The Youth, who daily farther from the east
Must travel, still is Nature's Priest,
And by the vision splendid
Is on his way attended;
At length the Man perceives it die away,
And fade into the light of common day.'

I THOUGHT that Roddy, who, for the last few years, had lived largely inside the hotbed of a London literary clique, might find Culdaviot very provincial and boring but when, the next forenoon, he said he would have to go on north after lunch and Shona said: 'So soon? Won't you stay over the weekend?' he accepted her invitation at once.

It warmed my heart that Jock and Shona had carried on the old Reachfar tradition of hospitality. At Reachfar, we never had 'visitors' but quite frequently and very suddenly often we had 'friends with us'. They might be neighbours like Danny the Beeman with his fiddle, come to spend the evening and have a *ceilidh* with us or they might be a family of travelling tinkers, camping in the barn until a blizzard blew itself out but they were all friends who were with us. If the word 'visitors' was used, it was usually in a derogatory sense, of people like the embarrassing and silly Miss Boyds who caused George and Tom to disappear out to the moor or into the barn until they had gone away.

George, Tom, Roddy and I were friends who were with my brother and his family and we were tacitly expected to take part in and contribute to the life of the household without special arrangements being made for our entertainment and we were warmly accepted by Jock and Shona in this way. The children had, as I had had at Reachfar, a life of their own within the larger life of the household.

When, in the early forenoon, therefore, George and Tom announced that they were going to pick strawberries in the garden, Shona said: 'Goodness me, this baby is badly timed. Janet, do you feel able to make the jam for me?' I agreed at once, whereupon she turned to Roddy: 'If I give you a list for the grocer, Roddy, will you run down to the village in your car?'

'Delighted,' Roddy said.

I went out to the garden with the strawberry-pickers, to whom the children had attached themselves. The garden, like the house, was an anachronism in the mid-twentieth century. It was huge and rich in fruit and vegetables of all kinds but there was also a large uncultivated area which had once been a shrubbery and landscaped flower garden and which was now an overgrown jungle. In this area, I saw, climbing over the stump of a dead tree, an old white sweet-scented rose, what we used to call a 'Granny Rose' and the last of its kind I had seen had been in the garden at Reachfar but when I stepped off the path to penetrate the jungle and look more closely at the rose, Liz said sharply:

'*You* can't go in there!'

'Why not?' I asked.

All three pointed ahead to a board, a large discarded black-board from my brother's school, on which was crudely painted in white letters: 'Keep out. Reachfar People only.'

'But I am a Reachfar person!' I protested.

Liz regarded me solemnly but suspiciously, her brothers on either side of her, supporting her. Their solidarity was palpable.

'Uncle Twice was,' Liz conceded.

'Yes. We remember Uncle Twice,' Duncan corroborated, although he did not remember because he was not born when Twice was at Reachfar. It was only Liz who remembered.

'Yes. Uncle Twice,' echoed little George.

Perhaps I looked as deeply hurt as I felt, for their faces seemed to soften. 'Maybe we'll tell you the password sometime,' Liz said.

'And if I go in without the password?'

'A horrible awful dreadful curse will come on you.'

'An *abominable* curse,' said Duncan.

'Yes, bebominable,' said little George.

'Then I won't go in,' I said and they looked pleased, granting me their approval as we went along to the strawberry bed.

Tom and George had rolled the net back from the first long rows of plants and now they surveyed the children and me as Tom said: 'Aunt Janet, I don't suppose you are much of a hand at berry-picking with being so long away foreign, so you had better just give Liz a hand with her row. Duncan, I will help you, and these two Georges can make a kirk or a mill o' a row o' their own.'

'And none o' this picking the big ones and leaving the wee ones,' George said. 'You have to pick clean. You can eat as many as you like, of course. That's what strawberries are for, eating.'

I thought that this, with the Hungry Generation, was a little reckless and, by the time George, Tom and I had picked the first twenty pounds of fruit, not a child had put a berry in a basket, but as George helped me to carry the fruit into the kitchen, he said: 'It won't be long now. Wee Gee is getting quite green about the gills, poor fellow.'

By noon, all three had been sick but had received no sympathy and at lunchtime they carried their food outside because they could not bear the smell of the jam I was now making.

'This happens every year,' my brother said. 'You would think that Liz at least would have learned by now. Sometimes I think they are just plain backward.'

'No, not backward,' said Tom. 'It's them that takes the longest time to learn that learns best. Look at George and me. We have never given any time to learning at all and we haven't learned damn all either.'

In the afternoon, Roddy too joined the picking squad while Shona sat with her knitting on a chair on the path and Jock helped me in the kitchen.

'That is the end of the strawberry sugar,' he said, as I put the last panful of the day on the stove. 'We'll take the rest of the strawberries down to the grocer.'

'Jock,' I said, with my back to him as I looked down into the jam, 'what is this Reachfar thing that the children have?'

'Just the ordinary fantasy thing that youngsters go in for,' he said. 'Why?'

'But why Reachfar?'

'It seems obvious. Don't you think so? It is the main thing on the borderland of Liz's memory. She is not sure if it is a real place or not, really and she has infected the other two with it. Their Reachfar is the old shrubbery in the garden but that is only a token of the Reachfar in their minds. Children have what Wordsworth called "a vision splendid" in the depths of their minds and Liz, Dunk and Gee call their vision Reachfar, but the vision is common to most children.' He pushed a tray of jars into the cool oven of the stove. 'Liz remembers Twice more distinctly than any other person at Reachfar,' he said then and, after a second, he added with a laugh: 'Twice was a man, you see, a man who was not a Sandison.'

My ten-years-younger brother seemed to know so much more about children than I did, seemed to take so many things about them as not-too-serious-matters-of-course that I felt that I would seem absurdly infantile if I tried to explain to him my hurt about not being accepted as a 'Reachfar person'. But I was beginning to understand a little about the workings of this fantasy. It was born out of that borderland in Liz's memory where Twice figured and I did not, so that Twice was a Reachfar person and I was not. The night before, I had gained a little ground by confirming that Liz had driven down the road in the car but I had not yet broken through the children's mundane world into their fantasy land and I did not see how I could ever cross this boundary which was an invisible line drawn in neither space nor time but in that strange and original dimension which was the memory of Liz.

Spitefully, the three children picked strawberries until their suppertime because, they said: 'We want to see them all boiled until they are dead like heretics in the Dark Ages' but when they had finished their early supper and were going upstairs to bed, they paused beside the baskets for the grocer which were lying in the back hall and Liz said: 'Look here, you two, I could eat a strawberry or so. Mum, may we have a few berries?'

'Six each. No more,' said Shona.

'And I hope you are sick again,' said Jock.

But they were not sick. They had already bathed but they now went up to clean their teeth and came down again to say good night.

'If I may say so,' Roddy said now, 'I think this uncle and aunt thing is very old-fashioned. I wish you people would call me Roddy. I don't feel like an uncle.'

'For myself, I never did hold with being an uncle,' said George.

The children laughed uproariously. 'George, you have never *been* an uncle!' Liz said.

'And *she*,' Roddy said, pointing at me, 'doesn't look like an aunt to me anyway. Aunts are either gay young women or fussy old ones with blue hair and pearls.'

But here the gentle Shona intervened with unexpected firm-

ness. 'No,' she said. 'They may call you Roddy if you like but — '
she reached over and laid a gentle hand on my knee while her
eyes looked at me appealingly ' – this is Aunt Janet and nobody
else.' She turned to the children. 'You have to have a few manners and a little respect for some things.'

It occurred to me now that, ever since I had arrived, George
and Tom had been calling me 'Aunt Janet' in the presence of
the children and I was certain that they were not doing this for
any reasons of punctilio so, in exploration of their motive, I
turned to them and spoke as I might have spoken forty years
before: 'You remember that, you two,' I said. 'I am Aunt Janet.'

'You needn't be telling *us* that,' George said. 'We know it
fine already.'

'Do you think we have gone foolish?' Tom asked me. 'Telling
us that!'

The slight emphasis on the 'us' gave me the clue and I at
once thought: So these children don't even want me as an
aunt? As I turned to look at the three, Liz was giving me a
long appraising look but she at once turned away from me to
Roddy.

'Roddy is better,' she said. 'You haven't got an uncleish face.'

The two boys shook their heads in agreement with her. 'So
you will just be Roddy,' Liz anounced and then her face altered
to assume an expression of conscious feminine flirtatiousness.
'Dad told us that you write stories, Roddy. Do you think you
have a story in you that we might like?'

'Now, Liz — ' Shona was beginning but Roddy broke in:
'What kind of stories do you like, Liz?'

'On the whole,' she replied, 'the ghastlier the better.'

'About hidyus monsters,' said Duncan.

'Yes, bebominable creatures,' Gee agreed.

'What about hearing about the ferret in Miss Tulloch's shop
from Aunt Janet?' Shona asked.

It seemed to be a convention in Shona's mind that the children might 'bother' members of the family but not other guests.
The three pairs of eyes turned to me with that scrutinising appraising gaze; from me they turned to George and Tom and
then the three children gathered round Roddy.

'We would rather have ghastly monsters,' said Liz, still looking at me, who was feeling so childishly hurt that I wanted to
run away out of the room and I was relieved when Roddy said:

'I am simply stuffed with terrible monsters that are dying to get out. Come along upstairs.'

'Roddy *is* a nice boy,' Shona said when they had gone, speaking as if one of us had accused Roddy of being the very reverse. 'Not many young men would bother with those three as he does.' She changed direction. 'I suppose you think I am a bit old-fashioned, wanting them to call you Aunt Janet. Maybe I am but I think it is good for them to have certain rules that they must stick to.'

'I think so too,' I agreed with her. 'I lived my early childhood inside a rigid framework and it made things very secure and happy.'

But, as on the evening before, as we sat round the fire the depression began to grip me again and in the midst of these people, all of whom, as I knew with my brain, were fond of me, I seemed to be shut off in a cold isolation. When supper was over and the group formed round the fire again I felt I could bear it no longer, so I got up and said that I was going to have a look round the garden.

It was a bright summer evening and as I walked slowly along the path with the shrubbery on my right, its dark tangled laurels and its sombre blackboard with the white lettering seemed so hostile that I began to think in a morbid way that, after all, I was on the verge of some kind of mental breakdown. I went away to the far corner of the vegetable garden beyond the strawberry bed and the raspberry canes and leaned against the rough stone of the boundary wall while I looked at the grey bulk of the house and at the nearer dark jungle of the shrubbery.

At its centre, I could see from here, there was a big old sycamore and behind it, on a rise in the ground, a group of dark firs. At one time, before the birds had sown the seeds of the rowans, dogroses, brambles and hawthorns which now grew all around, the sycamore and the firs must have made a pretty contrast, I thought. Looking at those tall straight fir trees, I was overcome with nostalgia as I thought of my Thinking Place among the high firs above the Reachfar well and, at this moment, a homing flight of rooks went overhead, giving their sad evening cry that seemed to say: 'Never more! Never more!' Blinking the tears from my eyes, I wished that I had never come to this place, that I were back in St Jago where I could live with memories and not among this thrusting frightening

31

actuality that seemed to be born out of those three children in the room upstairs.

I saw my brother making his way towards me along the path, his hands in his pockets with an air of studied nonchalance. I tried to smile at him.

'Janet,' he said, 'I don't think you are feeling well.'

This, I told myself, was bound to happen. George and Tom had an awareness of every mood that crossed my mind and although Jock himself knew me less surely, it would be their way to use him as an ambassador.

'What gave you that notion?' I asked. 'I am all right.'

'You are pretty thin and shaky and you are finding the kids a bit of a strain with all their Reachfar nonsense and everything,' he said, making me aware that he had been thinking of my questions of the afternoon about their Reachfar fantasy. Frowning, he looked down at the path and moved a pebble about with the toe of his shoe. 'They are going to be really difficult about you,' he went on and my heart went plummeting down. 'I was a fool not to foresee it but I didn't.' He looked so solemn that I suspected myself of inducing some extraordinary sort of psychological complexes in his children and my leaden heart now seemed to sink of its own weight into a yawning grave in the earth at my feet.

'Jock, what do you mean?'

He placed his back against the stone wall beside me and stared, like myself, at the house.

'Has it ever struck you,' he asked with seeming irrelevance, 'that when George and Tom speak your name, they pronounce it Channatt?'

'No,' I said with astonishment, 'it hadn't struck me but they do.' And they did. They spoke – they had always spoken my name with their Highland accent and intonation, the initial J softened to CH, the N in the middle doubled to make two syllables of equal stress and the final T doubled to make a more final ending.

'And it won't have struck you either any more than it struck me that when they say "Aunt Janet" they pronounce the words exactly as we do?' Jock gave a little laugh. 'I hate to admit it but it seems that even George and Tom have had their speech slightly standardised by communication with us university types and the mass media. The Channatt is a survival from the time of your birth.' He paused for a moment and went on:

'What I am getting at is this. George and Tom have the kids stuffed with stories about Channatt, just as they stuffed you and me full of yarns about Sandy Bawn and Uncle Kenny and Uncle Farquhar. There is Channatt and her ferret in Miss Tulloch's shop, there is the time that Channatt climbed on to the church roof, the time she fell into the Reachfar Burn in her Sunday clothes and a hundred more. To the kids, Channatt is a fantasy figure like Cinderella or Bo-Peep but, at the same time, Liz is suspicious that Channatt and Aunt Janet are somehow connected and she does not want to lose the fantasy Channatt. She is really afraid that you will explode the myth, make Channatt fade into the light of common day, as it were. She could not explain this to you, of course. It has taken myself a few hours to get at it. But this is what is wrong, Janet, honestly. And it will come all right. These things do. Liz is being horrible and taking the boys along with her as she always does, but try not to be hurt about it. It will come right.'

He reminded me of my father as he looked at me with worried eyes, while he tried to compose this difference between the children he loved and myself, the sister who, I think, he also loved a little.

'I am glad you have told me about this, Jock,' I said. 'I simply did not understand and I *was* hurt. I admit it. But not any more.'

'They are not easy to understand, even when you know them as well as I think I do. They are three completely new minds, you see. There has never been anyone exactly like any of them before.' The worried look left his face and he gave a happy chuckle of laughter. 'What really clarified this for me was when Roddy said it was old-fashioned to call you aunt. Did you notice Liz's face?'

'No. I didn't.'

'A look of stark terror went over it for a split second and her eyes seemed to be staring into an abyss as if her world were disintegrating under her.' I remembered how I stared at the uptorn tree the day after the earthquake. Again my brother gave that little laugh. 'But the thing I cannot explain is Shona. I don't think she saw that look, she would not have tried to explain it even if she had seen it but she has this remarkable instinct about what is right for them and she laid down the law that you were *Aunt Janet and nobody else.* Liz's relief was palpable, palpable to me, anyway. But then Shona goes on to say to you that she is probably old-fashioned with her little conventions and so on and this is how Shona really sees what she said – as a small training in convention. But it is more than that. The convention is there but there is also some deep-rooted mothering instinct that she had never bothered to formulate. Shona doesn't bother much with formulation; she follows her instincts and her emotions most of the time and she never puts a foot wrong with the kids.'

'She is indeed a wonderful mother, Jock.'

He smiled. 'Let's go in and upstairs and have a look at the three. They are at their most appealing when they are asleep and I want you to like them.'

'But I do like them! One can't help it. But one wants them to like *one*.'

'Don't worry. To like people comes naturally to them as long as they are certain that you are a real person and not someone who has stepped out of their fantasy world, thereby destroying it for ever.'

In the big bedroom, which I had not entered until now, the two boys were asleep in a double bed, the longer body of Duncan neatly curved round the shorter body of Gee as they lay close together. At the other end of the room, a single bed did not quite contain Liz who lay spread expansively on her back, her arms flung wide, her pigtails stretching from end to end of her pillow, one foot projecting from under the covers and dangling towards the carpet. Jock put a hand under the ankle, pushed the foot under the blankets and tucked them in.

'She is more trouble than the two boys put together,' he said softly, 'like you were. According to Tom and George, I was an angel and you were a positive devil.' We came out on to the landing. 'Females, I suppose,' he added.

'No,' I said. 'Dad had a theory that the first-born tended to be fuller of what he called "devilment" than the rest, partly through being first born and partly through the parents being anxious and inexperienced.'

'Maybe that is it but anyway, we bought a packet with Liz.'

'Jock, I think they are splendid. Aren't you proud of them?'

'That is not for me to say,' he replied with George's canny smile and I was struck by the fleeting cloud-shadow-along-the-hills way in which this brother of mine could remind me now of my father, now of George, now of my grandfather and yet

34

remained a separate individual who contained a little of them all.

'You were upstairs, John?' Shona asked when we went into the kitchen. 'Are they asleep?'

'Fathoms deep. Janet wanted to see them in bed.'

'I don't blame her. It makes them bearable, that they sleep, I mean. Sometimes, in the middle of the day, I comfort myself by saying that in another eight hours or so they will be asleep.'

'They have had a big day what with the berries and being sick and all,' Tom said. 'Roddy has been telling us about this Paradise place where you and Twice are, Janet. George and me were thinking that it would be a bit like Poyntdale in the old days with the Big House and all but it is a terrible size. I never heard of an arable place of thirty thousand acres.'

'And there are three big houses on it and about thirty of the size of Poyntdale Farm House,' I said. 'Olympus – that was Roddy's home – is bigger than the Big House at Poyntdale. The Great House of Paradise is enormous but Olympus is a much finer building, I think.'

'In a queer way, Shona,' Roddy said, 'the atmosphere at Olympus when I was a kid was very much like the atmosphere in this house. The drawing-room was always kept locked because the veranda off it was very dangerous.'

'The windows of that veranda open on to a hundred foot drop down a precipice,' I explained to Shona.

'And all the upstairs rooms on that side were locked too,' Roddy continued, 'like you people locking off the front of the house here.'

'We only do that to restrict the area of carried mud,' Jock said.

'I know, but it is the same sort of thing for the kids, a certain restriction, you know. And then there were always three or four of us in the nursery at a time. When one came home here to Scotland to school, the next one was shoved through from Mother's room to the nursery to make way for the new baby.'

'Seven boys,' said Shona, her eyes smiling as she dreamed of this bliss. 'What a regiment!'

'So the nursery lot were always a self-contained gang like your three,' Roddy said.

'Your mother had her hands full,' Shona told him as we sat down to supper.

'There were about a dozen servants, of course,' Roddy reminded her. 'But yes, things were pretty lively. It is odd when one thinks of it now. One regarded Mother and Dad as enemies most of the time, except when one had fallen off one's pony or had a sore tooth or something. We tested the locked doors every day, as a matter of principle, to see if we could look out of those windows and down into the gulch, just because it was forbidden, I suppose.'

'No. It is deeper than the forbidden, I think,' my brother said. 'Children *are* at war with the older generation. We are enemies as you said, in the way that the skin a snake is trying to cast off is an enemy.'

'Tom, George and I were certainly always at war with Granny,' I said.

'I wouldna call it war exactly,' said Tom, 'but with Her Ould Self you had to be going against her some of the time –'

' – or you wouldna have had a soul to call your own,' George broke in, 'but, mind you, it wasna that we werena fond o' Granny for we were.'

As George and Tom spoke, I remembered the unity that had prevailed between them and myself when I was a child, a unity that made of us a single entity, thinking and speaking as one person, especially in our constant attempts to outwit the authority of my grandmother. Today, I reminded myself, while I had been making jam in the kitchen, Tom and George had spent the whole day with the children. Had their allegiance been transferred from my brother and me to this new generation? If so, the transfer did not sadden me and I was not jealous of the children but it stressed my feeling of being odd man out in this household, the feeling that I was the only one with no securely integrated place in it. Tom and George were accepted by the children, as they had once been accepted by my brother and me, as two more of the child tribe who would aid and abet to some degree in the defiance of authority but who, at the same time, could define the limits beyond which defiance became unsafe. And Roddy had been accepted as one of the older generation, the generation of the mothers and fathers, someone pleasant enough, who could tell amusing stories at bedtime but someone who would not be allowed inside the child world proper. But my place had not been defined in this way. They still seemed to be in judgement upon me which gave me a feeling of insecurity, as if I belonged nowhere and was wandering again in some No Man's Land of outer space as I had wandered

36

after the chaos and disruption of the earthquake. I had never before in my life been so bitingly conscious of my need for a settled place in the scheme of things.

I felt a pang of homesickness for Twice and my own home again, that place where I really mattered to somebody, for the children asleep upstairs obviously were more important to my family than I was, but the main sadness lay in the fact that these children were more important to myself than Jock and Shona, even than Tom and George, but I had, apparently, no reciprocal importance for the children.

We were drinking tea before going to bed when my brother's glance sharpened and, looking across the semicircle, he said: 'Shona?' She smiled. 'I am afraid so. You had better give the doctor and the hospital a ring and tell them we are on our way.'

Roddy and I had both sprung to our feet, motivated by some sort of action-stations alarm and Shona now looked at us serenely. 'Sit down. Everything is all right. But would you go up for my suitcase, Roddy? It is beside the wardrobe in my room, all packed. I don't want to climb the stairs.' Calmly, she took charge of us all, including my brother who, I noted with malice had, for once, utterly and completely lost his head. Probably, I thought with enjoyment, the only times he ever lost his head were those occasions when babies became imminent. His unshakable calm and cool control were characteristics that had long irritated me.

'Now Fat Mary will look after the house, Janet,' Shona was saying, 'but she is not much of a cook. And George and Tom will keep the hungry ones out of your way. And – ' she smiled at Roddy ' – Roddy will do the shopping and odds and ends. John will stay in town with Mother and Dad. He will be not one bit of use here anyway until we bring this baby home and then he will come to his senses.'

My brother now came rushing into the room, each red curly hair on his head seeming to be quivering with a nerve of its own. 'Here's your coat,' he said breathlessly. 'I've got the car out. Come – '

'John, pull yourself together,' said Shona. 'Roddy is just going up for my case. There is plenty of time.'

'You had better be off out of here,' said George authoritatively. 'Tom and I have never fancied ourselves as midwives.'

'John, move the telephone into Janet's room so that you won't be bringing her downstairs in – '

37

'Roddy can move the bloody phone!' my brother exploded. 'Come *on*!'

Still issuing instructions for the wellbeing of her household and us all, we at last got her into the car which Jack drove away at breakneck speed in the middle of Shona's instructions about the sugar for the raspberry jam.

'God, I've never seen a family like this,' Roddy said as he and I came back into the house. 'But, Janet, I ought to go. I am simply one more for you to cook for.'

'If you dare to go away and leave me alone with this bunch, I'll never speak to you again,' I said.

We all sat up very late, talking spasmodically, jumping at every sound, all rushing to Jock's study together when the telephone rang and then, having reached it, we were all reluctant to lift the receiver. In the end, I spoke. It was Jock to tell us that Shona was safely inside the maternity ward. 'She is inside,' I told them all and we went back to the kitchen where we sat almost in silence except that, periodically, someone would say: 'Well, it is a good thing that she is inside.'

At last, we all went upstairs, Roddy bringing the telephone up and plugging it in beside my bed, but after all the other doors were shut, I turned on the light on the landing and went into the room where the children were sleeping. There was a strange comfort in their secure serenity, as they slept on unaware of what was happening and I found myself wishing that they would stay asleep, under some spell like the Sleeping Beauty or Rip Van Winkle until their parents came back to take charge of them. Thinking of them awake, with those keen critical intelligences working behind their large clear eyes, I felt hopelessly inadequate. I went to bed but I did not sleep. I wrote a long letter to Twice and checked the plugging of the telephone and its dialling tone several times, ate biscuits and smoked cigarettes until a little after five in the morning when the bell rang and my brother's voice, calm and proud now, with no trace of the hysterical crackle of the evening before, said: 'Janet? A boy. Six and a half pounds and a great thatch of red hair. And Shona is in cracking form. I think she sees herself catching up with Roddy's mother yet.'

I could not say much to him for his pride in Shona and the sheer joy in the baby made me cry but I had to brush the edge of the sheet hastily across my eyes as I put the receiver down for there came three light taps on the panel of the door.

'Come in!' I called.

The door opened about a foot and the three heads came round it in a vertical row, Liz's long pigtails dangling from the top to brush Gee's shoulders at the bottom.

'Mum and Dad are not in their room,' she said, 'and we heard the telephone – ' The six eyes seemed to accuse me of being in possession of part of their world.

'It was Dad ringing – ' I began.

Suddenly the door was thrown wide and they advanced towards me, an army in blue-and-white-striped pyjamas.

'What kind is it?' Liz asked.

'Kind?' My mind was fuddled.

'Boy or girl?' she snapped, as if I were an idiot.

'A boy,' I said. 'A boy with red hair,' I added, to show how clever I was. 'He weighs six and a half pounds.'

Liz turned to her brothers. 'Dunk pay up! I bet you a boy. Gee, pay up! I bet you red hair,' and they marched out of the room, leaving the door open and me in a stunned condition on the bed.

The door slammed shut in the draught from the open window and within moments it was thrust open again and Roddy said: 'The kids are awake. There is a battle going on in their room. Should we do anything?'

'Leave them to it,' I said. 'I don't suppose they will actually kill one another, the heartless little brutes.'

I told him what had happened and he began to laugh. 'Sorry,' he said then. 'I can see that you felt shattered but it is funny all the same. It is funny because they are so much more sensible about it than we are about this thing. They lay bets about the colour of its hair. They don't lie awake, as we did, imagining everything that could go wrong.'

But the battle in the other room was now rising in terrifying crescendo and there was a loud thud as some heavy object was thrown out and across the landing to bounce off the wall.

'Get in there and tear them apart,' I said to Roddy. 'I'll be with you in a minute.'

When I had put on my dressing-gown and reached the scene, Roddy was standing with Duncan and Gee held behind him, trying to fend off the enraged Liz, whose pigtails were undone, the long hair flying about her face and body while she danced with fury as Roddy prevented her from getting at her brothers. Momentarily, I forgot my fear of those three, forgot my desire

39

to do nothing to antagonise them, for there was something of the terror of the earthquake, of 'chaos is come again' in the abandoned rage of this little girl. In one movement, I seized her, sat down on the bed, turned her up and slapped her bottom so that my hand stung. 'Go for Liz' Shona had said and in very truth I went for her, as if she were the symbol of all the chaos, disorder and disruption which I hated so much and of which I was so afraid. When I loosed my hold, she darted away like a spring suddenly released, both hands on her stinging behind and, with her back to the wall, she glared at me, her blue eyes lit by red flames of fury. 'Just you wait till my Daddy comes home!' she yelled. 'Just you wait till I tell him about all your filthy cheatingness and your horrible unjustishness!' and then she threw herself down on her bed and began to howl more loudly than I had thought possible. Duncan and Gee, also howling now, tore themselves away from Roddy and hurled themselves on to the bed beside their sister as Tom and George, still in their night clothes, came into the room. 'Now, then,' said George with a stern air that was very unusual in him, 'what is all this row that you are making?'

Duncan pointed with angry accusation at me. '*She* smacked Liz!'

'Yes, *smacked* her!' said little Gee indignantly.

'Shut up, you pair of clypes!' said Liz, using the word for a tell-tale or informer that I had not heard since my childhood and, with the speed of a snake striking, she slapped their faces, one after the other, whereupon all three began to howl even more loudly than before.

'Bless my soul, this will never do,' said Tom. 'Come, Gee, lad, you come with me.'

He pulled the littlest one from the bed and led him out of the room, then George took Duncan away, Roddy going with them, so that I was left alone with the tear-stained Liz, who was not howling any more but heaving with great sobs.

'Liz,' I said, saying exactly what I felt, 'all this is quite horrible. Nobody has been cheating or unjust. You know quite well that we are not going to have you behaving like a savage.'

'They *were* cheating and unjust,' she said, staring out at the sky beyond the window. Dishevelled and tear-stained as she was, she had tremendous dignity.

'Who were?'

'The boys.'

40

'Oh? In what way?'

She looked around the room, then got off the bed and retrieved from the landing a battered, old leather attaché case on which were still visible the black initials J.E.S. for Janet Elizabeth Sandison, which identified it as the case that carried my books for six years to Cairnton Academy.

'This is the betting box,' she said with a sob. 'When we made the bets about the baby, I bet Dunk a week's sweets and Gee a week's sweets so – ' she sobbed, swallowed, ' – they put in a week's sweets each and I put in two weeks' sweets and today when I won the bets, the box was empty. They had eaten them a-a-all!' She dropped the old case on the floor and stood with the tears trickling down on to the long tangled hair, looking so forlorn that I wanted to cry along with her, so I pulled her towards me and said: 'The boys were very cheating and unjust indeed, Liz and I will punish them in the proper way.'

'No. It doesn't matter. But it was just – ' she shook her head, ' – I don't want them to be punished. It is that everything has gone all wrong. You see, if I had won the bets, I wanted us to have a special celebration sweets picnic in Reachfar for the baby getting born and now we can't have it any more. It was to be a surprise for Dunk and Gee, you see.' She began to cry again.

'But, Liz, they didn't know that. They are younger than you are and they thought that if you won you would eat all the sweets yourself, like they would have done, the greedy little pigs. People as young as Duncan and Gee don't think of nice things for other people like celebration sweets picnics.'

'I suppose not.'

'Now, if you will wash and get dressed and come into my room, I have something to show you.'

'All right.'

I went back to my bedroom, got out the shoe box full of sweets and chocolate and divided the lot into three heaps, half in one heap and two quarters in the others and covered them with the eiderdown. When Liz came in, dressed, calm, the hair in neat pigtails again, I called to George and Tom to bring the two boys.

'George and Tom,' I then said gravely, 'these two boys have done something very unfair and dishonourable.'

I told them about the betting box and the sweets while George and Tom looked down more and more gravely at their

41

charges. I then uncovered the sweets on the bed. 'I brought these sweets for everybody,' I said, 'but I have divided them like the bets in the box now. The big heap belongs to Liz. The smaller ones are for the boys.'

George stood back from Duncan, looked down at him and said: 'If I had done what you did, I couldna touch these sweeties on the bed. I would have to give them to Liz.'

'Aye and me too, forbye and besides,' Tom told little Gee.

The four eyes gazed at the paper bags, the foil-wrapped slabs of chocolate. They had never in their lives seen such a quantity of sweets other than behind the barrier of a shop window. Then Duncan gave a long sad sigh. 'Liz, you take them,' he said. 'Come on, Gee. We got to get dressed.'

They went out side by side and Tom shut the door.

'But George and Tom, I don't *want* all these!' Liz protested, her eyes filling with tears again.

'Of course you don't!' I said. 'But you can have your celebration picnic in Reachfar, silly.'

She brightened at once. 'Yes. Yes, so we can.' She looked round at the three of us uncertainly, unsure for a moment whether she was part of our world or part of the world of her brothers. 'I have to go and do Gee's buttons and sandal buckles,' she said then. 'He can't quite manage them all by himself yet.'

After a moment, we could hear the jerky little tune of 'We three have a certain solidarit-ee' from across the landing.

'Lord, what a morning,' I said.

'Och, it is just the excitement of the baby and all,' George said. 'Bairns can never say what they are feeling. Indeed, neither can a lot of grown-up people.'

'But people have to be letting off steam some way,' said Tom. 'Man, George, just think of you and me getting another bairn! We will have to get that poor devil Christian on the go again when we get home. He will be at the reading in no time.'

From myself onwards, George and Tom had taught every Sandison to read with the help of *Pilgrim's Progress*, the hero of which was always known as 'that poor devil Christian'.

'We must put Roddy down to the pub for a bottle,' George said. 'I canna wait to be drinking this new fellow's health out of a split new bottle.'

It was still not seven o'clock when I went downstairs, although it seemed to me I had lived through a long hard day since the moment when the telephone rang but when I entered the kitchen, the boys were laying the breakfast table and Liz, at the cooker, was stirring a large pan of porridge.

'If you are going to be in here, Aunt Janet,' she told me severely, 'you have to sit down and keep out of the way. We do our own breakfast and washing-up in the holidays but you people who want bacon and eggs and all of that stuff have to cook it for yourselves.'

I sat down obediently and said: 'When you have finished, I'll cook a little bacon for Roddy.'

'Yes. Roddy would like it I suppose.'

It was as if the scene upstairs, which had brought all the generations together on common ground for a short time, had never taken place.

This was my first experience of the kitchen at breakfast for, while Shona had been at home, she had been sending Roddy up with tea and toast for me. The children were very neat and efficient as they went about their work, Duncan handling the crockery and little Gee the cutlery, the latter pausing studiously while he decided at which side of each place to put the porridge spoon. While I cooked Roddy's bacon and egg, all the others had their porridge, the children having a large old-fashioned soup-plateful each and when I sat down to have tea and toast, they set about a loaf of bread, a dish of butter, a jar of marmalade and what remained from their porridge of three pint bottles of milk. In a very short time, all three got up and Liz said: 'We are going to feed the guinea pigs now. Call us when you are finished and we'll clean up.'

'That's the lot to eat, Janet,' Tom said approvingly when they had gone out. 'The Hungry Generation, as Jock calls them. That name comes out of some old bit of poetry, I am thinking, Roddy?'

'Yes, Tom. Keats,' Roddy confirmed.

'You and I will have to put the poetry on these rasps the-day, Tom,' George said. 'You will have to be at the jam again in the afternoon, Janet.'

It was a busy household, an up-to-date version of the Reachfar of my childhood and as soon as the children had cleared the table and were washing up in the scullery, I began to prepare the lunch of soup, meat and vegetables and pudding and as I worked I was comparing this kitchen, with its open fire for sitting by, its closed coke-burning stove, its electric cooker and all its other amenities with the old kitchen at Reachfar in which

43

the housewife's task had been so much harder and had demanded so much more skill. But this kitchen had one amenity which I could well have foregone, the telephone which was now plugged in here and sat on one of the window-sills.

My brother, like most country schoolmasters, was enmeshed in the social services of the community, as president of the local Youth Club, Secretary of the Community Centre, Treasurer of this and Chairman of that and a Justice of the Peace and it seemed to me that the telephone rang every five minutes. Here Liz proved invaluable.

'The Youth Club? Tell them to ring Mr Aitken – he is the secretary,' she would say or: 'A J.P.? If they are in a hurry for a signature, the nearest one is Commander Paterson at Overknowe.'

When the children had finished their washing-up, the boys went out to the garden but Liz came to me and said: 'I'll help you, Aunt Janet. Mum says you are not used to cooking with having people to help you all the time. I'll do the potatoes and carrots, shall I? Are they nice, your people, as nice as our Fat Mary?'

'But Mary isn't fat, Liz,' I said. 'She is as thin as a ferret. Why do you all call her Fat Mary?'

'It is nothing to do with fat or thin. It is because of *saying* fat.'

'Saying fat?'

With the patient air of an adult dealing with a slow-witted but persistent child, Liz stopped her work, looked solemnly at me and explained: 'In this countryside, we have two languages, Aunt Janet. We have ordinary English and we have the Doric but I was only five and a bit when we came here and I couldn't speak the Doric then.'

'Can you speak it now?' I asked.

'Och, aye, fairly that, an' ma brithers as weel,' she replied in a voice entirely unlike her normal voice which, together with the idiom and the altered vowel sounds – 'fairly' was pronounced 'ferrly' – made the words sound like a sentence in a foreign tongue.

'And I couldn't understand Fat Mary and she couldn't understand *me*, you see, and every time I asked her something, she would say: Fat? Fat is the Doric for what. So she came to be called Fat Mary.'

'Aye, fairly that,' said the owner of the name who had come

44

to fetch dusters. 'It's nae a'body that his a fancy name like mine.'

'And so are your house people nice like Fat Mary?' Liz asked again, returning with persistence to her point.

'Mebbe they're nicer nor me,' said Fat Mary, 'but Ah'll bet ye they're a' as black as the lum.'

'Black?' said Liz.

'Of course,' I said. 'They are St Jagoans.'

Liz clapped a dramatic hand to her forehead. 'Just fancy that!' she said. 'I knew about St Jagoans being black but I just hadn't connected up.'

For the remainder of the forenoon, in the intervals of answering the telephone, I told her of my home at Guinea Corner and of the servants, fat old Cookie, skinny old Minna, pretty young Clorinda and handsome shiny jet black Caleb. Each time I went to the telephone, I noticed that Duncan was sitting alone outside, nursing and stroking his brown guinea pig while Gee, George, Tom and Roddy picked raspberries at the other end of the garden and each time I put the receiver down, Duncan's head would pop round the edge of the door to ask: 'Was that Daddy, Aunt Janet?'

'Liz,' I said at last, 'why is Duncan so anxious for Daddy to telephone?'

'Oh, him,' she said, 'he's just all goofy.'

It was a far from satisfactory answer but I did not want to labour the point so I said no more. I was glad however when, about eleven o'clock, I did hear my brother's voice at the other end of the line.

'I meant to ring earlier, Janet, but I got tied up. Let me speak to Duncan, will you? He worries terribly about his mother.'

'So that's what it is?' I said. 'I'll call him.'

When the boy took the receiver from me, his hand was leaden cold and shaking and his voice trembled as he said: 'Hello, Dad,' but when he put the receiver back on the rest, he had a brave new authority, was no longer the little boy who had sought comfort from the smooth warm skin of his guinea pig. 'Dad says to be ready at half-past two, Liz, to go to see Mum.'

'I want to see that baby, me,' said Liz and Duncan ran out now, put his guinea pig in its hutch and went to join the others among the raspberry canes while I despised myself for not realising that a little boy could worry as much – perhaps more – than an adult could. I myself had worried as a child about the

45

health of my mother, now that I remembered it.

'Are you pleased that the baby is a boy, Liz?' I asked.

'Yes.'

'Wouldn't you have liked a sister for a change?'

'No.' She stopped work, her potato in one hand, the scraping knife in the other and with a devastating honesty of acute observation and also of sheer selfishness she said: 'Daddy likes girls best and he might like a girl baby more than he likes me,' and she set to work on her potato again.

When my brother came for them at two-thirty, they were dressed and waiting and they were a handsome brood. All three wore the kilt, white shirts, tartan ties and light blue woollen sweaters, Liz with blue bows at the ends of her pigtails.

'Are we going to see Granny and Granda as well?' she asked her father.

'Maybe,' said Jock. 'Get into the car,' and when the three had gone out, he said to me: 'Liz's eye never fails to sweep the whole horizon. Dunk is thinking of nothing but his mother, the wee fellow is bemused over the baby but Liz, along with everything else, remembers that Granda is always good for a bob or two and maybe more when a new baby has been born. Have you had any trouble?' he asked.

'Och, no trouble o' the world, man,' said Tom before I could speak.

'What kind o' trouble would we be having?' George enquired blandly. 'Tell Shona we are all asking for her.'

'I'll come and take the rest of you in to see her tomorrow,' he said.

That afternoon, when Fat Mary had gone home for a few hours, while the men worked in the garden and I made jam, the big house seemed to be very hollow and empty. The children, with their demanding young lives, had made it their own and when their presence was withdrawn, it lost reality and became a mere shell, that was sad with the echo of something that had gone.

46

Chapter III

'Not in entire forgetfulness,
And not in utter nakedness,
But trailing clouds of glory do we come
From God who is our home.'

THE NEXT afternoon, we all went into town, the children in
Roddy's car, Jock driving George, Tom and me but the children
were left with Granda and Granny today and did not come to
the hospital.

'Not even Duncan?' I asked my brother.

'No. He won't want to come again. None of them will. They
will tell you that they don't like the smell,' he said and laughed.
'No. Duncan only worries until he has seen his mother against
the strange background. After he has seen her, he can imagine
her, you see.'

'Jock, how do you know so much about how they tick?' I
asked. 'Duncan is such a silent little boy.'

'I suppose one gets some sort of instinct but I found this out
about Dunk when Gee was born. He went off his food, even
that time, although he was only eighteen months old. Then, on
the third day we all went in to see Shona – Granda and Granny
were here at the time. After that, after Dunk had seen her, he
was all right. They are queer little brutes and I never can get
over the fact that no two of them are alike. I have a hundred
and twenty on the school roll and they are all absolutely distinct
people. We look on this as a commonplace but it isn't really. It
is a miracle, this perpetual renewal in such infinite variety.'

When we reached the hospital and I stood looking down at
the new baby in the basket-cot, I thought again of what my
brother had said. Here was this scrap with red hair, like his
father and his brother and he had eyes, ears, a nose and a
mouth like everybody else and, yet, he was utterly unlike anybody. I felt over-awed by his majestic differentness and
individuality.

'Pick him up, Janet and have a proper look at him,' said
Shona from the bed.

'Shall I?' I hesitated, then bent over the cot and put my hands about the tiny body. In that moment, he opened blueish milky eyes, seemed to look at me and made a snuffly little noise before putting a tiny fist against his mouth and closing his eyes again. 'Shone, he spoke to me!' I said and they all laughed but they were not to know that I had fallen into an ocean of love of a kind that I had never known to exist.

'What is his name to be, Shona?' Roddy asked while I sat holding the baby.

'We won't talk about names as yet,' Jock said.

'John has a thing about names,' Shona told us, smiling. 'He won't talk about names or register their births until the very last moment.'

'Why, Jock?' Roddy asked.

I was only half-hearing what they were saying, the words coming dimly from beyond the trance that enclosed the baby and me but my brother's reply, spoken shyly and unwillingly, came through to me.

'As soon as you name them, they stop being mysteries and turn into people,' he said.

'People are pretty good mysteries, too,' Roddy said.

My brother got up, came over to look down at the child in my arms and spoke with his back to the others. 'Yes, but not wondrous mysteries trailing clouds of glory,' he said. Shona, feeling I think that Roddy was probing too deeply into Jock's reserves, now said: 'I heard that Liz had a smacking yesterday, Janet.'

I was astonished at this. Without being conscious of it, I discovered now that I had made an estimate of the characters of the children and this estimate did not include the likelihood of Liz 'clyping' to her mother of the débâcle of the morning before.

'They told you?' I asked.

'Not exactly. I asked who had had a smacking from Aunt Janet yet and the boys told me that Liz had but that you had made a mistake because it was *they* who should have been smacked.' She smiled. 'Dunk put forward the theory that maybe you would get better at knowing who to smack when you have had a little more practice.'

'But I gather that you caught up with Dunk and Gee in the end,' my brother said. 'There seemed to be a general satisfaction that justice had not only been done but had been seen to be done and that is the main thing.'

When we left the hospital, we went to the home of Shona's parents and, once again, I was overcome by that horrid feeling of being an outsider. My brother was dearly loved in this house which he had been visiting since his university days when he first began to court Shona. Mrs Murray was an older version of her daughter, a born mother, fat and comfortable in her older age, happy and smiling with her grandsons about her knees, but I felt that she loved my brother more, even, than her own daughters or the children. It might be that he had done something to replace for her the two sons that she had lost, one as a child and one in a flying accident shortly after the war. On the other side of the fire sat Mr Murray, with Liz leaning against the arm of his chair and if Mrs Murray looked on my brother with doting pride, there was no doubt as to where the big old man's allegiance lay. He had an arm about Liz and his big hand was gently stroking the pleats of her kilt while he smiled round at us all.

'Sheila is not back yet?' Jock asked.

'She should be here any minute,' Granny said. 'Liz, put the kettle on like a clever girl.'

Shona was the eldest of the family and Sheila was the youngest – the two boys had come in between – and when I had last seen her, she had been a girl at high school, so that I was unprepared for the trim young woman who shortly arrived. She was about twenty-five and my beautiful Aunt Kate at that age now flashed across my mind. Shona was pretty and had beautiful eyes but her looks were of the quiet unremarkable sort and her appeal lay in the sweetness and gentleness that emanated from her. Not so Sheila, whose dark red curling hair and svelte figure struck the eye like a blow, dazzling it so that she seemed to be surrounded by a nimbus of colour. She was a Queen's Nurse and the tailored navy blue coat and demure white collar of the dress underneath made her own colouring all the more intense and startling and my feeling of being outside was increased by the fact that all these other people, used to Sheila, their eyes dimmed by custom, seemed to find her quite unremarkable. But not quite all. I saw a hot light of appreciation, to put it euphemistically, burning in the dark eyes of Roddy Maclean and it was as if a little red warning light clicked on in my mind. Roddy, wealthy, gifted, handsome and loose-living was out of place in this cosy conventional household. I hoped that Sheila's quick wit would rise to her own protection.

I do not know how it was manoeuvred – there may have been no manoeuvring at all and the invitation may have risen out of the simple innocent hospitality of Granda and Granny who loved young people – but when it was time for us to come away, my brother drove us all home and Roddy stayed behind, although Jock would have to drive into town again to spend the night.

When the children were out of the way and my brother was about to leave for town again, I cornered him in the hall and said: 'Keep an eye on Roddy Maclean, Jock. That one is no good to somebody like Sheila.'

'Roddy? Sheila? Why not?'

'As old Mattha at Ballydendran would say: When it comes to the Sheilas, Roddy is all cock and no conscience.'

'Don't worry about that, Janet,' he said. 'You are thinking of her in terms of Shona. Sheila is as tough as old boots and as hard as nails. She will be all right.'

'Well, I have spoken the gypsy's warning anyway,' I said and went upstairs to the children.

They were already in bed and Liz greeted me with: 'We had baths before we went to town so we just cleaned teeth and washed hands. Look here, do you *really* know about Channatt and the ferret?'

'I think so,' I said.

'Then tell about the day in Miss Tulloch's shop.'

'Yes, tell.'

'Yes.' Little Gee had been nearly asleep but he sat up now, his eyes propped open and enormous.

'Once upon a time, long long ago, poor Miss Tulloch had rats in her grocery shop,' I began sitting down on the edge of the boys' bed, 'and Tom and George arranged that – that *Channatt* and Angus and Fly should go down to catch them for her.'

Liz frowned hideously, jumped out of her bed and came to stand in front of me, her eyes level with mine and full of doubt and accusation. 'Who were Angus and Fly?' she asked.

'Channatt's ferret and her dog.'

'The ferret was Angus and the dog was Fly?'

'Yes.'

50

'George and Tom didn't tell us that.'

'They just said ferret, *danged* ferret,' said Duncan.

'Yes, *danged* ferret,' Gee corroborated.

'Angus and Fly,' said Liz, sitting down beside me and staring dreamily at the opposite wall. 'Just fancy that. Go on.'

From her tone, I gathered that a concession had been made
to the effect that not only did I know about Channatt and her
ferret but that I also might know more about them than these
authorities Tom and George and with confidence I went on to
tell the whole absurd tale of that afternoon long ago when
Angus erupted from a hidden rathole inside the shop, which
was full of women, who all began to scream and climb on to
anything they could, including George and Tom who happened
to arrive at the peak of the drama. When I had finished, all
three sighed with satisfaction at what they seemed to think was
a good rendering of a favourite tale and then Liz said: 'Do you
know about any of Channatt's places?'

'Places?'

'Yes. She had a Thinking Place and a Picnic Pond.'

'Yes and a Bluebell Bank and a Stalwart Tree and a Strip
of Herbage,' I said, 'and lots more.'

The three pairs of eyes looked at one another, holding a
silent parliament and I said: 'She and Tom and George used
to hold Parlyments, too.'

'Tell,' said Liz.

I got up. 'No. Another evening. Gee must go to sleep now.'

'Tomorrow evening?' Gee asked.

'Yes, tomorrow?' said Duncan.

'Tomorrow,' Liz said conclusively, hopping across the floor
on one foot to her own bed. 'Good night, Aunt Janet.'

Before I went downstairs, I went to my room and sat in the
bay window that looked out over a monotonous undulating
countryside that was one vast sea of waving grain but, superimposed on this there was the view of the firth and the hills to
the north that could be seen from Reachfar. I felt now that I
was not one person but two, the Janet of the present and the
Channatt of long ago who had danced down the Strip of
Herbage. There was a deep enrichment in this but, at the same
time, there was a frightening consciousness of life's amazing
diversity and diffuseness along with an awed awareness of the
flexibility of time and space as held in the memory. Just as, in
the dimension of space, I could see the firth and hills of Reach-

far superimposed on the Aberdeenshire wheat and barley fields, so was I, at this moment within myself, the Channatt of long ago, the plain leggy child of seven or eight, superimposed on the matron of forty-six who sat on the window seat. With awe, I contemplated the number of places and people I had seen and known and, with wonder, I gazed on all this that was continued in my memory. I was not, even, only two people. I was the sum of an infinite number of Janets, a Janet for every second through which I had lived and these three children in the room next door were creating more and more Janets with every word they spoke to me. The Hungry Generation, my brother called them, who would eat their elders away if permitted but they were also a feeding generation, giving to us and re-creating us out of their own abundant, questing tumultuous life.

In the long light of the northern summer evening, George and Tom were out in the garden, busy with Dutch hoes in a large plot of cabbages. From the back door, I stood watching them for a moment. They were nearer to eighty than to seventy, I knew but, from here, looking at them from behind, they might have been two men in middle life. The light, although bright, had now the yellowness of evening and it was gilding the white hair that showed under their tweed caps as the spare, tall upright figures hoed side by side down the rows of cabbages, working with the effortless rhythmic ease that had always been theirs. Upstairs, I had been amazed and somewhat appalled at the fullness and diversity of my own memory but what was my memory compared with the memories of these two old men? Serene contentment was all about them as they worked among the earth and the growing things that they loved and some of that serenity and contentment flowed from them across the evening garden to wrap me all around. My mind moving from the three children in the room upstairs to those two old men among the cabbages, I felt myself to be among the most blessed of women, secure in my place in time between the past and the future.

George and Tom turned at the end of the plot to come up the next two rows, saw me and I went over to them.

'Is the clan sleeping?' George asked.

'Yes.'

'Were they asking about Reachfar?' Tom enquired.

'Yes. I had to tell them about the ferret in Miss Tulloch's shop.'

'Aye. They are very fond of that yarn. As fond as you used to be of the one about Uncle Kenny and Uncle Farquhar running down the hill in their night-shirts,' he said and I remembered what a shock it had been to me, when I was in my teens, to discover that Uncle Kenny and Uncle Farquhar had been real people, uncles of my grandmother. These men had been dead before I made this discovery that they had once lived and were not creatures of fable but for the children upstairs I, who had once let my ferret loose in Miss Tulloch's shop, had lived on to impinge on their own lives. But, in another and in the real sense, I had not lived on. They had decided that it was not I, Aunt Janet, who had let the ferrett loose but Channatt, who had lived once upon a time and long ago and they were right. The 'I' of today would not enjoy wearing a ferret round my neck like a small, live fur stole and would derive no satisfaction from slaughtering bolting rats with a stout stick.

Roddy had not come back when we went up to bed but, shortly after one in the morning, I awoke to hear him come quietly upstairs and go to his room. The night silence overtook the house again but, since Roddy had come in, the silence was less complete. There was an unease in it that had not been there before. I slept fitfully, waking in a succession of starts until about four o'clock when I sat up and put on the light. For a short time, I stared at the wall, reviling my rampant imagination but, in the end, I got up, went out on to the landing, switched on the light and looked around me. It was then that the unease identified itself. I heard a shuddering little sound from the children's room where the door stood ajar. I tiptoed in and switched on the lamp by the boys' bed. Liz and Duncan were lost in sleep but Gee's big eyes, wet with tears and wide with fright looked up at me.

'Gee, what is the matter?' I asked, laying my hand on the bedclothes.

With a wince and a suppressed scream, he jerked away from under my hand and tears began to flood down his cheeks.

'Gee, darling, what *is* it?' I asked.

'Aunt Janet,' he whispered and sobbed to me, 'I got the most terrible sore place.'

'Where, pettie?'

'On my bot.'

'Look, come to my room,' I said, turning back the bedclothes

53

and he came gently out on to the floor while Duncan slept peacefully on.

Holding the seat of his pyjama trousers away from his bottom, Gee limped across the landing and into my room where I put him face downwards on the bed and, horrified, I saw on his right buttock a pulsing festering wound about two inches long, with a livid purple stain spreading from it across the milky skin.

'Gee, why didn't you tell us about this?' I asked distractedly which made my voice sound angry so that he began to cry pitifully.

'Daddy said to be good and not bother Aunt Janet,' he sobbed.

'Darling, you are *not* bothering me. You should have told. How did you do it?'

'Dunk and me was sliding down the roof of the shed yesterday. There was a nail.'

I felt that my head was going to burst as I put a pillow on either side of him and put the eiderdown across them to make a sort of tent. If this had happened in St Jago, the child would be dead of tetanus by now and all because 'Daddy had said to be good'. I picked up the telephone. 'Ring Doctor Nancy,' Shona had said. 'She will come day or night. The gang and she are great chums. The number is on the built-in pad under the telephone.' Within fifteen minutes, the doctor was coming quietly upstairs, a small terrier-like woman with shaggy iron-grey hair above a shaggy shabby tweed suit – a very unlikely looking doctor, I thought, but there was nothing unlikely about her handling of the child.

'It is a terrible awful sore, isn't it, Gee?' she asked, looking at the wound.

'Yes, Doctor Nancy,' he sobbed as George and Tom, those light old sleepers, came into the room.

The doctor nodded a greeting to them as she took from her bag a rubber bottle with a spray nozzle.

'But I am going to let the sore out, Gee,' she said, 'and catch it and then we'll make a fire and burn it all up. Now, I am going to put stuff on it and it will be very cold. Ready?'

He was very brave. I sat on the bed with his head and hands in my lap and he gave a violent shiver and a little squeak as the anaesthetic struck his skin but as it took effect and the pain

54

was numbed, he gave a little giggle and wriggled as he tried to look round at his bottom.

'Hide your eyes in Aunt's lap,' Doctor Nancy said as she took a little scalpel from a case. 'These sores don't come out if anybody is looking.'

'Tom and George, shut your eyes,' Gee commanded. 'Aunt Janet, shut your eyes.'

But I did not shut my eyes. I watched as the scalpel came along and the pus came boiling out on to the gauze and very soon there was only a clean red scar, ready for the dressing. When this had been strapped on, Doctor Nancy handed me a little box of tablets with instructions to give him one every four hours and then she said: 'Now then, Gee, we'll burn up this sore, the horrible thing. George, have you a match?'

George handed her the matches from my table and she gave them to Gee while she carried the bundle of gauze to the fireplace and put it in. There was a sudden irruption and Liz and Duncan were in the room.

'You bunch of sneaks,' said Liz, 'having Doctor Nancy here behind our backs!'

'Yes, blooming sneaks!' said Duncan.

'What in the name of my Highland forefathers is the matter with Gee's behind?' Liz asked, seeing the bare bottom with its bulging dressing.

'It had a sore in it,' said Gee, 'but Doctor Nancy's got it out and we are going to burn it up, so there!'

'Strike a match and set fire to it, Gee,' said Doctor Nancy and as the gauze came alight, she chanted: 'Sore, sore from Gee's bum, Go to blazes up the lum!' All three took up the chant, dancing round in a ring on the hearth rug until nothing remained of the 'sore' but a few shreds of black ash.

'Now, get back to bed, the lot of you,' said Doctor Nancy and all of them, including Tom and George, melted away before that commanding eye.

'Would you like a cup of tea?' I asked her, feeling suddenly weak.

'I wouldn't mind,' she said, closing her bag.

Switching on the kettle in the kitchen, I said: 'I am sorry for calling you out like this, Doctor Nancy. Maybe I should have waited till the morning?'

'With children,' she said. 'never wait till anything.'

'I have none of my own,' I told her. 'I was nurse to a baby

for a few months and then governess to an older child for a time when I was young but that is all the experience I have had. This lot look like being the death of me.'

She laughed. 'No fear of them. They will keep you alive for their own sake, to cook their food and so on, although you may go a little short on sleep. Have you been in to see the baby yet?'

'Yes. He is a beauty.'

'Yes. Your brother and sister-in-law are very good at them.'

When she had gone, it was nearly six o'clock and there seemed to be no point in going back to bed for sleep would have been impossible, the three in the room next to mine being awake for the day. I dressed, got a glass of water from the bathroom and went in to give Gee his tablet.

'I told him,' said Liz smugly, 'that he shouldn't hide his torn trousers. This just shows you what comes of being cheating.'

'You shut up, Liz Sandison!' Duncan said. 'It was two against one for hiding the trousers. You are just jealous because Doctor Nancy didn't come to *you*.'

'Yes, jealous!' said Gee, turning his bottom towards her and caressing the dressing with his hand.

'I am *not* jealous! And this voting thing is all wrong. I am eight and you two are only nine between the both of the two of you. I should have *two* votes.'

'You should *not*!'

'No, *not*!'

'Aunt Janet, she can't have two votes, can she?' Duncan appealed.

'No. Democracy is founded on one person, one vote,' I said.

'What's democracy?' Liz asked.

'The form of government that we have in this country.'

'Democracy nothing! We have the Queen!' she protested. 'Me and the Queen – we have the same names!'

Looking down at her, I wondered if she could be the reincarnation of the bishop who had earned a royal rebuke for his use of the phrase 'Ego et meus rex' but before I could word a rebuke for her egotism, Duncan had put the lampshade on his head, had the eiderdown round his shoulders and was strutting along the floor, waggling his bottom so that his robe swayed behind him.

56

'Is it not passing great to be a queen and ride in triumph through Persepolis?' he declaimed.

Liz sprang at him, the lampshade crown went flying and the two of them were on the floor, clawing at one another in a tangle of eiderdown. I hauled them apart and threw one on one bed and one on the other.

'Stop that or I'll beat the daylights out of both of you!' I said.

'Him saying that!' Liz said, viciously like a cat spitting. 'Cheeky brat!'

'Yah, puddin' face!' said her brother.

'Now, look, get dressed,' I said. 'Gee, Doctor Nancy said to wear your kilt because it won't interfere with your sore.'

'My kilt? Not got a sore. Got a dressing. What if I tear my kilt? They are very expensive.'

'If you tear anything more or get any more sores, I – I'll run away straight back to St Jago,' I said with utter conviction but feeling that they would not care whether I ran away or not. They stared at me, Liz and Duncan who had taken their pyjamas off stark naked.

'But what about Reachfar?' Liz asked.

'Yes, Reachfar?'

'Reachfar?' came the second echo.

'We got a lot more to know about Reachfar,' came Liz again. 'Yes, a lot.'

'I'll wear my kilt. I won't tear it,' Gee promised.

'Although you can't expect life to be *entirely* trouble free,' Liz warned me. 'You have to take the good with the bad but we'll do our best.'

'I will tell you lots about Reachfar,' I promised and left them to dress.

When they had had breakfast, they fed the guinea pigs and then disappeared into the shrubbery where they spent the entire forenoon, Liz making no offers to help in the kitchen today, while George and Tom picked still more fruit. Fat Mary, having done her work upstairs, came down to the scullery and wheeled out the washing machine, which reminded me that, somewhere in the house, was hidden a pair of torn blood-stained trousers, so I went out to the garden path. I could hear the voices among the thick tangle of the shrubs and was arrested by the words, spoken solemnly in the voice of Liz: 'I baptise thee Angus. Amen' and then in her normal decisive tones: 'Put him back in his hutch, Dunk. It's not like having a real ferret but he'll have to do because Dad said no blinking ferrets.'

'What about Fly?' Duncan asked. 'What if Dad says no blinking dogs?'

'Yes, what?' came the voice of Gee.

'He won't,' came the decisive tone. 'He doesn't like ferrets but he likes dogs and with the baby and everything he would give us an elephant I shouldn't wonder.'

Liz, I thought, was already versed in the theory of gold-digging. 'Gee!' I called.

'Yes, Aunt Janet?'

'Where did you hide your torn trousers? Come and get them for Fat Mary to wash.'

The two boys came out of the shrubbery and Duncan put a guinea pig in its hutch while Gee went upstairs and returned with the trousers.

My brother came home to lunch that day and did not go back to the hospital until time for Shona's afternoon tea and I felt no surprise when, at a pause in the conversation, Liz put down her pudding spoon and became suddenly astoundingly beautiful and winning as she looked at her father and said: 'Dad, we wanted to ask you something.' It was a little like watching a fencing match for, after one sharp glance at her, my brother looked down at his plate and said in a dry, non-committal tone: 'Yes, Liz?' She knew her father well enough not to beat about the bush but all her persuasiveness was in her voice as she said: 'Dunk and Gee and I would like it very much if we had a dog.'

'Not a very big dog,' said Duncan.

'Not a expensive dog,' said Gee, who was eating standing up because of his dressing.

My brother looked up at them. 'Just a piece of dog, you mean,' he said. 'George and Tom, what do you think?'

'People are the better of a dog,' said Tom.

'I like to see a dog about a place myself,' George said. 'Tom and I have no dogs now and we miss them real bad sometimes.'

'Then I'll tell you what we'll do,' Jock said. 'After Mum and the baby come home, I'll take you all into town and we'll go to the dogs' home and choose a dog.'

'Not till then?' said Liz.

'A whole week?' said Duncan.

'But we *need* him, Dad!' Gee protested.

58

'Now, you must be reasonable – ' Jock was beginning when Roddy said: 'I'll come into town after lunch if you like, Jock. We could go to the dogs' home and I'll bring the clan back while you go on to Shona.'

'That is very good of you, Roddy,' my brother said but I said firmly: 'The clan has to be back by half past five, Roddy – not one in the morning.'

He turned a dark, mischievous knowing glance upon me. 'Keep your shirt on, Auntie,' he said. 'We'll be back by five,' but what he meant was: 'Yes, I am interested in Sheila and it is none of your business,' and he knew that I knew that this was what he meant.

'You two had better come too,' my brother said to Tom and George. 'You are the best dog choosers.'

'Tom will go,' George said. 'I will stop here and give Aunt Janet a hand with the berries.'

In the course of the afternoon, while George and I made jam, I said: 'You haven't a dog at Jemima Cottage now, George?'

'No. You know how Jean carries on about the house and her carpets. There wouldna be a moment's peace.'

'What happened to the dogs when you left Reachfar?'

'We only had Tom's old Fan and my old Moss by then. We gave them to one of the Dunchory shepherds but they died soon after.' He tilted the plate that held a sample of jam. 'I think this stuff will do, Janet,' he said.

I was silent while I potted the jam, while I tried to imagine George's and Tom's lives with my stepmother at Achcraggan since my father died. Jean was a woman of few likes or loves. Indeed, as far as I knew, the only person she had ever felt liking for was my father, because he had given her the security of marriage. He had always been able to keep her hysterical temper within bounds because, I think, she valued the security he gave her too highly to jeopardise it by annoying him but now that this one restraining influence was gone, I knew that her natural venom and malice would be having free rein.

When George and I had put yet another large pan of fruit and sugar on the stove and were having a cup of tea, I said: 'George, just how *are* things between you and Tom and Jean?'

'Och, don't you be worrying yourself about us, Janet. Tom and I can manage her fine. When she gets right past herself altogether, we just walk out and leave her and we get our dinner

59

with Mrs Shaw or Mrs Henderson or one o' the other neighbours.'

'Old bitch!' I said.

'She is all o' that right enough but, in a way, it is easier for Tom and me since she got the rheumatics. She needs us for carrying in the water and the coal and the like.'

'The water? What do you mean – carrying in the water?'

'Och, the tank bursted last February in the terrible frost we had so we carry in the water from the well now.'

'But George Reachfar that is nonsense! We must get the tank repaired. Is the pump all right?'

'Just so-so.'

'As soon as you go back, George, you will have the whole thing attended to and send Twice and me the account.'

'No, I will not do that and neither will Tom,' he said.

'Now, George, be reasonable. You can't –'

'Tom and I will not be reasonable with Jean that is not herself reasonable,' he said firmly. 'Your father left her well provided for and while she lives in *your* house she should keep it in repair but she will not spend a penny on it.'

'But it is you and Tom who are suffering!'

'Tom and I are not the suffering kind. When she gets past herself, we just walk out and leave her, as I told you, leave her without water or coal or damn' all. It fairly brings her to her senses. Janet, Tom and I could put in a new tank and pump tomorrow without help from anybody but we are not going to do it unless Jean goes shares with us and that she won't do.'

'Then *I'll* put in the new tank and –'

'No, Janet. You leave this to Tom and me. You and Twice have more to do with what you've got than spend it on that old bitch. Besides, in a year or two the County is going to bring a proper water main through Achcraggan and the sensible thing to do is to hang on and get connected to it.'

'George, I am not happy about this. Why don't you move over here to Jock and Shona and leave Jean to it?'

'We won't do that. Not yet, anyway. It would be different if anything came over either of us. But for the meantime, we will stop there and keep the place in order and we'll keep old Jean in order too. Do you mind on yon row at Reachfar the day the heifer was born? The day Jean threw the knife?'

As always with Tom and George and me, we broke away from serious thought of Jean by laughing over the various 'rows' she had made in the course of her bad-tempered life but I made a mental note to tell my brother about the burst tank although I had little faith that Jock could do more than I could to change the mind of George.

George and Tom had always contrived to give the impression that all was right with their world and because of this attitude of theirs, their good health and their seeming agelessness, I felt that I and my brother too had tended to lose sight of the fact that they were nearly eighty. Also, I had not seen Jean for years, so that I tended to forget that she would constitute a strain on men in their prime and much more on men like Tom and George who, all their lives, had lived in the well-balanced and what they would call 'reasonable' atmosphere of Reachfar. It was because the bonds of Reachfar were so close that they continued to live with Jean at Jemima Cottage, because the house was mine, inherited from a great-aunt but an even more valid reason for their staying there was that my father's much-loved garden might not fall away into ruin. For most of their lives, these two men had served the family first and themselves second and they were still serving in this way and I felt that I, with my full and happy life with Twice and Jock, with his happy and even fuller life with Shona and his children were guilty of selfishness. We had no right to speak of Hungry Generations. We ourselves had taken and were still taking a great deal from George and Tom. Punctually at half past five, Roddy's car stopped outside and the clan was in the kitchen, arriving in reverse order, Gee carrying a hairy black puppy, Duncan following and Liz coming last.

'Aunt Janet, George,' said Gee, 'this is him. And he belongs to me first and Dunk second and Liz last. Dad said so.'

'It's on account of Gee not being the youngest any more,' Duncan explained.

'And having a dressing,' Gee put in.

'And me being the oldest,' said Liz. 'Don't you like his collar and lead that Roddy bought for him? Tartan, we thought –'

' – because he's a sorta Aberdeen terrier,' said Duncan.

'But only sorta,' said Gee with pride. 'Dad says he is mostly just dog.'

'He is a fine fellow,' said George, 'but put him down on the floor and not be nursing him like a doll. The beast is due his proper place.'

The pup, put down, at once made a puddle on the linoleum, sniffed at it proudly and walked under the table, while the three children giggled, so I picked him up by the scruff of the neck, slapped his bottom, said: 'Dirty fellow' and put him outside and shut the door.

'Aw, Aunt Janet, you cruel thing!' came the protest as the pup began to whimper.

'Just leave him for a minute so that he'll mind on being shut out,' Tom said.

'Liz,' I said, 'get a cloth and wipe up that puddle.'

'Not me! He's Gee's!'

'You will take turn about at wiping up,' I said.

'And I was always hearing about it being polite to let ladies go first,' said George.

'If I wipe up then, I let him in again,' Liz said.

'Fair enough,' I agreed.

'What about a name for him?' Roddy asked.

There was a sharp silence until Liz, the spokesman in all crises, looked up over her floor cloth, 'We will take our time about deciding,' she said conclusively, 'like Daddy with the babies.'

'Supper,' said Fat Mary.

There was a threat of trouble at bedtime when I said that people went upstairs but puppies stayed down and that this pup would sleep in a cardboard box for the time being, in the back hall, but the family diplomats and peacemakers averted the battle.

'At proper places like Reachfar,' said Tom, 'beasts do not go up the stairs in a house.'

'It is only in nursery rhymes and such childishness that beasts such as geese go up the stairs,' said George, 'the dirty skittery brutes.'

'Reachfar!' the children shouted in chorus. 'Come along, Aunt Janet!'

When Gee had had his tablet and had discovered that he could lie down on his dressing without feeling any 'sore', I began: 'Once upon a time, long long ago at Reachfar, Channatt, George and Tom went down the burn to pick brambles. Now, quite often, when they had a special job to do, they made a special song to do it to and this time they had a song that went to the tune of "Onward Christian Soldiers". Do you know that hymn?'

'Yes. We have it at Sunday School.'

'All right. I'll tell you the song at the end.'

After I had told how Channatt went down into the deep gorge of the Reachfar Burn and made a noise like a bodach that scared Tom and George out of their wits so that they began to run for home, all of which was very well received, Liz said: 'And now the song.'

'At this time,' I said, 'Channatt was just starting to learn Latin so there are some Latin words in the song.'

'Channatt learned Latin?' Liz enquired.

'Of course she did, stupid!' said Duncan. 'She learned *every*thing. She was so clever, she – '

' – won a real golden brooch for cleverness!'

'She did not, you pair of muddle-heads!' Liz shouted indignantly. 'It was Aunt *Janet* here that won a gold medal and it will likely be left to *me* in her will, so there!'

Their tempers rising, they had forgotten my presence it seemed. All were in the boys' bed, Liz at the bottom, facing her brothers and they were leaning angrily towards one another, as Liz shouted that George and Tom had told her how one day the gold medal would probably be hers.

'Lies! All lies!' Duncan yelled, enraged at her superiority so that, suddenly, he took a fearful plunge. 'Channatt and Aunt Janet are the same person, you damn' fool!' he shouted and there was a second of charged silence which was broken by the low savage voice of Liz, speaking very slowly: 'By my Highland forefathers, I'll *kill* you!' she said but, quickly as she sprang, I for once moved more quickly and pinned her back against the end of the bed as Gee, frightened by a degree of rage greater than he had yet experienced, I think, began to cry.

Sitting in the middle of the bed with one hand on Liz's chest and the other against Duncan's, holding them apart, I said: 'You are both wrong. Channatt won the gold brooch set with pearls at school and I won the silly old medal.'

All six eyes blinked at me and then stared with disbelief.

'I can prove it, the medal I mean,' I added recklessly. They were stunned into silence now. 'Just a minute.'

I went to my room and to the drawer that held my small jewel case. I have little jewellery other than a collection of brooches, among these a small gold one set with pearls which I seldom wear but, under all the others, was the gold medal engraved with my name. Carrying it, I went back to the children's room.

'Here is the medal,' I said and handed it to Gee, while the other two heads crowded round it.

'Janet Elizabeth Sandison,' Gee read aloud from the obverse, 'Dux of Cairnton Academy, 1926.'

'Cairnton Academy?' Liz pounced on the essential factor. 'You went to Cairnton Academy?'

'Yes.'

Turning, she gave Duncan a quick slap on the ear. 'Channatt went to Achcraggan School!' she said triumphantly and to me: 'Didn't she?'

'Yes.'

'So Channatt and Aunt Janet are *not* the same!' she shouted at Duncan who was looking at me doubtfully still.

'No. Channatt and I are not the same,' I confirmed, trying not to sound regretful for it was sad but true and of the very essence of life that 'Channatt' who had attended Achcraggan School and the old Aunt Janet who sat on the bed were not 'the same'.

Duncan, convinced now, took the opportunity of his sister's diverted attention to clout her on the ear before he rescued a remnant of honour from the argument by asking: 'But she learned Latin, didn't she?'

'Oh, yes,' I confirmed, 'she learned Latin.'

'Just fancy that,' said Liz. 'I had kind of thought that I wouldn't bother with that old Latin when I went to High School,' she added thoughtfully and then broke in on her thought by repeating: 'Now, the song,' as if the intervening storm had never happened.

'Bella is a dealer's wife, bellum is a war,
    Magnum Bonum is a turnip growing on Reachfar;
    Puella is a girl like me, homo is a man,
    We are picking berries for making bramble jam!'

I sang to the tune of 'Onward Christian Soldiers' and then: 'Let's all sing it and when we get to "Puella is a girl like me" Liz sings that by herself like Channatt and Duncan and Gee sing "Homo is a man" as Tom and George used to do.'

When they had ended their chorus, Liz hopped across the room and got into bed. 'Aunt Janet,' she said, 'I think Reachfar is just wonderful.'

'A sorta miracle,' said Duncan.

'It clouds and clouds of glory, like babies,' said Gee.

'Good night,' I said.

Half-way down the stairs, I paused and recognised the deep general truth out of which their halting childish words arose. This myth of Reachfar that they were creating for themselves was something that they needed, something that had kinship with a deep need in all humanity. They felt the need for life to contain something that was wonderful, a sorta miracle that had clouds and clouds of glory and, above all, permanence. This myth that was rooted in the past, beyond the horizon of memory was a wispy tenuous thing that came and went in the mind like a rainbow in the April sky over Reachfar hill but it had, yet, the strength to be a bulwark which could defend the spirit and hold it unshaken amidst the erupting chaos of growing up and pressing on through day-to-day life.

Chapter IV

'The Rainbow comes and goes,
And lovely is the Rose,
The moon doth with delight
Look round her when the heavens are bare,
Waters on a starry night
Are beautiful and fair;
The sunshine is a glorious birth;
But yet I know, where'er I go,
That there hath past away a glory from the earth.'

I SLEPT very heavily that night, after the long tiring day and was awakened about seven the next morning by the tune of 'Onward Christian Soldiers' but very soon the song gave way to angry shouts and, wearily, I put on my dressing-gown and went into the room next door before a real scrimmage could develop.

'What in the world are you quarrelling about now?' I asked.

'It's her,' said Duncan, 'bossy brat!'

'Bossy brat,' Gee echoed, 'always singing *our* bit.'

'You are *not* Tom and George!' Liz countered.

'Then you are not Channatt,' said Duncan, 'is she, Aunt Janet?'

I felt that my head had begun to go round, gathering momentum and describing widening and ever widening circles. They seemed to take everything and endow it with a weird and unpredictable life of their own.

'I am Channatt!' Liz shouted, 'you two *can't* be Tom and George because Tom and George are across the landing in their beds and you two can't be them when they are here to be themselves.'

The boys looked nonplussed and no wonder. I was in something of a muddle myself, faced with this exercise in the logic of limbo as my brother called it when I was only half awake but, as well as looking nonplussed, the boys had a sudden defeated air while Liz looked smugly triumphant which annoyed me. I have never liked bullies and Liz had a marked tendency to bully these brothers of hers.

'If you mean the Reachfar Tom and George,' I said, 'the Tom and George across the landing are not them.'

'Don't talk stupid,' said Liz in an uppish tone, taking off her pyjama top and reaching for her vest. 'Tom and George were always at Reachfar.'

'Not those two through there,' I said. 'How could two old men like those two break in horses and do all the Reachfar things?'

With the vest in a ring round her neck, Liz looked at me with startled eyes and I pressed my advantage. 'The Reachfar Tom and George just *aren't* any more, just like Channatt isn't. They are all memory people. And Reachfar itself isn't any more either.'

'So Gee and I *can* be George and Tom, can't we?' Duncan asked, quick to see that Liz had been out-argued.

'Yes, can't we?' came the echo.

'Of course and Liz can be Channatt.'

'Yes,' said Duncan, striding over to his sister and slapping her on the bare diaphragm, 'and you will sing your own bit of the song and we will sing ours.'

Liz gave him a resounding clout on the ear and said: 'Don't you hit *me*, you little squirt!'

'And don't you hit Dunk!' said Gee, taking a swing at her.

'Don't anybody hit anybody,' I said, 'or I'll wallop the lot of you. Get dressed and hurry downstairs and let that pup out.'

They retired with their clothes to different parts of the room, their backs to one another but after a few seconds, Liz began to sing: 'Bella is a dealer's wife — ' and I retired to my own room to dress, leaving them in full chorus and accord.

The speed with which they went from rage to glee was in itself exhausting. I was brushing my hair when there were three thumps on the door and a cry of 'Open up!' and when I obeyed, Liz was there with a tray that held sugar, milk and a cup and saucer, Duncan with a small teapot and Gee with two biscuits on a plate. 'Do you like upstairs tea?' Liz enquired. 'Mum does.'

'I like it very much. Thank you.'

They arranged the things on the tray, went out and shut the door and as I looked down at the result of their unpredictable thought for me I felt, momentarily, that I was the most beloved and cared-for being in the world.

By the time I went downstairs, they were doing their

washing-up while the pup was tearing a newspaper to shreds in the middle of the scullery floor.

'You wouldn't think he could have held it all,' said Liz.

'Who? What?'

'Five puddles and two heaps he had in the back hall when we came down.'

'The pup? Yes, they can hold an amazing amount. Have you cleaned up?'

'Yes. Two lots each,' said Gee.

'And three for me,' said Duncan, 'but it's Gee's turn next.'

'And we smacked him but only a little bit and put him out but only a little bit,' said Liz.

'I had better give him something to eat,' I said.

'He has had breakfast. Porridge –'

' – and bread and marmalade –'

' – and milk and half a banana,' Gee ended, as the pup made a puddle.

'Gee, your turn,' I said. 'But maybe you had better let me feed him. I don't think bananas are very good for dogs.'

'Not?' said Liz. 'They are very rich in vitamins.'

'He seems to have plenty of vitality without,' I said as the pup fell upon Gee's floorcloth with savage growls. 'There is the postman. Bring in the letters, Duncan.'

When Duncan came back, they began to sort the mail. 'John Sandison, Esquire. Roderick Maclean, Esquire. Mrs Alexander. Mr Roderick Maclean –' I opened my letter from Twice, transported at once to St Jago where it had been written and did not hear the discussion among the children until Liz tugged at my arm. 'There is a letter here for Mr S. T. Bennett, Aunt Janet. We don't know any Mr Bennetts.'

'It is for Roddy,' I said and went on reading.

'How can it be for Roddy when it is for Mr S. T. Bennett?' she asked indignantly. 'I wish you would pay attention!'

'I wish *you* would let me pay attention to this letter from Uncle Twice,' I said impatiently. 'Now, be quiet for a moment.'

I read to the end of my letter and when I looked up they were standing in a row, staring at me, Liz holding the letter.

'S. T. Bennett is Roddy,' I said. They merely went on staring, disbelief emanating in strong waves from them. 'Roddy is a writer, as you know,' I explained, 'and he writes under the name of S. T. Bennett.'

The disbelief became even more palpable. 'All of us three

are writers, even Gee,' said Liz. 'Gee is a very good writer although he is only four and we didn't get a new not-our-own name when we started writing.'

I was the one to stare now, baffled for a moment by their angry logic until I was inspired to say: 'Roddy is S. T. Bennett sometimes like you being Channatt and Duncan and Gee being Tom and George sometimes.'

The disbelief disappeared. This made sense, apparently. 'It is his Just-fancy-that?' Liz enquired.

'We didn't know that Roddy had a Just-fancy-that,' said Duncan.

'No, we didn't,' Gee agreed but now Liz clapped her dramatic hand to her forehead and said: 'It isn't a Just-fancy-that at all. And he doesn't have it just because he can write. He is a writer of *books* and S. T. Bennett is his pissyoudohnim,' with which she put the envelope with Roddy's other mail and all three and the pup departed into the garden.

Feeling that one more crisis was safely over, I began to make the grown-ups' breakfast and when Roddy came downstairs, I nodded at the dresser and said: 'Mail.'

He went quickly through the pile but, when he came to a blue envelope, he merely glanced at the topmost of the several sheets it contained and then tore the whole into shreds and dropped them into the stove, a heavy frown on his dark brows.

'You don't like that one?' I asked.

'Why do they keep on and on when the thing is played out?'

'If I knew who and what they and the thing were, I might tell you.'

'As if you didn't know!' he scoffed.

I knew very well. 'If you mean women and love affairs, the women keep on and on because the thing is not played out for *them* and from the bottom of my heart, Casanova, I hope that one day fate catches up with you.'

'You spiteful old cow!'

As soon as breakfast was over, he went away into town, saying that he would not be back until late and I settled down to the day's routine of cooking while Tom and George set to work in the garden. Punctually at ten-thirty, the children came in with the announcement: 'We are hungry,' but they did not go out-of-doors with their mugs of milk and their slabs of bread and cheese as they usually did. They ate and drank standing in a row at the table and in complete silence. This was so unusual that I distrusted it, I felt the twittering uneasiness that characterises a flock of sparrows before a thunderstorm and, to break the silence, I said: 'Where is the puppy?'

'Fly?' said Liz. 'He is asleep in Reachfar, tied to the Stalwart Tree. Every time you take him inside anywhere, he makes a puddle.'

'He made one in the coal house –'

' – and one in the shed.'

'You are going to call him Fly?'

'Of course.'

'We christened him just after breakfast.'

'Yes, Fly.'

The silence descended again, broken only by sighs of repletion but they did not go out so, with a wary eye on them, my mind prepared for anything, I got out the flour bin in readiness to bake.

'You going to start baking?' Liz asked.

'Yes. A few scones, perhaps a cake, if I have time and nobody gets in my way.'

'Will you do something for us first?'

'What?'

She looked at the telephone by the window. 'Will you ring up Johnnie the Carpenter and ask him to come and build our house for us?'

'What house?'

'The play-house,' she explained with a touch of impatience. 'It is the little old garage, really, that Dad doesn't need any more now that he has the bigger one for the bigger car. Go on. Ring up.'

'No,' I said.

'Why not?'

The real reason why I would not make the call was that I felt that, since they had been so diffident in their approach, there was some prohibition against this call being made. One lives with this generation and learns, albeit slowly and painfully, I thought, as I measured flour into a bowl under their sullen eyes.

'If anything is to be built,' I said, 'only Daddy can arrange it. This is school property.'

'But it *is* to be built. Dad said so. And the concrete floor is there already. Dad got Mr Todd the Builder to make it.'

'Dad will be home for lunch,' I said. 'Ask him to call the carpenter then.'

'You are a proper stinking beast!' said the defeated Liz. 'Horrible!'

'Bebominable!'

'If you don't clear out of here and stop being impertinent, I shall smack all three of you.'

They glared at me, turned their backs upon me in a pointed way and went marching out of doors.

A few minutes later, I went out to fetch some coke for the stove and from the tool-shed next door, I heard the voices.

'We shouldn't have said that,' said Duncan.

'She is not bebominable, not *really*,' said Gee.

'She is!' said Liz loudly. 'She is a proper stinking beast. She thinks she is as clever as Dad and she has no business.'

'But Dad *said* not to bother Johnnie just now when he is so busy at the new houses,' Duncan protested.

'*She* doesn't know about Johnnie being busy, stupid.'

'I'm not stupid!' Duncan yelled.

'No, not,' shouted Gee.

'And if she didn't know about him being busy, why didn't she ring?' Duncan persisted whereupon there were no more words but the sound of a sharp slap before general battle was joined.

Acting upon Jock's advice to interfere between them as little as possible, I filled the hod with coke and carried it into the house while the angry scuffle gained momentum in the shed. It continued for a moment or two before it quietened to the sound of somebody crying and, thankfully, I shut the back door and went on with my baking. A few moments passed before Duncan and Gee arrived in the kitchen, their eyes big and solemn.

'Aunt Janet, I am sorry I said you were horrible.'

'And you are not bebominable,' Gee added.

'All right, I didn't think you really meant it.'

'And Liz is sorry too but she won't come in although she is all bloody.'

'Bloody?' I shook the flour from my hands. 'Go and bring her in here at once.'

'She won't come. We tried. She said if *you* had called *her* a proper stinking beast, she would let you bleed to death – ' said Duncan, 'and so she is out in the shed bleeding to death,' Gee ended.

71

'Oh, God help me!' I prayed and went outside.

Liz was sitting in the midst of a scattered heap of George's and Tom's split firewood, her long hair in wild disarray, tears running down her dirty face and she sobbed with pain as she nursed her bleeding arm. In a slant of sunlight from the doorway, the tears on her long lashes formed two tiny rainbows. I got her to her feet and rounded on the two boys in the doorway. 'How dare you attack your sister like this?' I said. 'You should – '

Liz snatched herself away from me, glaring at me defiantly while blood plopped to the floor at her feet. 'Let them alone!' she said. 'They didn't do it. We were fighting and I fell among the sticks.' She then bit her lip and began to cry again and the boys began to cry too.

Exasperated with their rainbow changes of mood and allegiance, I gave a sharp sigh and said: 'Liz, come inside and let me bandage that arm.'

'I can't,' she sobbed, 'not after what I said about you being a proper stinking beast.'

'You can un-say it, can't you?'

'Can I?' The big eyes stared at me. 'You are *not* a proper stinking beast, Aunt Janet and I am sorry I said it.'

'All right. Come now.'

George and Tom, with their sure instinct for genuine trouble among the young were now on the scene and the tears, under their influence, gave way to interest as I swabbed the cut and grazed arm with cottonwool while the water in the bowl turned pink. 'Oh lord, George,' I said, when all the dirt and sawdust had been removed, 'we'll have to get the doctor again. There is a great long splinter in here. Look!'

Under the fine palely-tanned skin there was a sinister grey half-inch of dirty wood.

'No, no doctor,' George said.

'Go out and get Fly, Duncan,' said Tom.

The children looked mystified but Duncan went to fetch the pup while my mind went whirling back to the kitchen at Reachfar long ago, where I sat on my stool with a long thin whin thorn embedded in my knee.

'Gee,' I said, 'get some butter and a knife.'

'This wee fellow will soon sort it, Liz,' said Tom when Duncan came in with the pup.

We set Liz on a chair, Gee applied a small sliver of butter to

72

the skin over the splinter, Duncan held the pup while he licked and then Liz and her brothers began to giggle.

'He tickles!' Liz said.

'Give him a bittie more butter, Gee,' said Tom. 'Keep him licking.'

George turned his back, took out his knife and opened the razor-sharp small blade which he held under the hot tap for a moment but the children were too busy giggling to notice.

'Let me see how he is doing,' George said then and, taking the arm firmly in his left hand, he peered closely at the splinter and said: 'Aye, I'll get a grip on it now. There's a good lass, Liz. It won't take a minute.' And before she knew what was happening, he had the blade under the end of the splinter which Fly's tongue had exposed, his thumb on top of it and, with a quick backward flick, he had the splinter out on the knife blade and dropped it into the palm of Liz's hand.

'Ow!' she said. 'Gosh!' and she looked with wonder from Fly to her brothers.

'Put some butter on Gee for him, Liz, for being a good dog,' said Duncan.

While I washed the arm again and bandaged it, the boys smeared about a quarter of a pound of butter on their hands and knees for the pup to lick but it was not in my heart to stop them. There was nothing in my heart but gratitude that another stormy crisis was over and the rainbow was in the sky again.

'I am sorry I have been a nuisance and have interfered with your baking, Aunt Janet,' Liz said when the bandage was in place. 'Dad won't half give me what for but it can't be helped.'

'Dad need not know anything except that you have hurt your arm,' I said as I emptied the pink water from the bowl.

She gave me that sad look that indicated more clearly than any words her certainty of my mental backwardness. 'That's what *you* think,' she said scornfully, 'but there are no flies on Dad.' She got up to go out. 'Actually, in some ways there aren't many flies on you either,' she added in parting tribute.

When my brother came home to have lunch and spend the afternoon with us while Shona had her nap, I told him of our forenoon and ended: 'But don't scold Liz when she comes in, Jock. It is all very strange for them with you and Shona away and Roddy hopping about like a flea on a blanket. The upset in their routine is the cause of half the trouble.'

'You are being very good about them and it is a god-send

to Shona and me,' he said, 'but it isn't much of a holiday for you. Yet, you seem to be thriving on it. You look a lot better than when you came.'

'I feel a lot better. I was more tired and rundown than I knew, I think. It is an odd thing. It takes a lot of energy to look after the clan but in a queer way they seem to feed vitality back to one. – Have you any idea what Roddy is doing?'

'Hanging around Roseville mostly, but he has taken Sheila up to his croft at Drumnadrochit today. It is her day off.' Roseville was the name of the Murray house. 'I don't think Granny knows what to make of Roddy. She can't help feeling his charm –'

'As Twice has said more than once, Roddy has too much bloody charm,' I interrupted.

' – but at the same time, she is wary of him. His whole background and way of life are too strange for her. She looks at him sometimes as if he were a peacock with two tails.'

'He is a lot more dangerous than any peacock. I wish to goodness I had never brought him here.'

'Oh, don't worry,' Jock said. 'Sheila can hold her own.'

'I hope so. But people tend to think in terms of people they know and it is a far cry from Roddy to *you*, the husband and father type. Only the other night, Roddy told me that a man of your scholarship was wasted in this way of life.' Jock laughed. 'I told him,' I continued, 'that one meaning of the word waste was emptiness and that, to me, your life looked less empty than his with only a novel or two to show.'

'The novels have their own value, though,' Jock said. 'One has to live the best way one can, doing the things one can do best. I happen to be better at being a father and teaching kids, I think, than at doing anything else. Talking about the things that people can do best, are you doing anything about your own writing?'

'My writing?'

'Now stop your capers, as Tom and George would say,' he told me. 'Dad told me that you had always wanted to write. I think you could do it, you know, Janet, if you really tried.'

I went to the window and stood looking out at the tangled shrubs of 'Reachfar' and, with my back to him, I said: 'I have a go at it off and on but don't let's talk about it, Jock.'

'All right. I don't want to talk about it as long as you are doing it.'

74

'Did Dad ever say anything to Tom and George about it?' I asked.

'I think not. He only told me about it when I visited him in hospital the day before his operation. I have thought since that he was giving me the only part of my inheritance that he could not mention in his will. He was handing on something that he regarded as a trust. "Janet needs a lot of encouragement about this," he said, so I just want you to know that I am encouraging you.'

'Here are George and Tom coming in,' I said. 'Keep an eye on those potatoes for me, Jock.'

I ran out of the room, burst into tears and locked myself in the downstairs lavatory. This family of mine, living and dead, in all its generations and ramifications of sensitive imagination and love was emotionally much too much for me.

When I went back to the kitchen and began to serve the soup, Tom said: 'Is Roddy not here for his dinner again?'

'No. He won't be back till late.'

'Roddy had another letter from his trollop this morning,' said Liz. 'Dad, what is a trollop?'

'You,' said Jock. 'A trollop is a rather messy female person with untidy hair.'

'Roddy's own hair is not all that tidy,' she commented. 'He tears the letters up without reading them. I suppose they are messy too. When Anne Masson handed in an essay with a squashed currant between the pages, Miss Gordon said it was messy and disgusting and tore it up without reading it. I wish Mum and that baby would come home.'

'Yes, I wish.'

'Yes.'

'The doctor says on Sunday,' said Jock.

'Aunt Janet, could we have a party for the baby?'

'What sort of party?'

'A cake – '

' – chocolate – '

' – with glop in the middle.'

'Is the party for you lot or the baby?' Tom enquired.

'He is a little on the young side for chocolate cake,' said George.

'But *we* would eat the cake to celebrate *him*,' Liz explained, 'and afterwards the three of us plan to offer you all a slight entertainment of a dramatic nature.'

'That will be most acceptable,' I said. 'I shall endeavour to fabricate a cake of the specified chocolate and glop nature.'

Just after my brother went away to the hospital, Doctor Nancy called to see Gee and when I went outside to fetch him, all three were busy carrying cans of water into the shrubbery, but they all came into the house to see their favourite friend. Liz tried to take precedence over Gee with her bandaged arm but Doctor Nancy told her firmly that she was Tom's and George's patient and that it would not be medical etiquette for another doctor to examine her wound. She then inspected Gee's bottom and put on a fresh dressing whereupon the other was ceremonially burned in the stove with the appropriate chant. Doctor Nancy then announced that she was going to the farm of Hill o' Badenoch to see a school friend of theirs who had sprained an ankle so, having asked if they might accompany her, the children went upstairs with wild whoops to tidy themselves a little while the doctor and I had a cup of tea.

'No more crises?' she asked. 'Except the arm?'

'It is one long crisis from my point of view but not from theirs, it seems. How Shona or any mother lives in the midst of all this all the time, I don't know.'

The doctor laughed at me. 'Parents have more resistance than you. I remember a young mother saying to me after I had delivered her baby that she was glad to have her stomach to herself again. What she really meant was: "I am me and the baby is she" and from now on we stay that way. But you have let this lot get into your stomach as well as all round the outside of you. Still, you are looking better today – less worn-out than you did in spite of everything.'

'I feel physically all right although a little mentally muddled,' I said. 'Before I came home, I tried to imagine these children but – ' I shook my head.

'They are not imaginable.' Then she repeated what my brother had said. 'And no two of them are alike.'

'Do you work a lot with children?' I asked her.

'Entirely with children now. There are four of us in the practice and I do the kids. They are very rewarding.'

Rewarding. As I watched her drive away with the three of them in the back of her car, I thought that she had used the precise word. But now the big house felt empty and at the same time claustrophobic, as if all the rooms around and above this big kitchen were caves of lifelessness that were about to

collapse and crush me so, with Fly lolloping round my ankles, I
went out into the garden.

At my home in St Jago, I was accustomed to spending hours
alone in the house while Twice was at work and my servants
were in the garden or in their quarters at the back and, there,
I had never experienced this stifling lifelessness. The children
seemed to have conquered this Victorian heap of grey stone,
making it curiously their own and when they withdrew completely from it and its garden, it lapsed into a spiritless anony-
mity.

I walked along the path with the shrubbery and its forbid-
ding blackboard on my right, tempted to go into the place, for
I have always been attracted by abandoned spots which nature
has taken over and made its own, but my feet were reluctant
to leave the gravel of the path, as if the shrubbery were inside
a fence of taboo. Instead, I went along to the far end of the
garden where George and Tom were working in a big bed of
carrots.

'You have a fine crop there,' I said.

'Aye. This the late lot that will help to keep the generation
eating through the winter,' Tom told me. 'Jock is very lucky
with the old sergeant in the village, having no notion of the
gardening himself.'

'The sergeant?'

'A retired policeman and a grand gardener,' George explained. 'He is off south to his daughter for his holidays just
now while Tom and I are here.'

'Jock has still no notion of the garden?' I asked. 'I thought he
would come to it when he was older.'

'No nor come to it,' George said. 'It is a funny thing. Sometimes I will be thinking that there is nothing at all in what
they call heredity. People are just themselves and quite different from anybody else. Do you mind on Betsy the mare that
used to dance the waltz at Reachfar? Well, not one of her foals
had the least notion of the music or the dancing. Tom and I
used to try them every way.'

'Yet there is something in heredity too,' I said. 'Wee Duncan
is very like my father, I think.'

'Aye, he is,' Tom agreed with me. 'He has the same soft
quiet sort of nature. He is far too soft for that limmer of a Liz.'

'You wait a year or two, Tom,' George said. 'Liz will get a
fright one o' these days. You must mind that you and I canna

77

manage old Jean the way Duncan could. He could put the peter on her with one look when she was threatening to go past herself.'

'What about a cup of tea?' I asked. 'The clan is off up to one of the farms with Doctor Nancy so there is a little peace. Shall I bring it out here?'

'It is a good while since we had tinkers' tea at half-yoking,' Tom said.

One of my jobs at Reachfar, on Saturdays and during the school holidays, had been to carry tea and scones and jam out to my grandfather and Tom at nine in the morning which was halfway through the first 'yoking' of the horses and again at three in the afternoon which was halfway through the second 'yoking' and when I was first entrusted with this job at the age of about four, I had called it 'tinkers' tea' because tinkers were the only people I knew who had their meals out-of-doors.

When I took the tray out to the garden, Tom looked at the sky before he put his hoe aside and said: 'Well, we have had a fine few days of good weather but it is making towards rain, I am thinking.'

'And these bliddy weeds will be up again as strong as ever,' said George.

'When I think of Reachfar long ago, I never seem to remember rain in the summer time,' I said.

'It used to rain now and again right enough but one doesna mind on it,' George said. 'One minds on fine hay weather –'

' – and the harvest,' said Tom, 'with a little frost in the air and the sun red at evening time so that the stooks seemed to be on fire.'

'But there was always rain at tattie-lifting time,' I laughed.

'Aye, the damned tatties,' George agreed. 'Clarting about up to our backsides in gutters. Do you mind on yon bit o' road at the bottom o' the Long Park, Tom? There was rising water yonder and with all the loads o' stones we put into it, we could never get the better o' it.'

'Aye, yon was a dirty bittie right enough,' Tom agreed but with indulgent affection.

'I shall be quite glad to see a little rain,' I said next.

'Aye. You must get gey tired o' the constant heat and sun in St Jago.'

'And St Jago doesn't do anything in moderation. When it rains, it is always a flood.'

The children now came round the corner of the house, having been dropped at the gate by Doctor Nancy and each of them was carrying a small parcel wrapped in white paper.

'Look what we got from Johnnie's father,' Liz said. 'Real proper honey all sealed up in wax by the bees – '

' – and not the stuff the shops put into jars.'

'And we each told the bees our news,' said Gee.

'It is a good job you did that,' Tom told him. 'Danny the Beeman at Reachfar always said the bees made more honey if you told them the news.'

'Especially if it is good news,' George added.

'What did you tell them?' I asked.

Liz looked cross. 'Johnnie's father said: "Lat Geordie the wee-est loonie spik first",' she said in what she called the Doric, 'and so of course *he* went and told them about the baby.'

'And I was next and I told about George and Tom staying,' said Duncan.

'So all I had left to tell about was *you* being here,' Liz informed me scornfully which made me feel very small until she added disarmingly: 'An enormous great happening like you coming all the way from St Jago isn't just *news* like a baby getting born or George and Tom staying. News is just ordinary things that happen all the time, like in the newspapers, Shocking Crash at Spinners' Corner Three Killed,' she explained, 'so I told them as well about Roddy taking Aunt Sheila to Drumnadrochit and that they were probably going to get married. Look here, we're hungry.'

When they had filled themselves with a dish that they called 'Oven Garden', which consisted of cut-up potatoes, onions and any other available vegetables cooked in a casserole in leftover gravy and when they had drunk the inevitable mugs of milk, their minds were liberated for further exploration of the outside world and Liz said: 'So there were bees at Reachfar?'

'Och, yes. About thirty hives o' the stingin' little booggers,' Tom replied.

Of all the livestock at Reachfar, Tom and George had least liked the bees and their next dislike had been my Aunt Kate's flock of ducks and geese.

'They were very ill-natured bees indeed,' George said. 'Maybe there wasna enough news about Reachfar for them.'

'We always have plenty of news,' said Liz. 'Come on, Dunk.

Come on, Gee,' and all three went out and I watched them disappear into the shrubbery.

I turned to Tom and George, drew in breath to say to them that it might be advisable to conceal from the children certain aspects of Reachfar, for I felt it possible that not only bees but perhaps pigs and cattle would arrive in the garden outside but I found that I could not speak the words. If, by the power of the children's dream, bees, pigs and cattle arrived, which I felt to be possible, some appropriate steps must be taken at the moment of the arrival but it did not seem possible to take prohibitory steps against the elusive gossamer of the dream itself. What I did decide to do, however, was to call them in to bed, by way of taking the power of their minds off the bees and when I went out to the path where a little tunnel led away into the laurels, I heard the three voices chanting:

> 'Spell, spell, magic spell,
> Make true this wish we wish so well!'

and I could smell the smoke of burning twigs. Even if they are wishing for bees, I found myself thinking, I hope they get them and I almost felt like praying in the words of my childhood: 'Please God, send them bees!'

'Liz, Duncan, Gee!' I called. 'Bedtime!'

Obediently, they came at once and I went up with them to wash Gee while he stood in the bath, then went to their room with him to wait for Liz and Duncan to come.

'Tonight,' Liz commanded, 'tell about Danny the Beeman.'

'Once upon a time, long long ago at Reachfar, Channatt had a friend called Danny the Beeman. He was long and thin and dark with a leathery skin and black eyes like a gypsy and he played the fiddle,' I began and went on to tell of how Danny had taught Channatt to dance the Highland Fling and how she had danced to entertain the people at the Harvest Home. When I had finished, Liz hopped slowly and thoughtfully across the floor and into her own bed whereupon she said: 'The farmers around here grow lots of oats and wheat and barley but they don't have Harvest Homes.'

'How do *you* know they don't?' Duncan asked from the other side of the room. 'Maybe Mum and Dad go to lots of Harvest Homes while Fat Mary sits in downstairs.'

'Yes, maybe,' came the echo, sleepy but loyal in support of his brother for the annoyance of Liz.

'By my Highland forefathers – ' she was beginning in war-like tones when I interrupted her: 'No. They don't have them anywhere any more, I think. Harvest Homes are long ago and far away things.'

She slid down under her covers. 'It isn't fair,' she said. 'It seems to me that a lot of the very best and most wonderful and glorious things are far away and long ago and people don't have them any more.'

'Yes, it isn't fair.'

'Not fair.'

'Oh well, good night, Aunt Janet,' said Liz.

'Good night, everybody,' I said and, as I went out on to the landing, I was thinking that, even at this early age, those three children, through their greed to experience everything life had to offer, were aware of that basic sadness that lies at the heart of life, the sadness that comes from the knowledge of a glory passed away from the earth.

When I went downstairs, George and Tom had gone out to the garden again and I joined them there. The sun still shone, mellow and warm but there was a cool little breeze coming in fitful gusts and the clouds were piling sullenly on the horizon beyond the fields of grain. We were just about to come indoors when George said: 'Wheesht! What's that?'

'It's a swarm o' bees,' said Tom, pointing with his hoe over the roof of the house. 'Dang it, they are going to settle too!'

Transported, I looked up at the little black buzzing cloud which was now directly above us, watching it wheel round in a circle, describe a closer circle above the shrubbery and then cascade down where the white rose grew over the tree stump.

'I suppose they are from Hill o' Badenoch,' George said. 'Johnnie o' the Hill is the only one about here that keeps bees as far as I know. Maybe you would speak to him on that tele-phone, Janet?'

'Surely. What is his name?'

'Johnnie Gibson.'

I looked up the number, Mr Gibson answered and I ex-plained who I was and about the swarm.

'Noo, that's richt funny,' he said. 'It's nae but twinty meenutes back that that wee Liz queanie wis on this verra phone tae me, askin' me fat wis the price o' a hive o' bees. Well, Ah'll be richt doon, mistress, me an' Hughie.'

They arrived in a Land Rover about twenty minutes later and

81

lifted out an assortment of sacks, gloves, veils and other equipment and then a green-painted box hive.

'They can ha'e this auld hive,' Mr Gibson said, 'an' stop i' the yaird here. It's a fine placie for them. Whaur i' they?'

I pointed to the rose-covered tree trunk. 'They are somewhere around that rosebush. Could you take the hive in there perhaps?'

'Aye, fairly that, mistress.'

'But mercy, Johnnie,' said George, 'you canna go giving us your bees!'

'Not at all!' Tom added.

'Ach, Ah've had sic a year o' swarms Ah dinna ken fat tae dee wi' them,' he said and, picking up the hive, he pushed his way into the laurels, Hughie following him.

'Janet,' said George sternly although in a low voice, 'we don't want these stingin' booggers here among the bairns! Are you out o' your head?'

'And the baby coming home forbye and besides,' said Tom.

'You had bees at Reachfar all the time I was a bairn and I never got stung. Why should this lot? Never look a gift bee in the sting,' I said. 'Bring Mr Gibson and his man in for a dram when they are finished.'

It was the middle of the next forenoon before the children discovered the beehive. It was raining and they had spent the early part of the day in their playroom across the back hall but at the first fair interval they went out and disappeared into their favourite place. Within minutes they were back in the kitchen, breathless with excitement.

'Aunt Janet, guess what? There's a beehive in Reachfar!'

'Yes, a real one with a little door!'

'And bees peeping out! *Real* ones!'

'Yes,' I said. 'They came last night, after you were in bed.'

Liz suddenly flushed, looking very guilty. 'I think a mistake has got made,' she said, bit her lip and began to cry.

'Liz, what is the matter? Don't you like the bees?'

'Yes. Oh, yes. But last night, when these two were sleeping and you were in the garden, I rang up Johnnie's father and asked him how much a hive of bees would cost. I only asked the *price*! He said they cost a pound a bee. There's hundreds in a hive! *We* can't afford bees. *We* haven't got hundreds of pounds!' She was now shouting in protest, banging her fists on the table in her despair.

'Oh, Liz,' said Duncan.

'Oh, Liz *Sandison*!' said Gee.

'Listen, Liz!' I said, 'Mr Gibson didn't bring the bees here. They came here of their own accord. Remember how George and Tom told you last night that they swarm around their Queen and follow her wherever she goes? Well, the Queen of this swarm decided that she wanted to come here and her faithful followers came with her.'

George and Tom, who had been out in the shed chopping firewood, knew instinctively that the children's world had gone wrong and now came into the kitchen. Liz turned her tear-stained face to them and they had to tell of the arrival of the bees all over again. ' – and then we spoke to Johnnie's father on the telephone and asked him to come and take them back but he brought the hive and put them in and said they could stop here,' Tom ended.

'But mind,' said George, 'if anybody touches that hive, Johnnie's father will come and take it away. You can watch them working from a bittie off but you are not to go near them. Channatt was the one that had sense about bees. She never went near them at Reachfar and she never got stung either.'

'But the honey?' said Liz, her eyes now dry and sweeping the full horizon.

'Johnnie's father will take the honey off for you,' said Tom, 'if they make any, that is. They are unreliable booggers a lot o' the time and not very reasonable. Still, George, that was a big swarm for the time o' year. The old people used to say:

"A swarm o' bees in May is worth a load o' hay,
   A swarm o' bees in June is worth a silver spoon,
   But a swarm in July is not worth a fly."

But late in the year as it is, that lot will be worth more than a fly, I am thinking.'

Chanting this new rhyme, the children went back out to the shrubbery, no doubt to watch the bees and from a safe distance, I could only hope, for I was now less certain of the desirability of the bees than I had been on the evening before. As I went on with the household routine of the morning, I marvelled at the surging ebb and flow of feeling that the children created round themselves, so that the light was always changing, making the bees at one moment a glorious fulfilment of a heart-felt desire, at the next a buzzing menace, a mere hive of 'stingin' wee booggers'. This shifting light in the mind made me think again of the rainbows of a windy April on the hills to the north of Reachfar, as they appeared, wavered, glowed, disappeared and appeared again, clothing the hills and the sea in a wondrous living light.

Chapter V

'But for those first affections,
Those shadowy recollections,
Which, be they what they may,
Are yet the fountain-light of all our day,
Are yet a master-light of all our seeing;'

I WAS now beginning to feel that the children no longer distrusted me, that I was established in their minds as Aunt Janet, a member of the family who knew more about Channatt and Reachfar than all the other members and who was, for this reason, interesting and acceptable but, as my grandmother had been fond of saying: 'Pride goeth before a fall.' I had not calculated that, by telling all three about Reachfar each evening at bedtime, I was undermining the former supremacy of Liz, out of whose faint early recollections the fantasy had been born and I had also underestimated her determination to maintain that dominion of hers over her brothers.

On the second evening after the bees arrived, I had finished the bedtime tale of Reachfar and Liz had got out of the boys' bed to hop across to her own when she stopped in mid-floor, standing on one leg and said: 'Aunt Janet, you remember Granda Sandison before he died and went away, don't you?' She was speaking in the superior grownup tone that she used when she wished to demonstrate her superiority in age and experience over the boys, the tone that never failed to rile them and, in a second, Duncan and Gee were out of bed too and in battle formation in the middle of the floor.

'We all remember Granda Sandison!' Duncan shouted.

'It was only last Christmas-time that he went away!' shouted Gee.

'Belt up, you kids,' said Liz with disdainful inelegance and turned pointedly to me. 'Remember the Candle Creatures?' she asked in a smiling intimate voice, as if she were speaking of an aspect of my father that only she and – possibly but not probably – myself could know. Indeed, she was visibly hoping that I did not know of this aspect of my father so that there could be a little bit of 'Reachfar' that was hers alone while the boys were visibly hoping that I would display a complete knowledge of this new thing and be able to let them share in it but, before I had become aware of the situation in this clarity, I had looked puzzled and had said: 'The Candle Creatures?'

'So you *don't* know about them?' Liz asked, raising her eyebrows, crossing her pigtails under her chin and throwing them over opposite shoulders as if they were a mink stole. She was more irritating than I can ever describe. She then turned her back to us and sailed with dignity towards her bed instead of hopping as she usually did. My hands itched to get at her blue-and-white-striped pyjama seat. Her power to irritate was almost indescribable, as I have said and, although I managed to control myself, control was now beyond the boys who, with a concerted rush, fell upon her and bore her to the floor where, sitting on her stomach, Duncan began to pummel her and shout: 'Never *were* any bloody Candle Creatures! Never were – '

'Weren't!' yelled Gee, kicking her buttock. 'Weren't ever any bloody Candle Creatures!'

Liz was howling, the boys shouting and yelling and I was trying to tear apart the writhing Laocoon group when my brother arrived in the doorway.

'Duncan, George, get into bed. Elizabeth, get up.'

The boys seemed to melt and trickle across the floor into bed while Liz, crying, struggled up into a sitting position.

'Daddy, Dunk punched my nose and Gee kicked my – '

'You probably deserved it. Get into bed at once. Good night, all of you. Come along downstairs, Aunt Janet.'

Very much as Duncan and Gee had done, I trickled downstairs in his wake but in the hall I said: 'I am sorry, Jock. I just don't seem to have your authority.'

He laughed at me. 'You treat them with too much respect. I know there are reasons of some sort behind all their outbursts and rows but one can't spend one's life studying *their* reasons. By seven in the evening, the adults have a right to be despots.'

'You are home early,' I said as we went into the kitchen.

'I have some letter writing I must do and I don't like this situation in Egypt.'

I noticed now that the television set, which had its normal home in the playroom, had been moved into the kitchen tonight and pictures flickered on its screen but no sound came from it, the volume having been turned down. During my busy days, I had no more than glanced at the headlines of the newspapers but, now, while the chorus of some musical film danced soundless on the screen, I remembered that one headline had said: 'Nasser seizes the Suez Canal.'

'The Suez thing?' I asked now. 'Is it that serious, Jock?'

'It isn't too good. I am going through to the study. Keep your eye on that thing and if any news comes through, give me a call.' Jock went away, Tom and George were still in the garden, Fat Mary was ironing in the playroom. Feeling suddenly cold, I sat down at the fire for a little before I began to prepare the evening meal. Suez Canal. International Crisis. Twice was four thousand miles away. My brother was only thirty-six and still a naval reservist. There were Shona and the new baby in the hospital. There were the three upstairs – It was all too big and frightening. I remembered August and September of 1939. It was all too big. I got up and began to clean the vegetables for supper as George and Tom came in from the garden.

While I prepared the meal, they sat by the fire smoking their pipes but we did not speak much because the silent flickering figures on the screen in the corner were a distraction. Tom and George did not have television at Achcraggan, I had never seen it until I came to my brother's house and none of us liked it very much. The flickering figures in the corner were an intrusion on the privacy of the family circle and it was only my brother who could ignore them and behave as if the lighted screen did not exist, but he was aware of our discomfort and said, as I cleared supper away: 'Just put up with it until the news comes on at nine, if nothing comes through before that. Oh, George and Tom, you may like this thing that is coming on now. It is some of the old music-hall stuff.'

He turned the knob that controlled the sound and he and I washed the dishes while a raucous voiced comedienne sang 'Down at the old Bull and Bush'.

'Jock,' I said, 'have you ever heard of the Candle Creatures?'

Frowning, he stared at me over the saucepan he was drying. 'Candle Creatures?'

'It is something to do with Dad. Liz produced it. That was part of the reason for the row upstairs.'

'Dad? Candle Creatures? It doesn't sound like Dad. She must have it wrong, surely.'

'I don't know. It doesn't matter. I just wondered if you knew.' But the Candle Creatures did matter to me and when we went back to the kitchen to watch the rest of the music-hall show before the news, I sat with my physical eyes on the flickering screen but with my mental eyes I was searching back through my memories of my father for some clue to this secret that Liz was with-holding from her brothers.

In the strange and unpredictable way that help often comes, it came to me from the most unexpected quarter, for the second-last act of the music-hall show was announced as 'Ton Singh, Magician of Chiaroscuro' and there appeared a man in Indian dress who stood beside a small lighted screen within the television screen and began to create the shapes of men and animals by casting shadows with his hands.

'That television is very clever,' George said, as a Chinese with long drooping moustaches took form in shadow play, 'but when I stop to think that I am watching a shadow making Chinamen out of shadows, it seems to be time to turn it off.'

'The Candle Creatures!' I said suddenly. 'Jock, Dad used to make shadows with his hands like that.'

'Did he?' Jock was not very interested.

'On the wall of my attic,' I said excitedly, 'by the light of my candle. Didn't he ever do it for you when you were small?'

He shook his head. 'No.'

I remembered that my father had been at Reachfar only for short periods when Jock had been young enough to be amused by shadow play, so I said no more but went through to the scullery cupboard, purloined a candle from the box I had noticed on the highest shelf, took an old saucer and smuggled both out of the kitchen and up to my bedroom while George, Tom and my brother watched the final act of the music-hall show.

When I came downstairs again, the news was over and Jock seemed to be relieved, to feel that the Suez Crisis had passed its most dangerous peak and when George spoke, he became interested in the smaller family things.

'Janet,' George said, 'can you truly mind on your father making those rabbits on the wall at Reachfar?'

'I had forgotten, George, but Liz made me remember.'

'But you couldn't have been more than two when he used to do it!' Tom protested.

'Yes. It was pretty far back. But I remember them. There

was a rabbit, a duck, a goose, a deer and a hare. Maybe there were more but those are the only ones I remember.' I turned to Jock. 'But they weren't called Candle Creatures. Liz must have named them that.'

'I didn't know about them at all,' Jock said. 'What an extraordinary man Dad was, when you think of it. He always used to go up to see Liz before she went to sleep. I suppose that is when they had their shadow shows. I say, *that's* where that queer little book came from!'

'What book?'

'It is in the study. It came with the Reachfar stuff. I'll get it.' When he came back, he handed me a cheap, little old book, with pages stained brown at the edges, covered in faded orange buckram on which, in black lettering, were the words: 'Home Magic. A Compendium of Tricks for the Amateur. Price ninepence.'

'There is a bit in it about making shadows,' Jock said.

'How priceless!' I laughed at Tom and George. 'But Dad never spent ninepence on this, I am prepared to swear. I bet it came home to Reachfar in one of the bargain boxes that you two used to buy at farm sales. Still, it is odd that I have never seen it before. You are sure that it came with the Reachfar stuff, Jock?'

'Certain.'

'Just let me have a look at that bookie, Janet,' said George with sudden interest and I handed it to him. After a moment, he turned to Tom and said: 'My memory is not as good as Janet's Tom, but I am minding something about this. This bookie didn't come from a farm sale.' He turned back to me. 'It was given to your father as a present at an Inverness Horse Show long ago.'

'I have the very night in mind this minute!' Tom said. 'A little ago, when that mannie with the turban was making the shadows in the television boxie there, I was feeling I had seen something o' the kind before but I couldna mind where but I have it now.' Tom turned to Jock and me. 'I think this is a story that we have never told you before, maybe. God knows, George and I have told you many an old yarn in our time but not this one. It was the spring o' the year 1912. I am not much of a hand at dates, as you know, but George and I will never forget that year, for it was the year that the first Betsy o' Reachfar, the foal that was born on the same day as yourself, Janet, won the championship o' the Show as a two-year-old filly. It was a fine day early in May and your father took Betsy into the ring in her own two-year-old class and George and I could see right away that she was going to be first, although all the best Clydesdales in the north were there. Yon filly had the best temper and the bonniest manners I have ever seen in a horse – '

'And that is more than could be said of her namesake at that time,' George put in with a smiling glance at myself, 'the namesake', for I was christened Janet Elizabeth and the foal was named Elizabeth Janet and Betsy for short.

'Mind you, everything about her was first-class,' Tom went on, 'but there were others in the ring as good as she was in that way. It was the way she behaved herself under your father's handling that got her the prize. Of course, I have never seen a horse that wouldna work right for your father. But when, anyway, she came out of her own class with the first, Sir Torquil was speaking with the judges and then he came over to Reachfar, your grandfather that is and George and me and said we ought to enter her in the Open Class. The Commy-*tee* would take last minute entries he said but it cost a pound to put her in and Reachfar was a little doubtful but Sir Torquil would put up the entry money himself so in she went.'

'In a way, it spoiled the whole pleasure o' the day,' George took up the story. 'Tom and I only went to shows to have a dram with our cronies mostly but from eleven in the morning until three in the afternoon, when the Open was judged, we couldna leave the filly for long enough to have a drink, we were that anxious. Indeed, we never even had any dinner that I mind on.'

It seemed to me that we were getting further and further away from the faded old book that was lying in my lap but this did not matter, for Tom and George glowed with the happiness of their old memories while I could visualise the show field with the trees all around, the refreshment tents, the entertainment booths and I could hear the pipe band as it played among the crowd of excited children and farm hands and their wives out on a spree for the day.

'Anyway,' Tom went on, 'dinner or not, three o'clock came and Duncan took Betsy into the ring. The Poyntdale Stallion, Tarquin, her own father was in there against her and a fine dapple grey mare from over Easter Ross way and I thought Sir Torquil had put up his pound for nothing but after a long time the judges signalled for Duncan to lead Betsy forward, George and I couldna believe it – '

'– and neither could your father,' George took up the tale. 'He let the rein go slack, he was that surprised and Betsy set off over to the judges on her own before he got himself together and took charge of her. It was Himself that taught her to come forward when somebody crooked their finger at her and off she went to the chief judge, looking for a bittie carrot. And so she got the cup. It is still in my old kist at Castle Jemima. What started us off on this old yarn, Tom? Och, aye, that wee bookie. Well, with Betsy winning the cup, your granda went clean past himself and gave your father and us two a pound each and said he would take Betsy home in the train himself and we were to stay at the Show and make a night of it. There used to be dancing and concerts and merry-go-rounds and all sorts of capers after it was dark, you know.'

'So we made a proper spree of it,' Tom continued. 'We had a go at the sledge-hammer and the three of us took half-a-crown each off the mannie that was in charge of it and he wouldna let us try again. Then we went to the shooting gallery and the mannie asked us if we were soldiers or ghillies before he would let us shoot and we told him no and then George shot seven bulls in a row and the mannie had to give him a big china flowerpot on a stand that was the fanciest prize in the place. He wasna a bit pleased and he was less pleased still when George told him he was a ploughman now but had been a Seaforth once and was for calling the police. But George said to go and call them and he would tell them that the sight on the rifle was crooked so he didna send for the police after all and we went off with the flower pot.'

'We made the round o' the place right enough,' George said, 'and then we decided to finish up at the concert in the big tent and it was in there that we saw the Indian making the shadows on a bittie screen like that fellow on the television boxie this evening and when it was over we went into one of the refreshment tents to take a last dram before catching the late special train for Fortavoch. We had just got our drams from the barman when the Indian that had made the shadows came into the tent and went forward to the table. He was a proper Indian, not a cockney dressed up like that one on the television boxie, a slim-built fellow and his face was a greenish sort o' colour, with the cold likely, poor fellow. The place was well filled and a lot o' the men were gey drunk and two of them took exception to the Indian and were for throwing him out. Jockie Croonach was sitting on a barrel near us and your father gave his glass to Jockie and said: 'Hold that for a minute, Jockie,' so Tom and I gave Jockie our glasses too and followed your father. By this time there was a good few gathered round the poor Indian but your father took the nearest two men, one in each hand, by the collars o' their jackets. They were wee craiturs, compared with himself, town men, likely. "If anybody goes out of here," he said quite quiet-like, "you two will go first and, still holding them, he said to the barman: "Never mind sending for the police. Give the Indian gentleman a drink." All them that had been shouting got quite quiet, the Indian got his drink and your father and him and us went back over to Jockie in the corner.'

'And it was then,' Tom ended the tale, 'that the Indian opened his pack and gave your father that wee bookie. He had a dozen or so of them and he tried to sell them after the concert but I don't think anybody bought one. So we had another dram with him while he showed your father how to put his hands to make the rabbit and then we came home to Reachfar and that is where the bookie came from.'

As the story ended, I felt as I imagined the children must feel when I had told them what Gee called 'a real clouds of glory about Reachfar'. I wanted time to end for the moment just here, on this note of satisfaction and contentment and I wished that, like the children, I could put the light out, draw up my covers and go to sleep. Carrying the little book, I went up to their room to see that they were safely asleep after their scolding from their father and, having covered up the sprawling Liz, I went into my own room and laid the little book on the dressing-table. But, seeing the purloined candle and the saucer, I was tempted to try my skill so, since it was still daylight, I drew the curtains, dripped some wax on to the saucer and set the candle upright. It was years since I had seen candle-light other than as a decoration on a dinner-table and the high square room was at once filled with flickering shadows like partially recollected memories.

With the help of the little book, I found it easy to make 'Candle Creatures' appear on the wall. In a very short time, I could conjure up the rabbit, the duck, the goose and the deer, antlers and all but it took a little more time to make the long-eared hare stand up on his hind legs and caper as I remembered him capering across the gable wall of my attic at Reachfar. However, in the end, he was there, ears erect, forelegs batting the air while he danced forward and back on his hind legs and I sat down, the book between my hands in the fitful light of the candle.

There came to me a sudden thought of the universality of men like my father, ordinary men who go about their daily business and have their little holidays like my father's day off when he took Betsy the filly to the Horse Show. It was possible, I thought, that somewhere in India at this moment, some old man was telling his grand-children or great-grand-children of his long-ago travels beyond the seas, of the time when, in a hostile Scottish town, one man had risen up to see that justice prevailed because he believed that all men had a right to the drink that they could pay for. History, it seemed to me, was as simple as this. It was made by what ordinary individual men believed and were prepared to stand up for and not by men such as the very important one who had made the anouncement over television about the Suez Crisis. Indeed, not only did ordinary people like my father and us of this ordinary family make history, we also bent its crises to our family uses, for it was because of my brother's sense that history, in the accepted sense, was being made in Egypt that we had watched that absurd programme which had given me the thing I most wanted to know for the sake of Liz, Duncan and Gee. The 'Candle Creatures' were part of our family history, a part that I had forgotten and out of a world-wide historical crisis the memory of them had come back to me. There was a tap at the door, it opened and Jock's red head came round its edge. 'Janet, are you all right?'

I felt rather silly, sitting there in the candle-light with the daylight showing at the edge of the curtains. 'Yes,' I said. 'I can make Candle Creatures! Look!' I made the hare dance along the wall.

'You are ruining these kids,' my brother protested but laughing none the less at the comical hare. 'You mustn't let them devour your time and thought like this.'

'They are not devouring my time. They give back far more than they take from me. Jock, wasn't that a wonderful story of the Horse Show tonight?'

'It was but it makes one wonder how many more wonderful tales are going unrecorded.'

'But for the kids, this one would have gone unrecorded too. The trouble with people like George and Tom – indeed, the trouble with all of us – is that we don't know what is important, George and Tom have never recognised that anything *they* may know is of any importance but all sorts of odds and ends of family history and all sorts of skills too are dying with them because they don't think them important enough to record. Oh, well,' I laid the little book aside, 'we have rescued the Candle Creatures.'

'In themselves, they are not important but I am glad that they brought out the Horse Show story,' Jock said.

'I am glad about the story,' I agreed, 'but the Candle Creatures have importance for *me*. I want Duncan and Gee to start even with Liz about Reachfar, Jock. That girl, if you will forgive me for saying so, is a wicked little devil.'

'I am reliably informed that she is the spit and image in character of yourself at that age.'

'Nonsense! I was a simple slow-witted child. Heavens, I was *there!* I know. I never had that guile, that practical inventiveness, that wicked charm. I didn't have those looks to start with. Liz has Shona's lovely forehead and eyes.'

Jock sighed. 'You never had to deploy what you might have had. You were ten before I was born, remember. Liz had the competition of Duncan when she was not quite four.' He was standing in the middle of the floor looking down at me and he smiled. 'Actually, you and Liz are remarkably alike in a queer way. You are both feminists. You both resent the socially accepted superiority of the male and you are both out to crack it if you can. You have been bashing at it all your life – Dad encouraged it in you – and you have cut quite a hack in the post for feminine freedom, when I think of it. And Liz has been bashing at it since the day Dunk was born. I have to watch her very carefully in school, you know. I am not blowing a tin trumpet when I say that she is the brightest one in her class. There are nineteen of them but she might well be the brightest one – the other eighteen are the children of busy farm-workers and don't have the home opportunities that she has. But there is a wee fellow, Johnnie Veitch, the son of a shepherd, who can make her run for her money. As you said, she has practical inventiveness and she knows that Johnnie is weak in history. Before

94

history class, in the late forenoon on Wednesdays and Fridays, Liz puts Johnnie through a demoralisation course in the play-ground at the interval – at least, she would if she got the chance. She did it twice before I caught up with her but now she spends the Wednesday and Friday forenoon intervals with Shona in the kitchen and Johnnie shows up quite well at the history class.'

I had noticed that one of the few things that made any lasting impression upon Liz was a stern word or two from her father and, the next morning, she was very amenable and agreeable, as she and her brothers prepared their own breakfast while I produced a meal for the adults. When Jock had left for town and Roddy too had driven away, George and Tom went out to the garden and Liz asked: 'Is there anything you want us to do to help you? If so, speak now or for this morning hold your peace because we are about to be rather busy.'

'In that case, I shall hold my peace, thank you,' I told her. 'What are you about to be rather busy with?'

'The theatrical entertainment for Sunday.'

'Is it coming along well?'

'Absolutely dire.'

'Lousy.'

'Rotten.'

'But it will be all right on the day,' said Liz, crossing the hall and opening the back door. 'Rehearsal call!' she shouted. 'Five minutes! Gee, you been to the loo? If not, get in there at once and hurry up. Dunk, take the Number One dress box into Reachfar. I'll bring Number Two.'

The boys jumped to obey the self-elected playwright-producer-stage-manager and I saw no more of them until they lined up at the table at eleven o'clock for bread, cheese and milk, when they spoke hardly at all and seemed to be rapt away in some world of their own.

With intervals for meals, they spent the whole day in the shrubbery and remarkably peacefully too and when I called them for supper, they were staggering with exhaustion as they carried their dress-up boxes full of old curtains and rags into the playroom. There was no question that, whatever their theatrical entertainment might be, they were putting all their energies into it.

'Dad is not back?' Liz asked, slumping into her chair at table.

'I am afraid not. Did you specially want him to be back?'

'Not specially. I had an idea that he might hear our lines but I don't think I could bear to speak that stuff again today.'

'Me either.'

'Or me.'

'Perhaps Dad will hear you in the morning. If not, maybe I could do it?'

'No.' She gazed at me with gentle gravity. 'No, thank you. Nobody ever hears us in rehearsal except Dad.'

'Then I am sure he will make time to attend to it. Shall I mention it to him when he comes home?'

'Yes, please.'

They were so tired that they ate less than usual and went upstairs as soon as they had finished, without the customary lark with Tom and George and with no requests to stay up to see if their father would come home.

'Just do your teeth and wash faces and hands and knees,' I said. 'I think you have worked a little too hard at your play.'

'Ah've worked masel' tae a shaddah, fairly that,' Liz said in her Doric and then with her towel as a cloak about her, she declaimed: 'I am but a poor player, a walking shadow, that struts and frets his hour upon the stage and then is heard no more.'

'Talking of shadows,' I said as I scrubbed the yawning Gee's knees, 'I thought that instead of Reachfar tonight we would have a little shadow-play. It is nice sleepy stuff.'

'Shadow-play? What's that?' Liz asked, becoming alert.

'An old Reachfar thing. When you are in bed, I'll show you.'

They became less listless, very soon they were all three lying in the boys' bed like spoons in a box and I drew the curtains and fetched my candle.

'You must keep your eyes on the wall to see the play,' I said. 'Ready?'

Standing between their backs and the candle, I caused the rabbit to appear on the wall and there was a compulsive heave of the bedclothes as Liz threw an arm and a leg over the bodies of her brothers and squealed delightedly: 'It's a Candle Creature! It's Rory the Rabbit! No!' The arm came up and squashed the boys' heads into the pillow. 'You mustn't look backwards or they disappear. You have to watch the wall and call their names and then they come. Johnnie Duck!' she called and, as I made the duck appear, I hoped that my father's

96

repertory had not been greater than mine. This game, in Liz's time, had obviously been more sophisticated than when I was two years old for I remembered no names for the shadows. My father, I thought, had been catching up with a more sophisticated age.

'Not fair!' Duncan protested now. 'Gee and I don't know their names!'

'Not fair!' Gee echoed.

'I'll whisper. Gee first,' said Liz, leaning over her elder brother's head to the ear of her younger brother, forgetting in her enthusiasm that the Candle Creatures had been one of her small superiorities.

'Gawpy Goose!' Gee called now and I made the goose.

'Me,' said Duncan, Liz whispered and he called; 'Dandy the Deer!'

'And there is just one more,' Liz said to my relief, 'but he is the best one of all. Marmaduke the Mad March Hare!' and all three became one convulsion of giggles as Marmaduke went capering to and fro along the wall.

I opened the curtains and blew out the candle. 'You must go to sleep now,' I told them and Liz got out of the boys' bed but she did not hop over to her own. She walked quietly and dreamily, as if she were moving among gossamer tendrils that clung about her, as the happy shadows from the past wavered and floated about her mind.

'The Candle Creatures are a very baby thing, really,' I told the boys as I tucked them in.

'I liked them and I am not a baby,' Gee said solemnly.

'I liked them too, although they are only shadows from a candle and not creatures at all,' said Duncan.

Liz, in the middle of the floor, came out of her gossamer dreams and into battle as she hurled herself at the boys' bed. 'They *are* creatures!' she shouted, slapping the hump which was Duncan's bottom. 'A candle by itself can't make them! They only come for Granda Sandison! And for Aunt Janet!' she added. 'And they don't come unless you *call* for them!' She began to cry pitifully and, guiltily, I realised that I had underestimated the emotion that these shadows out of the past could call up in a child as tired as Liz was that night. 'I wish I had never told you their names, you horrible disgusting stinking beasts that you are!'

I took hold of her and began to lead her over to her own bed, half-asleep on her feet as she was but the two boys sat up, wide-eyed when Liz was sitting in her own bed and Duncan said: 'I take it back, Liz. They *are* creatures.'

'Yes, creatures,' Gee averred solemnly.

'They are – are – '

'Created?' I suggested.

'Yes, created, so they are creatures.'

'Created with the help of a light from a candle,' I said, 'so they are Candle Creatures.'

'Yes, Candle Creatures,' the two voices said together and then: 'Aunt Janet, will you show me how to – to create them?' Duncan asked.

I have often heard it said that women tend to favour male children more than female children, just as men, like my brother, tend to favour girls but of myself this was not true. My allegiance was with the devilish Liz, so much more unpredictable and less manageable than the boys and although I had gone to some trouble to break her superiority over the boys, I now handed her back that small superiority one hundredfold. 'No, Duncan,' I said, 'but I shall show Liz and if she likes to show you and Gee, she may.' I tucked in Liz's covers while the big eyes looked proudly up at me. 'Will you make Candle Creatures for the baby when he is old enough, Liz?' I asked.

'Yes. I'll make them for him all the time. I'll make them for him for ever and ever,' said Liz, her voice dying away on the last word as she fell asleep.

Chapter VI

'Behold the Child among his new-born blisses.'

THE tide of excitement rose high at six o'clock on Sunday morning, threatening to overwhelm the house, although my brother would not be arriving with Shona and the baby until about four in the afternoon. By eight o'clock, the three children had had several bouts of loud song, two bouts of fisticuffs, had overflowed the bathroom wash-basin all over the floor and Gee had fallen downstairs. To add to my difficulties, it was pouring with rain outside and they showed no inclination to take to their haunts in the shrubbery, for which I did not blame them but when they had had breakfast, I said that they must put on Wellington boots and mackintoshes and go out of doors.

'We have to do our washing-up first,' said Liz.

I would gladly have done the washing-up, if only they would go away but I hesitated to interfere with their routine, fearing that this would only make matters worse. However, when there came a loud crash from the scullery and I went through to find an asortment of crockery in splinters on the floor, I decided that something desperate would have to be done. But they forestalled me.

'That's torn it,' said Liz. 'We've gone right past it.'

'By miles,' Duncan agreed with her.

Gee looked up at me. 'There is only one thing to be done with us,' he told me in his solemn wide-eyed way. 'Put us in the playroom and lock the door on us.'

'Then that is just what I shall do with you. Come on, march!' Obediently, they marched across the back hall into the playroom, Fly following them and when I shut the door there was a tense silence which, as soon as I turned the key on the outside, broke into a raucous burst of song.

My brother had spent the night in town and when George, Tom and Roddy, who had cowered in their beds during the early morning activity, came downstairs, there was a fight going on in the playroom but when George went towards the door I said: 'That door is locked and don't you open it. They told

99

me themselves that the only thing to do with them was to lock them in there.' As I went about my forenoon work, making among other things the chocolate cake with the glop in the middle, I had one ear cocked at the locked door, from behind which came all sorts of crashes, loud laughter, howls, bursts of song with short intermittent periods of silence but there came no appeals to be let out.

In there they seemed to feel safe from themselves and from a world that had suddenly become overpowering to them on this day that their new brother was coming home. I began to understand that, only now, was the baby assuming full reality for them. Until today, he had been part of the strangeness of the hospital, of their mother and father being absent from home. He had not really impinged on their lives but, today, with his coming to this house which they had made so much their own, the miracle was suddenly complete for them and was hardly to be borne. In the face of this tremendous thing, they had to declare themselves in all their puny stridency in case it would overpower them. At ten-thirty, there came three rhythmic bangs on the inside of the playroom door, accompanied by a chant of:

> 'We three have a certain solidarit-ee
> And we feel
> Hungar-ee!'

I let them out to have their bread and cheese in the kitchen but they showed no inclination to talk to any of us. As soon as they had finished, they filed back to the playroom and waited for me to lock the door, as if it were a bulwark between them and the great world outside which had suddenly swelled beyond their encompassing.

They came out again for lunch, went in again as soon as the meal was over and about three-thirty, when I opened the door and said: 'You had better go up and get tidy and come through to the drawing-room now,' they looked at me tensely and then looked round at the clutter of the familiar room as if they were loth to leave it while, in the big, unfamiliar festive-occasion drawing-room, where Tom and George had made a large fire, they crowded silently together, all three in one armchair. Their tense uneasiness communicated itself to the rest of us so that we made stilted remarks to one another and it was with relief that I heard a car stop outside for I felt that if something decisive did not happen soon, the house would explode into fragments. The car, however, contained only the grandparents and Sheila, which merely made matters worse. The old people began to ask the children if they were looking forward to seeing their brother and various questions of this sort and, after giving one or two monosyllabic answers, all three suddenly left the room on a common impulse and scampered back to the playroom.

'Brats!' said Sheila, 'They are jealous of the baby! Pleased, Father? Pleased, my eye! Remember how Liz *bit* Dunk the first day he was home?'

Sheila was very conscious of Roddy, I noted and he, in her presence, was very subdued so that even his robust colouring seemed to be dimmed. Jock had been right. Roddy was not having his customary ease of conquest over Sheila. 'Kids,' she went on. 'If you ask me, Jock and Shona are demented. They have no life of their own. Everything is given over to that lot through there in the playroom. And soft! Why did they have to go trailing away over to the other side of town today to see that old Aunt Hannah?'

George, Tom and Granda were talking together at one end of the room and this tirade was directed ostensibly at Granny and me but, in actual fact, at Roddy. Sheila was announcing her independence of the entire sex and marriage situation and all that it entailed but she need not have troubled, I thought, for Roddy Maclean was extremely unlikely to offer her marriage. It was a measure of her innocence that she should think he would but it was a measure of her wariness that she could recognise him, almost subconsciously, as a danger.

'Oh, hush, Sheila,' Granny said comfortably. 'You know how insulted Aunt Hannah gets if she thinks she is being neglected and she does like to see the babies.'

'Who is Aunt Hannah?' I asked by way of making the conversation less intense.

'She is *my* auntie, really,' Granny explained. 'She is nearly ninety and a bittie cranky –'

'Cranky?' Sheila interrupted impatiently. 'She is a proper old cow, Janet, and a mean old skinflint into the bargain. When I went to see her last New Year, she gave me a bit of the shortbread that Mother gave her the year before. It was like a damp flannel!' At this moment, Jock's car arrived outside and in the general hubbub Sheila's need to assert herself was diminished but, although we all crowded from the drawing-room to the front door, the children did not appear. I felt embarrassed about this, felt that it was a reflection on my foster-parenthood during which I should have tried perhaps to prepare them in some way – but how? – for this tremendous event in their lives. Jock, however, got out of the car and greeted us all as if everything were normal and we all went to gather round Shona, very slim and neat in a cotton suit and then we all looked into the back of the car which held the basket-cot with the baby who was sleeping very hard, yet seeming to me to have a secret knowledge of his importance to us all.

'Liz, Dunk, Gee!' Jock called and the three appeared in the doorway. 'Oh, there you are. I wish you would give a hand here.' He lifted the cot out of the car and laid it on the damp gravel. 'Take this baby into the house, will you?' He spoke as if the basket and its contents were a parcel. 'Let Liz and Dunk take the handles, Gee and you hold the end under his head.'

Fascinated, I watched them carry the baby carefully up the steps and into the house but when we went into the drawing-room, there was not a child to be seen. They had taken the basket-cot straight through to the playroom.

'It is all right, Janet,' my brother told me. 'He belongs more with them than with us, you know,' but after a little he led me through to the back of the house. The cot was on the floor among the clutter of toys and the three children were sitting round it, staring with wonder at the sleeping baby.

'Will you let Aunt Janet have a look at your brother?' Jock asked.

'Yes, come in, Aunt Janet,' said Liz but not one of them took their eyes from the baby for even a second and I found that my own response was very much like theirs. There was nothing to be said about this creature in the cot. One could only look. He was utterly complete in himself and yet, at the same time, utterly dependent on us all and in the face of this paradox one could only look with wonder and not think or say.

Sheila, assisted by Roddy, who had not so far assisted me to the extent of washing a saucer, made the tea and the children carried the baby through to the kitchen, putting the cot on a chair while they attended to the cake with the glop in the middle but, as soon as they had finished, they picked the cot up again and went back to the playroom. Shona, I had noticed, had drunk a cup of tea but had eaten nothing and I said: 'Not even a biscuit, Shona?'

'I couldn't, thanks, Janet. I am stuffed with Aunt Hannah's corned beef sandwiches. They had so much mustard on them that they were almost uneatable but I ate them.'

'The more fool you,' said Sheila.

Shona merely gave her gentle smile and turned back to me. 'Aunt Hannah knows I don't like sweet things very much and she made the sandwiches specially. You know how it is, Janet.'

'I know,' I said, 'like old Granny Fraser at Rosecroft giving me Abernethy biscuits with butter and sugared caraway seeds on them when I was a kid. My back teeth go under water even now when I think of those caraway seeds but I used to eat them.'

We left the table and Sheila and, of course, Roddy volunteered for the washing-up so that Fat Mary could enjoy the party. When we were sitting down in the drawing-room, the children came with the baby and put the cot on the sofa beside me. 'You keep him, Aunt Janet,' said Liz, 'while we make up for the play and when we knock on the door, put him right down here, see?' and she patted a spot on the carpet.

'Has the baby a part in the play?' I asked.

'Of course!' said all three together and left the room.

'I don't know whether you know it,' Jock said to me, 'but you are greatly honoured, being given that baby. It means that, at the moment, you are the only trustworthy person in this house.'

'You must have had a real time of it with them, Janet, what with sore bottoms and grazed arms,' Shona said. 'It is easy for me and sometimes I find them wearing enough.'

'They have a queer sort of logic of their own,' I said, looking at the sleeping baby and I told how, that forenoon, they had suggested that I lock them in the playroom. 'It was as if they felt safe from themselves when they were locked up,' I ended.

'I don't know about their logic,' Shona said, 'but I lock them in there fairly regularly. Sheila says it will give them claustrophobia and all sorts of things but sometimes it is a choice between their claustrophobia and my going mad.'

'Claustrophobia, rubbish!' said Jock. 'If a kid knows that you mean well by it, it will be all right. They have a keen sense of justice and the fitness of things if they are allowed to exercise it and away in their own place and out of range of driving somebody crazy is a fine place to exercise it.'

There now came the three taps at the door and I put the cot down on the appointed spot. Liz leading, the three children came in slow single file into the room. They were dressed in long robes of old curtain material, on their heads were paper crowns and Liz's long hair was ingeniously stuck to her chin with adhesive tape to form a beard that reached to her waist. Duncan's face and hands were coal black, his blue eyes staring oddly from this mask of soot and Gee's face had a pair of black shoe laces fixed to his upper lip, trailing down over his chest like the moustaches in old pictures of Chinese mandarins. Each child carried a package done up in coloured paper and, as they came forward, they sang: 'We three kings of Orient are –' They proceeded to enact round the basket on the floor a Nativity Play. 'A slight entertainment of a dramatic nature,' Liz had called it. I found it far from slight and very dramatic, dramatic to the point where they bore me along with them on the wave of their palpable sincerity. They were utterly convincing about the star they had seen and followed and their worship of the baby was more convincing still as they placed their gifts at the foot of his cot and none of us in the audience could breathe while they knelt, repeating the Lord's Prayer. 'Amen,' they said, one after the other, unclasping their hands and opening their eyes to look at the baby who, as if inspired by them into playing his part, opened his eyes, waving his small hands in the air as if in applause.

'Mum, he liked it,' said Liz, undoing her beard.

'Yes, Liz. We all liked it. Thank you,' Shona said.

'Mum, will you take off my mackstache?' Gee asked.

'I doubt Tom and I will have to take that black fellow out to the garden tap to wash him,' said George, 'or will we just send him out to St Jago?'

'Mum, open the baby's presents,' said Duncan.

Shona unwrapped the talcum powder, the baby soap and the little celluloid duck and the baby again did his part by trying to push the head of the duck into his mouth.

'The actors have got to be paid,' said Granda, passing out the half-crowns.

'And now the baby has to be washed and fed or he will eat his new duck,' Shona said and, taking him out of the cot, she handed him to me with a casual: 'Here you are, Janet. Take him through to the kitchen for me.'

Granda, Granny and Sheila were now going home and

104

Roddy decided to drive into town behind them so while Jock and Shona, Tom and George saw them off, I sat by the kitchen stove nursing the baby while Liz directed the two boys in the laying out of his toilet materials from the basket that had come home with him. As she draped the tiny night clothes and the napkins over the warm rail of the stove, I said with an envy that I hoped she would not notice: 'You are very expert, Liz.'

'Been helping to bath babies since God come Wednesday,' she said and picking up the little bath, she went through to the scullery for water.

When the others came through to the kitchen, Jock said: 'Leave them to it, Shona. Take the help while you have the chance,' and grinned at me with the baby on my lap. I was about to protest but suddenly I became conscious of George and Tom looking down at me, smiles on their faces that were half-happy, half-teasing and I felt, I think, a little like the children must have felt that morning when they told me to lock them in the playroom. I felt overawed and overcome but I felt also that I had a certain responsibility to this older generation which now must take the form of justifying their oft-expressed belief that: 'Janet will tackle any damn' thing at all whether she knows about it or not,' so I said: 'May I wash him, Shona?'

'I wish you would,' she said. 'I shall have to do it often enough. Come, Gee. You be *my* baby and let Aunt Janet have that new one.' Pleased, Gee climbed on to the lap which would now be less his own than before but, from his vantage point, he looked at his father and said: 'But not to keep, Dad?'

'Oh no,' Jock said. 'Aunt Janet has only a share in him like the rest of us.'

I could have wished that there were fewer eyes upon me as I went about my unaccustomed task but all went to the satisfaction of everyone, it seemed, including the baby. When Liz and Duncan had put the toilet things away, Shona put Gee down and said: 'Now I have to go up and give the baby his supper. You will all go to bed quietly and not disturb him, will you? Dad and I will be in to see you later on.'

They watched her as she took the baby from me and as they looked at him in their mother's arms, their own lives, which he had absorbed entirely since he came home, flowed back around them.

'You and Dad can stay with the baby,' Liz said. 'Aunt Janet will be coming up for Reachfar.'

'Yes. Every night we have Reachfar.'

'Yes, Mum. Reachfar.'

Had I been Shona or Jock, I thought, especially had I been Shona, I would have been petty enough to be hurt by this curt dismissal of part of the routine of the children's lifetime. It had about it the flagrant opportunism of sheer selfishness, but Shona was evidently less petty than I was for she merely said: 'Very well, but don't keep Aunt Janet too long. I am sure she has had plenty of you today.' Her love for her children was so great and she was so secure in their love for herself that she could afford to be lavish and lend them to me although through that love of hers she also knew that, when I went away, she would be called upon to serve them at bedtime as she had done every evening since their birth.

While they had their baths, I sat in my bedroom and I could hear what they said.

'One of the things about this baby,' said the decisive voice of Liz, 'is that it will get us staying up later if we work things properly.'

'How?' Gee asked.

'Helping to bath it, stupid.'

'I'd like just as much to be in bed with my book,' said Duncan.

Listening to this, I remembered the three worshipping kings of the dramatic entertainment and wondered whether they saw their brother in that light or merely as a means towards declaiming even more stridently their own thrusting, independent wayward life. And then I remembered the sooty face of Duncan which, along with his hands, had been only roughly washed before he handled the baby's things and I went to the bathroom to get him clean. There was nothing, I felt, that I could do about them except mean well by them, as my brother had said and it seemed to be axiomatic that to see that they were physically clean was an act of well-meaning.

That evening, the entire household with the exception of Roddy who might not be back until the small hours retired to bed about nine o'clock but I was still awake and reading when, at ten-thirty, my brother came into my room. Dressed in blue-and-white-striped pyjamas, wide-eyed and distraught, he looked like a Gargantuan parody of one of his own children in one of their moments of crisis.

'There is something far wrong with Shona,' he said and, implicit in the words and in the fact that he had come to me, there was the childish demand: 'I am in trouble. Do something!'

He followed me as I ran across the landing to the other room. As I bent over the bed, Shona, who had been about to speak to me, suddenly writhed and pulled her knees up nearly to her chin in agony and when the spasm passed, she panted for breath as the sweat broke over her forehead and upper lip.

'I have called the doctor,' Jock said.

'Want to be sick,' Shona gasped.

I grabbed the baby's little pot and sat on the bed beside her but although she retched violently in a long and painful spasm, she did not vomit.

'Have never been able to be sick much,' she panted and then her body contorted itself in a convulsion of agony again.

It was no more than ten minutes before Doctor Nancy and one of her male partners, the one who had delivered the baby, were in the house but the short period contained more physical pain for Shona than I had ever witnessed in the course of my life. The doctors merely watched one spasm before Doctor Turner said: 'Ring the hospital, Nancy. Tell them we are coming in.'

'But what *is* it?' my brother asked frantically.

'Not certain. Soon find out though. Don't worry. Get dressed.'

Very soon, they were ready to go, Shona with her winter coat over her night-clothes; but now an anguish greater than the physical pain had been able to bring upon her showed in her eyes as she panted: 'Oh Janet, my baby! Janet, look after my baby!'

'I will look after him, Shona,' I promised as Jock began to half lead her half carry her downstairs.

'A cup of tea, I think,' said Doctor Nancy as she shut the door on the departing car. I looked up the stairs towards the room that held the cot and saw the door of Tom's and George's room close quietly. They had decided to keep out of the way. 'Don't worry,' Doctor Nancy was saying, 'for if that one up there in the cot wants anything, he will let us know,' and I followed her through to the kitchen.

'Doctor Nancy, what *is* the matter with Shona?'

'Not sure,' she said shortly but I felt that she was almost sure although she would not tell, because the case was Doctor Turner's. She herself, I suddenly realised, was here because of the baby, because in taking Shona away, they had cut off the baby's food supply. 'She will be all right. Bill Turner is pretty able,' she added, by way of comforting me. 'The cups are in here, aren't they? I must say you are not having much of a holiday but it seems to be agreeing with you.'

'What shall I feed that baby on?'

'Diluted cow's milk. Stop worrying. He will be all right. They are tougher than you think.'

It was all very well for *her,* I thought, equipped as she was with all her medical knowledge, accustomed as she was to infants and crises of all kinds but she did not know how frightening it was to feel as inadequate as I did. Much as I liked her and trusted her, I was glad when she went away and I was free to go upstairs and look at the baby. Shona had described him, that first day I had seen him in the hospital, as 'one of the peaceful unobtrusive sort – not like Liz, thank goodness,' and this, I thought now was true for Shona but not for me. He was peaceful, certainly, lost in sound sleep but the moment when he would wake was already obtruding itself on me. At ten days old, was one pair of arms as good as another?

I lay on the bed but I could not sleep, what with watching the baby and listening for the telephone and at four o'clock I went downstairs and fetched the tray that the doctor and I had prepared – the milk, the sugar, the electric kettle, the measuring cup and the bottle and teat found on the top shelf of the cupboard. But this journey when the sky was getting light was enough to wake George and Tom and as I reached the top of the stairs, they met me on the landing. In Shona's room, I told them what had happened.

'We thought it best to keep out o' the road last night,' George said. 'I wonder what in the world came at poor Shona?'

'I think it must be appendicitis,' I said. 'Maybe Jock will ring soon,' and now the baby stirred, woke, seemed to take thought for a moment and began to cry.

By the time I had made up the bottle, he was scarlet in the face with fury in spite of the best efforts of Tom and George and my hands shook, as I poured the mixture into the narrow neck of the bottle, with trepidation that, at any moment, the other three would arrive to augment the howling chaos.

'Right,' I said, sitting down on the bed. 'Give him to me, George, for pity's sake.'

I thought I had nothing to do but put the teat between his lips which were sucking between yells but the baby had other ideas. As soon as the rubber teat touched his lower lip, he swiped with his tiny furious hand, almost knocking the bottle to the floor and with redoubled fury he made himself into a rigid bow and emitted a howl that could have been heard at the other end of the parish. This neutral cool bit of rubber was not what his lips were accustomed to, he informed us loudly and at length. George bent over and squeezed a few drops of the watery milk from the teat into the howling mouth and, after an astonished insulted second, the baby spat straight up into George's face.

'The wee devil!' said George.

Naturally, now, my worst fears were realised and the other three arrived in the room, becoming very wide-eyed and silent and huddling together when I told them that their mother had had to go 'back to the hospital' during the night.

'And now you three will come with Tom and me,' said George and they led them away.

The baby howled and howled. I walked round the room with him after I had changed his napkin; I tried to put the teat in his mouth again and he howled even more loudly until, at last, he pushed his fist into his mouth and cried himself to sleep, sobbing pitifully at the injustice of the world. At seven o'clock when the telephone, which I had muffled with a shawl, rang at last, it did not wake him and I snatched up the receiver with a shudder of gratitude, for I did not want my brother to hear those yells. 'Jock? Do they know what is the matter?' Incongruously, my brother gave a high-pitched laugh. 'Yes. Aunt Hannah's corned beef sandwiches.'

'God, it isn't funny!'

'It isn't really,' he said, his voice shaking now, 'but she will be all right now. She has had a bad go, though. We'll be in here for a day or two.'

I looked at the cot. 'A day or two?'

'Yes. They have to be sure she can't infect the baby. And then there is her milk. That will have to be dried up.'

'Dried up?' I was staring at the cot now.

'Janet, are you all right?'

I pulled myself together. 'Yes. Yes, of course. But I am short on sleep and stupid.'

'How is the baby?'

'Fine,' I said heartily, hoping I was not overdoing it. 'He came awake and I made up a bottle as Doctor Nancy said and now he is asleep again,' and I managed to get away with this literal truth that was so fundamentally untrue.

At eight o'clock, the baby woke. I made up another bottle and we had another prolonged battle but he would not suffer the teat in his mouth, so I laid him, roaring, on the bed and rang up Doctor Nancy.

She assured me that the child was not poisoned like his mother, that the infection could not pass through the breast milk but that they were keeping Shona in hospital because there was a risk that she could infect the baby by handling him. Doctor Nancy also brought with her a jar of some proprietary infant food and she made up a bottle of this for me and when we had put a few drops on his tongue, he at last accepted the hated teat and drank the feed.

'He will be all right now,' she said. 'As I told you before, they are much tougher than you think.'

She went away and, sighing with relief, I sponged the baby and laid him, already asleep, in the cot, then dressed and carried him downstairs to the sofa in the kitchen.

The other three were very subdued and wanted to do nothing but cluster in their solidarity round the baby. Little Gee was very pathetic, frightened by the strangeness of it all, Duncan was obviously worried at his newly-returned mother going away again and I saw something of my own temperament in Liz. She was afraid to speak or move in case she would explode into frustrated rage at her world going wrong like this.

I was starting to prepare the lunch when Liz said suddenly: 'Aunt Janet, the baby is throwing up!' and throw up he did until the entire feed he had taken was in a pool on the floor. Then he began to cry again but it seemed to me to be more of a pathetic wailing than the lusty howling of the early morning. I carried him upstairs, sent Fat Mary down to do what she could about the lunch and, when he had fallen asleep again, I telephoned Doctor Nancy, chasing her round the several farms she was visiting.

'Make the next feed a little weaker,' she said. 'He will settle to it,' but the baby did not settle to it. He fed, was sick, howled, slept fitfully, howled again and when Doctor Nancy came at six in the evening, he was sick in her presence, as if to indicate to her how wrong she was.

'He will come to it,' she said, however. 'It is the bottle or nothing and he will come to it. Feed him again at ten o'clock and ring me in the morning.'

At ten, he drank the feed greedily, yelling when I took the teat from his mouth for short pauses but the yells were peevish now and already the little hands were different. They had lost their blind strength and their chubbiness and between the tiny fingers there were horrid little webs of grey skin. And at ten-fifteen, he was sick again.

George and Tom did not go to bed. They stayed with us all night, dozing at short intervals while the baby slept and when at seven in the morning, he awoke, fed and vomited again, I wanted to give way to tears of despair but Tom and George, who had been sitting on the edge of Shona's bed, suddenly stood up, side by side, very erect. They seldom asserted themselves; they were modest men who thought that everybody knew better than they did but this was one of their few moments of assertion.

'The old people used to say – ' Tom began.

'Does anybody about here keep goats?' George asked.

Exhausted and despairing as I was, with the weakly crying infant on my lap waving his tiny searching webs of hands, it took a few seconds for their meaning to penetrate my mind.

'But Doctor Nancy said – '

'To the devil with doctors!' said Tom.

'And to hell with that shop stuff out of that can!' said George.

I capitulated. 'Wake Liz and ask her,' I said. 'She will know.'

Sleepily, Liz came into the room with them. Normally, Liz and her brothers would have been awake and at battle by this time in the morning but the three of them were as exhausted as the rest of us, worried and frozen in an inarticulate misery.

'Goats?' she said, looking from the crying baby round the three of us. 'Ring up Mr Murchison. He is the Agricultural Officer. He will know,' she said and trailed sadly away back to her room.

While George held the now frail exhausted infant, I found out that a small marginal farm fifteen miles away had a herd of goats.

111

'Go and get Roddy,' I said. 'We'll send him up there.'

Roddy too had been up all night, making cups of tea and doing what he could and I think he was glad to get into his car and do something more active.

'I'll come with you, lad,' Tom said. 'George will stay with Janet.'

'As quickly as you can, Roddy,' I said, thinking of my brother coming on the telephone as he would be sure to do between nine and ten o'clock.

'You bet,' Roddy said and they went away.

The baby slept again but now his eyelids were almost transparent and the sleep was very fitful and uneasy. I wondered if infants dreamed, had nightmares, as I watched the spasms that momentarily puckered the tiny, now aged-looking face and I was almost certain when he awakened with a horrid start that it was out of some nightmare of sickness, starvation and cruelty. As he began to cry, the three children came into the room, their faces very solemn as they formed themselves into a row facing George and me where we sat side by side on the dishevelled bed.

'We three have a certain solidarit-ee,' they said quietly in unison,

> 'It was kind of you all to come,
> But our brother
> Needs our Mum.'

I was weak with worry and exhaustion and the tears started from my eyes, ran down and dripped on to the baby's nightgown. What the children had said was true. We had all done all we could but the baby needed his mother and nobody else. Quietly, the children now began to cry too until George got up, put his hands on two shoulders of the clinging sobbing little huddle and began to propel them out of the room.

'Now, now,' he said, 'Tom and I and your Aunt Janet are going to see that your brother is all right. Come now. We will go down below and make a drop of porridge.'

He glanced back over his shoulder at me, I nodded and he went out, shutting the door.

I began to pace the floor with the baby, talking to him as I went: 'Oh, Alexander Thomas Sandison, like this goat's milk will you?' And then as I went on pacing, I prayed: 'Please, God, make him like the goat's milk. Please God, don't let Tom

112

and George do something harmful for the first time in their lives! Alexander Thomas, you are going to like this goat's milk, aren't you?'

When Roddy's car came back, everybody, including Fat Mary, came upstairs but the only operative people were Tom and George and we all watched while they boiled the kettle and mixed the milk, sugar and water in the measuring jug. When they handed me the bottle, I was almost praying aloud as I put the teat in the infant's mouth and, without protest, he began to suck. And then I noticed that he was feeding in a different way. The hungry desperation had left him. It was as if he were enjoying what was flowing into his mouth. When I removed the teat, he made an angry little noise, belched and groped about with his hands but no longer in protest and when I returned the teat to his lips he gave a satisfied little snuffle.

'He likes it,' said Liz. 'He's pee-ochering!'

'He is *what*?' Roddy asked.

'Pee-ochering!' Liz said and imitated the baby's snuffling noise.

'Aye, he is fairly pee-ocherin', fairly that, the bonnie wee darlin',' said Fat Mary.

But I was still wary after the bottle was empty, ready with my towel for the vomit which had always ensued but it did not come. The baby sent a final belch over my shoulder, making everybody laugh and then lapsed into contented sleep, just as the telephone rang. Liz picked up the receiver. It was Doctor Nancy.

'God knows,' said George, coming between the receiver and my hand, 'I have no liking for that bliddy unnatural telephone, handy as it is but I will speak to her.' And then into the telephone: 'The baby? Och yes, he is fine. He has settled down fine now. Herself says you needn't bother to come up and you so busy. Yes, we will do that. If we will be needing you, Doctor, we will call.'

'George,' I protested as he put the receiver down.

'Ach,' said Tom, 'what she doesna know canna hurt her.'

At ten o'clock the baby woke again, indicating that a little more of this goat's milk would be in order but, this time, I bathed him first, getting rid of all the sour-smelling clothes which Fat Mary plunged into a bucket of water. And just in time for, as I began to feed the child, my brother walked into the kitchen. He looked down at the baby snuffling over the bottle and said: 'He is all right? Shona is worrying about him. She fed all the others herself, you see and sometimes they are difficult about bottle feeding – '

'Ach, he didna care for the cow's milk or the doctor's stuff,' said George, 'but since we got him on to the goat's milk he has been no bother.'

'No bother o' the world,' Tom confirmed and with their genius for telling the important half of the truth, neither he nor George indicated how short had been the time since the 'bother' stopped.

'Goat's milk?' Jock said. 'Did Doctor Nancy – '

With one accord, George and Tom raised their right hands and gave the backs of their necks a rub as they had always done when they found themselves in an embarrassing situation.

'Well, now that you mention Doctor Nancy – ' Tom began.

' – she doesna know about it yet,' George said and then added defiantly, 'but he *likes* the goat's milk and he didna like *her* stuff.'

'I suppose it is all right,' Jock said hesitantly, torn, like myself, between modern science and the ancient wisdom of Tom and George which had always served us so well.

'Of *course* it is, Dad,' said Liz.

'Of course!'

'Acourse!'

'You seem to be fairly solid for the goat's milk,' Jock said, accepting the verdict of the generations.

When Roddy had taken the children away up to the farm to see the goats and arrange for future supplies of milk, Jock said to me, 'I feel that you have all been through more than you are admitting in the last thirty-six hours.'

'The frightening thing is one's appalling ignorance,' I said, after we had told him something of what had happened. 'Shona would have had some sort of instinctive grip on the situation I feel, but I had none at all.'

'She had enough grip never to take her eyes off that bairn, Jock,' Tom said.

'Aye,' George agreed. 'You said the other day that she had a share in him. Maybe she has a bigger share than you will ever know.'

'It was supposed to be a holiday, this,' Jock said apologetically.

114

'And it is,' I told him. I was anxious to lighten the tone. 'It is what is called a nice change but, everything being equal – ' I looked at the cot ' – that one and I will retire upstairs for a snooze this afternoon. Fat Mary, will you make us a cup of coffee, please?'

When the children came back from the farm, they went out to the shrubbery, only to come rushing into the kitchen again: 'Aunt Janet, the bees are out gathering honey from all over the garden!'

'And bringing it to the hive –'

' – and going in with it!'

'Bees?' said Jock, frowning.

The children, looking guilty, gathered round me. 'Oh lord,' I said, 'didn't we tell you that we have a hive of bees?'

Excitedly, the three told him how the bees had arrived and dragged him out to the garden, George, Tom and I following. I was suddenly aware that it seemed to be a terribly long time since I had been out of the house.

'Come back, Daddy!' Liz shouted. 'You mustn't pass the sign!' There was a painted board hung from a laurel that proclaimed: 'Bees! Stinging danger! Do not pass this point!'

'You watch them through here, Dad,' said Duncan.

'Yes, through this hole,' Gee added.

After lunch, I retired upstairs with the baby, fed him and then went to sleep myself and I did not wake until after four when my brother came to my bedroom with a cup of tea for me. The baby came awake for a little while and Jock picked him out of the cot and sat with him in the crook of his arm. 'You wicked fellow,' he said, 'worrying your poor old aunt nearly out of her wits.' There was something irresistibly comical and yet tender about Jock's handling of the child. Long narrow hands with long thin fingers are a characteristic of our family and I noticed now that Jock's hand was about as long as the baby's body from neck to hips and Jock handled him surely and expertly but in a way that was quite unlike the way that any woman would handle an infant.

'By the way, Jock,' I said, 'I hope you don't mind too much about the bees. George and Tom wanted Mr Gibson to take them away but I said not.'

'The kids seem to be very sensible about them.' He smiled at me. 'But why did you say not to take them away?'

'The children had been up at the farm with Doctor Nancy

and when they came back I heard them chanting a spell in the shrubbery. I was sure that they were wishing for bees and then, when the swarm arrived, it seemed – well, it seemed not right to send it away again. There is so little nice magic in the world.' I felt embarrassed and changed the subject. 'Incidentally, when they made their spell they had a fire going. I could smell wood burning. Are they allowed to have matches?'

'Yes, but only in Reachfar. And they never use them now except for what they call spell-fires. Fire had a fascination for Liz. She burned herself several times but it made no difference so, at the beginning of this holiday, I presented her with a box of matches and said shrubbery only. It is always pretty damp and drippy in there. There has been no trouble since.'

I then told him how Liz had tried to persuade me to have the carpenter build the playhouse and he laughed. 'You are beginning to catch on to the fact that Liz seizes any and every opportunity for the furtherance of her own ends,' he said. 'They all do but they don't all have such a degree of thrust as Liz. They will get their playhouse before the winter. They don't need it just now anyway.' He looked down at the baby. 'So you are bored and have gone off to sleep again, you anti-social little morsel, furthering your own ends like all the rest,' he said and put the child back in his cot.

Chapter VII

'Our birth is but a sleep and a forgetting;
The Soul that rises with us, our life's Star,
Hath had elsewhere its setting,
And cometh from afar:'

SHONA was in hospital for five days altogether but, after our
nightmare thirty-six hours were over, all was plain sailing, or as
plain as was possible with Liz, Duncan and Gee among the
crew. When they understood that their mother was sick 'because
of something she had eaten,' but was getting better now,
they ceased to worry about her – even Duncan – for to be sick
from over-eating, which was how they interpreted it, was something they completely understood.

'It is very stupid but there it is. We all do it now and then,'
Liz said, sighing tolerantly over human frailty, 'but *Mummy!*
Just fancy that!'

On the whole, they were pleased rather than otherwise that
their mother had demonstrated that she was like themselves in
this way and more pleased still that she had indulged herself
to an extent that they had never done, to the degree where she
had had to be taken away to hospital.

In the intervals of eating and helping me with the baby,
they were very busy in the shrubbery and unusually at peace
with one another. I often wondered what they were doing in
there among the tangle of laurels and rhododendrons but every
time I thought of entering the place, that memory of their
first hostility would return and my curiosity would wither away
before the wind of taboo. The children were no longer hostile
to me, of course. They were obedient and co-operative and I
felt it to be no more than fair that, if they respected the laws
which I laid down, I should respect their law about their private
territory. But I was curious, none the less, as I saw an old
wooden washtub from the garden shed being rolled into the
wilderness, as I watched them carrying cans of water in, as I
listened to the sounds of hammering, bursts of song and sudden
recitations of speeches from Shakespeare. My brother in his

117

university days had been something of a scholar in English literature and they seemed to have inherited something of his love for the language, while they had certainly inherited his aural memory. They recited the soliloquies of Hamlet, the political speeches from Julius Caesar, interspersed with bursts of popular song and they recited parts of Chaucer and Tennyson, interspersed with the songs from the Shakespeare comedies. Like myself as a child, they had a predilection for the sonorous and sad in verse and one forenoon when I put the baby out in his perambulator, I was amused to see them sitting like a row of sparrows on a high branch of the sycamore tree, their faces tragic, while they intoned:

'O Mother Ida, many-fountain'd Ida,
Dear Mother Ida, harken ere I die.
Hear me O Earth, hear me O Hills, O Caves
That house the cold crown'd snake!'

They had themselves almost in tears with the sad grand sonority of it all and in the next second the mood changed as Liz said: 'Look here, you two, I got an idea!' and they all scrambled along the branch and down out of sight among the shrubs. Again, they made me think of the fitful comings and goings of the rainbows as the shadows of the clouds fled along the hills across the firth from Reachfar.

On the day before Shona was to come home, my brother said: 'I shall have to register the baby tomorrow. It is the last day.'

We were alone in the kitchen and I looked out of the window at the perambulator. 'What name?' I asked.

'Except that Tom has to come into it, we haven't made up our minds even yet.'

'I christened him, sort of, that awful night when he was starving.'

'Did you?' Jock asked quietly. 'What did you call him?'

'He wasn't a mystery that night any more, Jock,' I apologised. 'He was just a little person who seemed to be threatening to slip through my fingers because I couldn't find the right food for him and I have to have a name for him — to call him back by, sort of. Alexander Thomas, I called him.'

'Then that is his name,' Jock said. 'Shona mentioned Alexander as one of her fancies and she will be delighted.

Remember the old book on the Greek mythology at Reachfar?'
he asked suddenly.

'Yes. Why?'

'It always made me wish my name was Alexander when I
was about Dunk's age.'

'I don't remember that bit,' I said.

'Alexander was really Paris, the one that caused all the
trouble among the goddesses with the golden apple, but that
wasn't why I wanted the name,' he assured me hastily. 'He was
a god exiled among the shepherds on Mount Ida and he was so
brave that they named him Alexandros which meant Defender
of Men.'

'Oh, yes. He was the one Oenone was in love with,' I said.
'I remember that bit. By the way, I wish you had seen the
children the other day. They were perched in a row on the
branch of a tree out there, with faces as long as fiddles, reciting
Tennyson's *Oenone*.'

'That is a favourite one,' he told me, 'and they are also quite
blood-curdling with *The Ancient Mariner*.'

He seemed to take their young knowledge of classical poetry
very much as a matter of course and I said: 'You know, it is
a little odd to hear a child of Duncan's age tearing off a line
or two of *Tamburlaine* and very aptly too.'

'*Tamburlaine?* I didn't know they had been into that. I have
never read any of it to them. They learn the poetry by ear,
you know, by my reading it to them. I am not a story-teller
like you and Roddy but I have discovered that if you read
poetry to them, they become fascinated by the rhythm whether
they understand the sense or not, so I read poetry and everybody is happy. What did Dunk say?'

'It made Liz furious. She was going it a bit, laying down the
law, you know and Duncan put the lampshade on his head and
strutted across the floor saying:

>Is it not passing great to be a queen
>And ride in triumph through Persepolis?'

'Oh, he got that from me. I often use that couplet to bring
Liz down to size.'

The next day, when Shona came home, she took the baby
from me and said: 'George and Tom, this is your new grand-
nephew Alexander Thomas Sandison and Sunday first is
christening Sunday at church and he will be baptised.'

119

'My, but I am pleased with his name, Shona,' Tom said proudly, 'and Uncle Twice is another man that will be pleased.'

'And we'll have a christening party?' Liz asked.

'And chocolate cake – '

' – with glop in the middle?'

'Yes,' I said.

They formed into line. 'We three have a certain solidarit-ee – '

'Stop that,' Jock interrupted. 'It is only a big lie anyway. You are not three any more. You are four.'

The six eyes stared at him as this great new truth invaded their minds. 'So we are,' said Liz. 'I hadn't connected up. Just fancy that, four!'

'Four!'

'Fancy that!' and by an unspoken but communal decision, they ran away and disappeared into the shrubbery.

Now that Shona and Jock were permanently about the house, I saw a great deal less of the children, who spent most of their time inside their own secret world, coming out of it only to demand food, look at the baby for a little while or hear a story about Reachfar from me at bedtime. Although it was, in theory, holiday time, my brother was involved in various activities that kept him in his study for part of every day while George and Tom spent most of their time in the garden and I helped Shona with the baby and the cooking.

'This is a shame,' she said one day. 'You are supposed to be on holiday.'

'I *am* on holiday,' I said, 'my sort of holiday. I have never in my life had what people usually mean by a holiday. I always went home to Reachfar and took part in the life there from where I left off.' I laughed. 'I remember once, at Cairnton, Jean indicated that the proper way to have a holiday was to go to Rothesay for a fortnight and stay in a boarding-house. I was sick with apprehension that Dad might take her seriously and send me to Rothesay. He didn't, though. I went home to Reachfar as usual.'

'I am worried about Jean,' Shona said. 'I think it is terrible her being up there all alone when she has quarrelled with nearly everybody in Achcraggan. But what can one do? I wanted George and Tom to bring her down here with them but they wouldn't do it and maybe it is just as well. Even last December, when we were north for Dad Sandison's funeral, she was absolutely horrible to John by the end of the week. We had left the kids with Mum and Dad and Sheila and John used to go out to the kiosk every evening to ring up and see that they were all right. Jean said we went on as if nobody in the country except ourselves had ever had children. Janet, why does she have to be so nasty?'

'Why ask *me*?' I said.

'She does herself so much harm. Though why I am going on about Jean being nasty, I don't know. Aunt Hannah is nearly as bad although she is not so plain *wicked* as Jean. The worst thing about Aunt Hannah is that she is so mean – mean with things like money and food, that is. She isn't mean *about* people as Jean is.'

'Well, you watch out for her sandwiches after this,' I said and Shona smiled.

'I bet she has had a proper rocket from Sheila about those sandwiches,' she said. 'Sheila will have gone through her food cupboard again, throwing everything in the dustbin.'

'Sheila gave me to understand that she never went near Aunt Hannah.'

Shona laughed again. 'Sheila visits Aunt Hannah every day. That is where Aunt Hannah is so much better off than Jean. Jean has nobody of her own. Sheila loves Aunt Hannah but she doesn't like anybody to know it and think she is soft. Janet, Roddy is interested in Sheila, sort of, don't you think?'

Shona spoke in a tentative way, with the voice of one who is stepping out into a sphere wider than her own and where she had no confidence in herself and it occurred to me that, probably, in the world of relationships, she was situated as I had been when she was rushed off to hospital, leaving me with the baby. I had little experience of children; Shona had little experience of relationships.

Even now, with her four children and her complete control of her domestic world which contained them, Shona was only in her mid-thirties. My brother had begun to court her when he was nineteen and she only seventeen, she had remained faithful to him throughout the long years of the war and they had been married early in 1946. Shona had had few relationships outside the happy well-balanced home circle into which she had been born until she married my brother and they had created this full, satisfying home circle of their own which spread its boundaries to contain Shona's parents and sister,

George, Tom and me. This house, with the three children in the shrubbery and the baby in the perambulator, was the new centre of the Sandison family.

'Yes,' I said. 'Roddy is interested in Sheila, sort of.'

Shona looked at me with the wide innocent eyes of one of her own children. 'He is such a nice fellow,' she said. 'I was hoping that Sheila might – ' She lapsed into silence.

'Roddy is not all that of a nice fellow, Shona,' I said gently. 'He is very wild and reckless and a bit ruthless, quite honestly. If Sheila is watching her step with him, I think she is quite right.'

'It isn't that. Sheila isn't watching her step in that way.' She paused, her eyes worried and sad. 'The way things have gone, life has been very unfair to Sheila. When I got married, Dad and Mum were so much younger. I didn't think of the day when they would need looking after. And my brother Andrew was alive then too. But now, here I am with this lot – ' she indicated the clothes-horse, draped with children's clothing which I was ironing ' – and Sheila is left with Mum and Dad and Aunt Hannah. It all seems very selfish.'

'Selfish? Don't be silly, Shona. Can you think of anything you could have done that would give more pleasure to your father than Liz? Or anything that your mother would like more than Duncan and Gee?'

'Yes,' she conceded. 'They are fond of the children. But what about Sheila when I have so much? She ought to be married with children of her own.'

Shona was still innocent and inexperienced enough to believe that Heaven is the same for everybody and, because she had found her Heaven in this cumbrous house and over-grown garden with Liz, Duncan and Gee squabbling round her feet, she thought that Heaven for Sheila must be a simulacrum of this. I myself was less sure of the nature of Sheila's Heaven but I was completely sure of another thing, although I did not say it aloud to Shona and this was that if Sheila wanted Roddy Maclean, she would carve out some compromise whereby she could have him and look after her mother and father and Aunt Hannah, too, if she felt for them as Shona said she did. For Shona, all the sailing had been plain throughout her courtship and marriage to my brother and she had no conception of the ruthlessness that comes to mariners on the sea of life who find themselves in waters that threaten to stop them reaching the

122

harbour of their desire. And there was no point in telling Shona of this or in trying to explain it to her. No description or picture of a storm at sea can convey the actual experience of the storm and so I said: 'Roddy Maclean is not the marrying or having children sort, Shona.'

She looked at me without comprehension. She obviously thought that all men were of this sort. 'You mean because he is a writer and a – an intellectual? But *John* is an intellectual – '

'No, that is not what I mean. It is not because of anything that Roddy is on the outside. It is because of what he is in himself, in his own nature. Roddy had a very strange childhood, Shona.'

She sat like a child listening to a tale with disbelief just suspended and no more, while I told her of Roddy's parents, my friends Rob and Marion Maclean and the extraordinary love-hate relationship that had existed between them. 'And I think Roddy as a child must have overheard some of their terrible quarrels,' I ended, 'and they have left a mark on him.'

'Poor little boy!' Shona said.

'But he is no longer a little boy,' I said firmly. 'He is a man and a very passionate and ruthless one and, in my opinion, Sheila is better clear of him.'

'You would know better than I do,' she said. 'I just thought – Hush! Yes, that's the baby, I'll fetch him in.'

In the presence of her baby, Shona forgot about Sheila and Roddy and all the problems that might lie outside this warm cocoon of napkins and talcum powder as she crooned: 'Alexander Thomas, you are a leaky, messy little boy.'

'Fly isn't leaky any more, Mum,' announced Liz, coming in. 'He has a special place now – '

'– On George and Tom's weed heap.'

'When will Sandy Tom stop being leaky?' Liz asked.

'Who?' I asked.

'Sandy Tom, we thought.' She nodded at the baby. 'You can't go Alexander-Thomasing about the place all the time.'

In this ruthless way did Liz and her brothers speed on towards the future, when they would be calling for their brother 'about the place,' and in this ruthless way did they try to shape the future to their hearts' desire as they sped.

That evening, at bedtime, when I went up to their room, I noticed that there was a heap of coins on Liz's chest of drawers but the little porcelain bank that had held this money was gone.

123

It had been a pretty little Victorian piece, given to her by Granda Murray and I said: 'Where is your little bank with the flowers on it, Liz? You haven't broken it, have you?'

'No, I haven't broken it. I require it in another place for another purpose,' she said repressively.

'Then that is all right. It is so very pretty.'

'You like it, Aunt Janet?' Duncan asked.

'Yes. Very much.'

'So do we,' said Gee.

'Come along, Aunt Janet. We are ready,' said Liz.

'At Reachfar, long long ago, there was this place among the fir trees of the moor that Channatt called the Juniper Place – ' I began. I told them how, in this green place near the spring, the juniper bushes grew in fantastic shapes, some like animals, some round like cushions, some like goblins and some like carved stone pillars and how Channatt had private names for them all. When I ended, they sighed in their customary satisfied way but, before I left their room, Liz's mind came out of the dream of the Juniper Place and went roving on to the future, to the baby's christening, the next event in her life to which she was greedily pushing forward.

'Aunt Janet, Dunk got christened and so did Gee. Did I get christened or is it only for boys? I don't remember getting christened but I remember Dunk and Gee – '

'*I* don't remember getting christened,' Duncan broke in suspiciously with a wary eye on his sister whom he obviously suspected of claiming some superiority in that, as a girl, she did not require the blessing of the church.

'Nor I don't remember it either forbye and besides,' said Gee aggressively, in the idiom of Tom.

'Nobody remembers getting christened,' I said sweepingly, to quell the incipient quarrel. 'When people are christened, they are too young to remember.'

'It's not fair,' said Liz. 'Getting born and getting christened and everything is very important and people should be able to remember it.'

This was even worse than what Jock called 'the logic of limbo'. This was the entire problem of human personality and human memory that had vexed the philosophers down the ages and, while they gazed at me as if I ought to wave a magic wand and make them remember their births and their christenings, all I could say was: 'It may not be fair, as you call it, but that is how it is.' I was then inspired to add: 'A poet said: "Our birth is but a sleep and a forgetting" and that is the best description that I know. And you must all go to sleep right now and forget about everything until tomorrow.'

With an air of satisfaction, Liz hopped across the floor and into her own bed while the boys slid down into theirs.

'Reachfar is like a sleep and a forgetting,' Liz said.

'Yes, a forgetting –'

' – and a sleep,' said Gee with a big yawn.

I went to my room for a little while and, when I came back to look at them, they were all sound asleep. Shona was fond of saying that they were at their best when they were asleep but, to me, they now looked more mysterious than ever. How was it that these three questing minds had been born out of a physical union between Shona and my brother?

On the forenoon of Sunday I made the chocolate cake with the glop in the middle and, at three in the afternoon, we all went to the christening service and Alexander Thomas Sandison was baptised, the last of four babies that afternoon, because his surname came alphabetically last. Sitting beside me, Granny began to shed tears at the first christening and she whispered to me under the indignant yells of a little girl who was being named 'Marleen': 'I can never come to a christening without crying.' I patted her knee but what I found more moving than the baptism service was the attitude of the three children who sat between George and myself. They became tensely watchful as the minister took Sandy Tom in his arms and did not relax until he was safely back in the arms of his mother, whereupon they sighed and leaned back in their seats. I remembered the questions they had asked at breakfast that morning and came to the conclusion that they might be thinking that, in this moment of being received into the church, the baby would take wings and disappear through the vaulted ceiling into the vaster vault of Heaven and they were exerting all their will to anchor him to the earth. It might have been however, only that they were afraid the minister might drop him. In either case, what moved me was the purity, the sincerity of their thought for their brother. In those few moments, they had no existence except in relation to Sandy Tom. When we came back to the house, Roddy and Sheila made the tea, the chocolate cake was eaten and the children, losing all likeness to the devout creatures they had been in church, went away to prepare

125

for the theatrical entertainment that we had been told to expect.

In their unaccountable way, they had chosen to enact for us the Witches' Scene which opens the fourth act of *Macbeth*, than which nothing, it seemed to me, could be less suited to the occasion but it had the great merit of giving them the licence to make their faces hideous with streaks of blue and yellow crayon, walk grotesquely doubled up like hair-pins and it required no stage properties except the big, old black pot in which the birthday dumplings used to be boiled at Reachfar, which they brought in with them as their cauldron.

> 'For a charm of powerful trouble,
> Like a hell-broth boil and bubble –'

Duncan, as second witch, had just declaimed in an eldritch voice when a car drew up outside the window of the drawing-room.

'I'll go to the door,' Shona said and went out but, as she went, Roddy, whose chair faced the window, spoke the one word: 'Hell!'

'Yes,' came Shona's pleasant welcoming voice as she opened the door to come in again. 'He is here. Come in.'

'Hi, Rod,' said the young woman in the doorway and we were suddenly plunged into absurdity greater than the children's representation of Shakespeare's witches.

Framed in the doorway, she was like a page from a glossy magazine, a page depicting a young woman who was obviously a denizen of the city dressed for an excursion to the country. She was expensively coiffed, made up perfumed and dressed and she had a great deal of self-assurance when, at first, she looked round at us of this stuffy family party but, yet, in all our dowdiness, we were too much for her. There were too many of us, we were too diverse in age and appearance and we culminated in the three crayon-streaked witches around their cauldron in the middle of the floor. Poise fell away from her as she explained: 'I came up to cover the opening of the Festival at Edinburgh so I just came on.'

'Miss Lane, Mrs Sandison, Mr Sandison,' said Roddy, his face dark as thunder.

She looked round at us all and her eyes came back to rest on Sheila, who sat by the fireplace in her home-made cotton dress and Sheila, with an air of withdrawal, looked away from her and Roddy and into the fire. Discomfort spread through

126

the room like fog and Shona picked up the teapot. 'I'll make some fresh tea. Sit down, Miss Lane.'

'I'll make the tea,' said Sheila and, with a quick, mischievous knowing glance at Roddy, she went towards the door but he arrested her in mid-floor.

'No,' he said. 'No tea, thank you. We'll go, Shona, if you will excuse us, and the children can go on with their play. Come, Deb,' and he propelled the young woman in front of him out of the room. We were all silent until the two cars had driven away out of the gate, when the First Witch said: 'Deb, he called her. That is his trollop. She didn't look very messy, Dad.'

'Let's go on with the play,' Jock said.

'No. We have lost the feeling for it, haven't we?'

'Yes,' Duncan agreed.

'Yes,' came the echo.

'Then go and wash your make-up off,' Jock told them.

'Trollop!' said Sheila when the children had gone out. 'What a bloody nerve that Roddy has!' She began to collect the tea things noisily on to a tray.

'I never heard of a young woman running after a young man like that before!' Granny burst forth.

'You are just old-fashioned, Granny,' Jock told her.

'My goodness, did you see that suit?' Shona asked. 'Wasn't it beautiful?'

'I couldna see anything for the paint on her face,' George contributed.

'And were you seeing the length o' these red nails 'o hers?' Tom asked.

'She is just a very ordinary denizen of Roddy's world, I should think,' I said waspishly, 'and I wouldn't like to be in her shoes this minute. Roddy has the sort of temper that is better left uncrossed.'

'Him?' said Sheila scornfully over the loaded tray she was holding. 'He is nothing but a big soft lump!'

Again, as on that first afternoon I had seen her, she made me think of my Aunt Kate and I followed her through to the kitchen and began to dry the cups that she washed, but I did not talk to her about Roddy. With that phrase 'a big soft lump', she had given away the truth of Roddy as he was in relation to herself just as, earlier, she had given away her knowledge of

127

his sex-nature with the phrase: 'What a bloody nerve that Roddy has.'

I had known Roddy for some time and through a series of situations and I knew from experience that he could truly be described as a big soft lump in one sense and in a similar way I knew that, at the same time, he had plenty of what Sheila called 'bloody nerve' where women were concerned. But I had also learned that before one can learn any truth about the nature of some other person, it is necessary to be in some way emotionally involved with that person. The nature of other people can be discovered most completely through love for them and what Sheila had discovered of Roddy's nature argued, at the least, some liking for him and some sympathy, however unwilling, with him. She might not love him but neither was she neutral about and totally unaffected by him. Of this I was sure. I then remembered how Shona had confessed to a sense of guilt about Sheila being abandoned to look after the older generation of the family and once again the thought of my Aunt Kate came into my mind. Kate had been the youngest of my grandparents' family and she had remained at Reachfar with them until they died, losing, in the process, the only man she had ever wanted to marry. That Aunt Kate had married somebody else, had been widowed and, then, late in life had married Malcolm, the first man of her choice who was now a widower, was beside the point. The young life they might have had together, the children they might have had, were lost irrevocably.

'Have you been to see Aunt Hannah lately, Sheila?' I asked.

'Have I not! That morning when John rang us from the hospital about Shona, I went right round there and let her have it.' She told me with spirit of how she had cleared the entire contents of Aunt Hannah's cupboard into the dustbin, of how she had restocked it and then she said: 'Ach, I carry on as if I were angry with her and she and I do have rows all the time but I am really sorry for her. Janet, she had a family of four sons but they all emigrated – two to Canada, two to Australia – at the time of the Trade Depression years and years ago and they have never been back and she has never seen her grandchildren. Heavens, she has *great*-grandchildren and there she is, all alone in that wee house, still stinting herself and feeding Shona rotten corned beef because stinting became a habit when these sons that don't give a damn for her now were young. It's so unfair! And yet she is a thrawn old monster and always was. Maybe it is partly her own fault that her family all cleared out but – ' she broke off and then added: ' – oh, I just don't know.'

The analogy between her and my aunt returned again. At one time, I remembered, my aunt had elected herself the protector of Flora Smith and her idiot sister Georgina, who irritated her as Aunt Hannah did Sheila and Kate used to talk of the Smiths in just this impatient, scornful yet compassionate and understanding way in which Sheila spoke of Aunt Hannah.

'Kids!' she said now, as a loud burst of song came across the back hall from the playroom. 'Where did Liz pick up that word "trollop", do you suppose?'

'From Roddy himself. That girl Lane – at least, like Liz, I suppose it was she – has been writing to him almost every day and it seems that he told Liz that the letters came from his trollop. It is just the sort of answer that Roddy would give.'

'Shona told me that Roddy and his brothers were brought up in a very queer way,' she said next, after a short pause.

This, to me, was another indication of her interest in him, this desire to know about his young life.

Twice has no living relations except a stuffy old lawyer cousin in Edinburgh who has always irritated me by never being able to tell me anything of Twice's life before he and I met. The doting mother who shows the photograph of her son, aged one year and lying naked on a rug, to his fiancée is not entirely at fault psychologically. The fiancée, for reasons of her own, may not admit her interest in the photograph but she is interested nevertheless.

I described to Sheila Roddy's former home, his parents and their way of life which, in this mundane Victorian scullery with its modern appurtenances, sounded very remote and exotic but I did not tell her the little I knew of Roddy's exuberant, ruthless and lawless sex-life. I remembered now that I had heard the name of this girl who had arrived today some time ago. She and Roddy had had a quarrel in December of the year before, as Roddy himself had told me and, significantly, the quarrel had taken place in the morning, in Roddy's London flat.

At this point in my acquaintance with Sheila, I knew that in the course of her work as a visiting nurse in a seaport city, there were few of the more sordid ways of life that had not come under her notice but I did not know her against the background of the slums, just in the way that Duncan did not know his mother against the background of the hospital and, until he saw her there, felt that he had lost her. The Sheila that I knew was the girl washing dishes, against this solid family background of people chatting in the front of the house and children singing in the playroom and I saw her more clearly still driving her little car, helping her fat mother to descend from it or being the cheerful helpful daughter in her own cosy conventional home in town. I felt that, when she came home and put off her trim uniform, she came home literally into her true background of cosy convention and respectability, leaving the slums, the venereal clinics and the neglected children of drunken parents behind her. She recognised that the latter were the background and furnishings of a certain way of life which she, in her choice of work, had dedicated herself to ameliorate but these things had no reality within Sheila's personal dimension of life. Her mother had 'never heard of a young woman running after a young man like that' she had said but what she had meant was that this was outside the conventions of her own way of life and, in a similar way, Sheila knew that many young men had all sorts of sex liaisons but she did not expect to meet such a young man in her sister's home and, partly for her own sake, partly out of some inexplicable loyalty to Roddy, I was not going to expose this side of him to her. I had warned my brother and that would have to suffice but, also, I thought now that Sheila had her own wary estimate of Roddy and did not see him as a paragon of respectability.

When I called the children to have supper, Sheila and her parents went back to town but not before Granda had paid the children their 'acting money' for the interrupted performance of the afternoon.

'It costs only two shillings today, Granda,' said Liz, 'because you saw only half of it.'

'My, but you are a right honest wee queanie,' said Granda dotingly.

'In my book,' said Jock, 'half of half-a-crown is one and threepence.'

'Och, be quiet with you!' said Granda, as Liz led him away into a corner.

'Liz,' said Shona sharply, 'what are you asking for? Come back here! Dad, you are not to give it to her!'

Granda patted Liz's head. 'I'll see to it, pet,' he said. 'Run ben to your supper.'

'Dad,' said Shona sternly, 'whatever it was, you are *not* to give it to her. She is never done – '

'Hold your tongue for pity's sake,' the old man said. 'It's nothing much and ye know fine the biggest pleasure I have is giving them wee bitties o' thingies.'

The car drove away but Shona was not finished with the subject, and came through to the kitchen and read the riot act over the table where the three sat at supper.

'Mum,' Liz said, when she paused for breath, 'there was a spot of sick on Sandy Tom's pillow.'

'What?' said Shona and was off through to the front of the house as Tom and George began to laugh.

'Shut up, you two!' I said. 'Liz Sandison, you are a sinful little brat!'

'Aunt Janet,' she said solemnly, 'you don't seem to see how difficult it is to do what everybody wants when they all want something different. Granda *wants* to give us things but Mum doesn't want him to want to and it gets you in such a muddle – '

' – that you don't know where you are – '

' – and feel like going out of your head.'

'Sandy Tom was *not* sick,' said Shona, arriving with the cot. 'I ought to smack you, Liz Sandison.'

'Ach be quiet, woman, and wash the bairn,' said George.

'And give him his supper,' said Tom.

Sandy Tom enjoyed his bath routine except for the washing of his face and, as I approached it with the small sponge, he threw himself back and yelled, looking up at Tom and George who at once said: 'Dang it, you don't have to be rubbing at the bairn's face as if it was the scullery floor!'

'Where would his face be dirty and him lying sleeping all day?'

Sandy Tom, I knew with my reason, was too young as yet to practise consciously, as Liz did, the age-old diplomatic trick of 'Divide and rule' but, on principle, striking a blow for the middle generation of which I was a member, I took a firm hold of the back of the struggling little head and sponged the angry red face.

When 'Reachfar' in the children's room was over, I went to my own room for a time, ostensibly to get tidy for supper but in reality because I was reluctant to break out of this world

131

that the children and I shared. While they sat in the boys' bed, listening to what I said, imagining what I described, I had an extraordinary and satisfying sense of total communication for I seemed to see what was mirrored in my memory reflected again in their eyes so that, while they received this dream which they desired and which I wanted to give to them, they were, at the same time, giving it back to me in a richer deeper form.

I was just about to go downstairs when there was a tap at my door and Roddy came in. 'When did Sh – the Murrays go?' he asked.

'About five-thirty.'

His face was very heavy and sullen as he sat down on the window-seat so that his back was to the light, making him look darker than ever.

'Damn Deb,' he said.

'I don't feel in the least sympathetic,' I told him. 'How did she know you were here anyway? You must have written to her.'

'I did damn all of the sort. She got the address from my bloody agent.'

'Where is she now?'

'On her way back to Edinburgh. Janet, what happened after we left?'

'Nothing much. We washed up and put the kids to bed. Tom was a bit taken with Deb's finger-nails and George with her make-up.'

'Oh, Christ!'

'There is not a bit of good cursing and blaspheming. If Deb hadn't caught up with you, one or more of the others would.'

'She hasn't caught up with me!' His eyes blazed with rage. 'She is on her tearful way back to Edinburgh. I wish she was in hell!'

'She has caught up with you in the sense that she has made clear to everybody that you don't belong in this milieu,' I told him. 'And while we are talking about who and what people really are, I might as well record the fact that I don't think much of your pass at Sheila as a social gambit. It must be obvious from what you have seen here, that the people of my family have no part in life as you live it, Roddy.' He sat looking up at me from under the heavy black brows, silent but more enigmatic, now, than angry, as I went on: 'Your way of life is your own affair but you cannot pursue it in this circle without causing unhappiness.'

'You want me to leave,' he said.

'Not necessarily but if you stay, I would like you to conform, if possible. Maybe you agree with me that this is a very happy community, although simple in its ways and it would be a pity to disrupt it.'

He made no comment on what I had said but spoke as if to himself. 'I ought to go anyway. I have known this for the last week' and, now, he reverted to what I had said. 'This is a very happy simple community, Janet, as you say and you have said your piece about my way of life but you may remember that I told you out in St Jago that I didn't know that the way of life you have here existed until last December. I have never lived anywhere except in the jungle – the jungle of St Jago or the jungle of cities. To get out of the jungle, I used to take to the sea but I am beginning to learn that I am a land animal, although not the jungle sort.' He gave me his impudent grin. 'I am a land animal that could be domesticated, given the right treatment by the right person.'

'I doubt it,' I said and he turned away from me to stand looking out of the window.

As a rule, Roddy had a decisive positive look, his shoulders always squared back, borne on a strong pliant spine, his eyes always looking straight ahead in rage or anticipation or gladness but, now, he drooped against the light of the window, his dark head bowed in thought. He looked, suddenly, young and pathetically vulnerable, which made me remember that he was not yet thirty and also remember the tragedy of his patents' death that was only about a month behind us. With his established position as a writer, his sheer physical size and his force of personality, I had found it easy to think of Roddy as much older than he was but now the perspective shifted. He slid away from me down the generation so that I suddenly saw him closer to Liz, asleep next door, than he was to myself. And I remembered, too, that evening in London when he had said: 'It is not so much a question of you finding your way as of me finding mine.' Growing up is not a smooth progression like the days and the years through which we live. We grow up in sudden flashes of light, sharp stabs of agony and through a mist of tears, like the tears Liz shed when she discovered that her brothers had eaten all the sweets from the betting-box because they were too young to imagine her grand design of a feast of sweets to celebrate the birth of the baby.

'I'll go to the croft,' Roddy said into the silence. 'It is quite habitable and I ordered a bed and some odds and ends in Inverness when Sheila and I went up that day.'

'You don't have to go unless you want to, Roddy. I am not showing you the door.'

'I know that but there is a door I have got to find for myself. You remember I told you it was seeing your father's funeral that made me buy a croft up here in the first place? That was a turning point in a longish process, Janet, a process like waking from deep sleep into a new sort of life. When we came here, I thought the process was complete but it isn't yet.' He turned about and walked past me to the door where, holding the handle, he spoke with his back to me: 'Who was the chap in the Old Testament who served seven years for Rachel?'

'Jacob,' I replied in an automatic way.

'You can call me Jacob,' he said and went out, shutting the door.

But, as I tidied my hair at the glass, I told my reflection that I would wait till the seven years had passed before I credited Roddy with the faithfulness of Jacob.

Chapter VIII

'Hence in a season of calm weather
Though inland far we be,
Our Souls have sight of that immortal sea
Which brought us hither,
Can in a moment travel thither,
And see the Children sport upon the shore,
And hear the mighty waters rolling evermore.'

THE next morning, Roddy and my brother came down to the children's early breakfast, Roddy packed up and anxious to be away now that he had made his decision, Jock ready to go into town to an early meeting.

'Wait till I take this tray up to Shona,' I said, 'and I'll cook you some bacon.'

'I'll take the tray up,' Jock said.

'Where are you going today, Roddy?' Liz enquired.

'I have to go back to work,' he said. 'My holiday is over.'

'You are going really away?' she asked shrilly.

'For good?'

'Not coming back tonight?'

'Perhaps you will invite me to come back sometime.'

'But we wanted you today or tomorrow or sometime convenient but quite soon,' Liz protested. 'We have a very very important plan but we can't do it by ourselves. We need a *man*,' she ended with emphasis.

'Won't your father do?' Roddy asked.

Liz bent upon him that long, sad patient look. 'Don't you know that you have to take the good with the bad with people?' she asked.

'Liz, what in the world do you mean?' I said.

She gave me an impatient glance and pushed a large spoonful of porridge into her mouth. 'This is building and hammering,' she said, which merely added to the confusion.

'Building and hammering?' I repeated.

She put her spoon down on the table in an exasperated final way and the boys followed suit. 'Daddy,' she said, as if the lack of intelligence in Roddy and myself disgusted her, 'is very good at poetry and football and making toffee and just nearly everything but he cannot hammer a nail in – '

' – without hitting his thumb or breaking something – '

' – and *every*body knows that,' Gee added finally, picking up his spoon again.

'So, Roddy, will you stay for just this morning even?' Liz coaxed, as her father returned to the room.

'No,' I said. 'Roddy has important plans. George and Tom will help you perhaps.'

'But this is an important plan that *we* have,' Liz argued, sweeping all other plans made by all other people aside with her porridge spoon, 'and George and Tom are no good because this is *secret*.'

'*Top* secret.'

'Yes, *top*!'

'So, Roddy, please will you stay?'

'Certainly not,' said Jock. 'If Roddy has decided to go, your plans don't come into it, Liz. You will just have to think again and make new plans. Now, be quiet and get on with your breakfast.'

A sullen silence descended on all three and did not lift until breakfast was over when Roddy got to his feet and said, 'I'll go up and say good-bye to Shona and get my bag.' Now that his going was inevitable, the children accepted it and their faces brightened towards giving their friend a cheerful send-off but, as he opened the door to go out, Liz turned her big eyes up to the ceiling and gave a long sigh.

'O – oh-oh,' she said, 'for a *falconer's* voice, to lure this tassel-gentle back again!'

Roddy, holding the door ajar, looked back at her over his shoulder, arrested as if frozen there. As a rule, Roddy never seemed to be still. Compounded of so much strength and energy and colour, the air around him always seemed to vibrate and this sudden arrestment had the effect of time suddenly standing still. The children began to look scared and, after a second, Liz, thinking that inadvertently she might have said something displeasing, asked in a small voice: 'Daddy, Roddy *is* a little bit like a falcon, isn't he? A *gentle* falcon?'

'Maybe he is,' Jock agreed smiling.

Roddy shut the door. 'I have changed my mind,' he said. 'I can go after lunch. What is this hammering you want me to do?'

136

All three sprang up. 'You sit down,' Liz said, 'and have another cigarette and a cup of coffee, Roddy. We'll get things ready – '

' – and call you.'

'Yes, quite soon.'

They rushed out and then Liz pushed her head back round the door. 'Dad, where are all the iron bits and hinges and things for the little old garage?'

'Now, Liz,' Jock said sternly, 'Roddy is not going to build that for you. Don't be ridiculous. Johnnie will come – '

'Aw, Dad!' the three voices protested together.

'But I *am* going to build whatever it is, Jock,' Roddy said. 'Where is the stuff?'

'It is all in a sack in the tool shed, Liz,' Jock capitulated and they went away.

'If I have heard one rendering of *Romeo and Juliet*, I have heard fifty,' Roddy said, 'but I have never heard a better reading of that line. God, it made my heart stop and the hair rise on the back of my neck!'

My brother looked shyly down at his plate. 'The thing is,' he said slowly, 'it wasn't a reading. It was the full expression of Liz's desire that you should stay and help her. She happened, by pure accident, to hit upon the perfect words. And to get her own selfish way, I would remind you,' and he looked up, smiling at Roddy.

'How did she ever come to know these words anyway?' he asked.

'There was a programme about falconry on television a little time ago,' Jock explained. 'The kids don't like TV much but they like anything to do with birds or animals and they like words.' He grinned. 'Heaven knows they use plenty of them as you may have noticed and falconry is full of words they had never heard before. It was myself who quoted Juliet's line about the tassel-gentle to them.'

Roddy gave a little shudder. 'That may have been an accident, that line, as you say, but it was a moment I shall never forget.'

My brother went away to his meeting, the children called Roddy out to the shrubbery, Tom and George came down for breakfast, Shona came down with Sandy Tom and the pleasant family round of the day began.

'Roddy has decided to stay to lunch and go away afterwards,' I told Shona. 'He is out in the shrubbery with the clan.'

'He is such a nice boy. I am sorry he is going.'

'I think he is badly smitten with Sheila,' I said, 'but one doesn't know how long it will last. I think it is the lure of the unattainable, as much as anything. I gather that Sheila has played it very cool and he is not used to that.'

'Sheila is a queer mixture,' Shona said. 'There is a very tough streak in her but she would have to be tough to do the work she does. Some of these homes she visits and the people she has to deal with would give you the creeps. And then she has always had a lot of men after her but she has never seemed to feel much about any of them. Sometimes I think she hasn't any feelings much, except for old people.' Shona now looked at me as if she were about to say something which was true but which I could not possibly believe. 'She doesn't even have any real feeling for the children,' she said, looking away from me towards the shrubbery beyond the windows. But the shadow soon passed from Shona's serene brow as she returned to her own world and to her family, while she listened to the sounds of hammering from the shrubbery and when they all came in at ten-thirty, with the usual announcement of being hungry, she said: 'What are the four of you doing out there?'

'Secret,' said Liz. 'And nobody is to go in there – ' she turned to me ' – 'specially *you*!' she said fiercely.

But I did not feel excluded now as I had done that first time she had pointed to the notice: 'Keep out. Reachfar People Only.' I had a feeling that all this activity in the shrubbery was building up into something connected with myself.

When George and Tom came in, George announced with pleasure: 'I see that Johnnie o' the Hill has put down a few bonnie black stirkies to graze the glebe.'

'Aye, they'll soon clean it up,' Tom said.

The 'glebe' was a large field, over the garden wall beyond the shrubbery, that belonged to the school, having been gifted by a local landowner during the last century to provide a school garden, in the days when gardening was part of the curriculum of these Scottish country schools. Even when I went to school in Achcraggan, I remembered, we had spent several hours of the school week in the garden.

'It is a good job they have done away with the gardening in the schools nowadays,' George said. 'Jock would have made a poor fist of teaching the bairns to garden.'

138

'Aye,' Tom agreed, turning to Roddy. 'It is a queer thing about Jock. He was brought up by George and myself mostly, after his mother died, but he never had any notion o' the horses or the ground. There was nothing in his head but playing golf up through the moor with an old stick or listening to the cricket on the wireless boxie or reading books.'

'John is ham-fisted about everything – ' Shona began but Liz interrupted in defence of her father: ' 'Cept tying knots, Mum.'

'Aye, that is an odd thing,' George said. 'He could always, even as a bairn, put a better splice in a rope rein than Tom or I could.'

'It is not so odd,' I said. 'One of his grandfathers was a sea captain under sail, after all.'

'And Jock picked on the Navy in the war, when you think on it,' Tom said.

There was a thoughtful little silence as if everyone were listening to the march of the generations until Liz said: 'One of *our* great-grandfathers was a sea captain, Aunt Janet? Tell!'

'I don't know much about him but I'll tell you this evening,' I promised.

'I wish we still had gardening at school,' Duncan said. 'I like to garden.'

'Dunk is the best gardener,' Gee told us. 'It's not fair. Dunk's bowl of hyacinths was out long before Liz's and mine last winter-time.'

'Maybe Duncan is going to be like his Granda Sandison,' I said. 'Granda Sandison could make anything grow.'

'George,' Liz asked, 'why is Aunt Janet so much better at making long-ago faraway people really real than you and Tom are?' She frowned, struggling with the mystery of time and memory. 'You are older than Aunt Janet, a whole *generation* older!' she brought out triumphantly. 'You ought to remember better than she does.'

'I was never as good at minding on things as your Aunt Janet, though,' George said.

'No, nor me forbye and besides,' said Tom. 'Some folk are a lot better at minding than others.'

'Well, you three, come along,' said Roddy. 'We still have quite a bit to do out there.'

When my brother came back in time for lunch, he brought with him four small packages, one for each child and Shona

139

frowned and said: 'From Dad again?' She picked up the one marked with Liz's name and gave it an angry little shake. 'Liz has got to be stopped asking for things, John. Granda is never done giving them money and presents but *she* is at the bottom of it. She asks for things and then he buys things for all the others too.'

Jock sighed. This was obviously a weary problem of long standing. 'I don't see what we can do about it,' he said and turned to me. 'Granda often asks Liz if there is anything she wants. Do you see what one can do, Janet?'

'I don't see why you need to do anything. As Granda said, giving them little things is one of his great pleasures. And you know, Shona, I think they are very good about their money. They don't rush off to the village for sweets when Granda gives them their acting money as lots of kids would do. They put in their banks.'

Shona looked at me as scornfully as her serene face could look, made a noise that was almost a snort. 'They are saving up to buy a pony,' she told me, 'and every half-crown that goes into those banks brings that trouble a bit nearer.'

'Look, Shona,' Jock said, 'half a crown a week from Granda to each of them is nineteen pounds ten a year. It is going to take them at least three years –'

'Two,' said Shona. 'They have already been at it for a year and it isn't only Granda's half-crowns. It is every penny they can lay hands on and now Sandy Tom is getting acting money too.' She glared at me. 'Don't *you* go giving them any money!'

'But why shouldn't they have a pony if they save up for it like this?' I asked. 'You've got the glebe to keep it in and –'

'Guinea pigs and now a dog are enough,' Shona said. 'You haven't seen this kitchen in the winter, what with the guinea pig food and the worms and stuff for the bird table. They are doing all that out-of-doors just now. I tell you I just can't *do* with a pony in the kitchen!' The last words were almost a wail which made me laugh, so that Shona herself began to smile.

'We won't have it this winter anyway,' Jock said, 'and we'll cross the pony bridge when we come to it.'

When the packages were opened, Liz's was found to contain a little china bank with pink roses painted on it, there was another china bank in the form of a pig for Sandy Tom, similar to those that Duncan and Gee had while the latter had a miniature toy car each.

140

'Liz,' said Shona sternly, 'you asked Granda for that yesterday? Why? He already gave you one.'

'I have other plans for the other one, Mum. I explained to Granda.'

'What plans?'

'Secret.'

'You are a very naughty girl, Liz and you should be ashamed of yourself.'

'Mum,' Duncan said, 'this is a good plan. You will like it in the end.'

'Yes, in the very end,' Gee confirmed.

'I don't like any plans that make you ask Granda for things.'

'We wanted him to keep our yesterday's acting money to pay for my new bank but he wouldn't,' Liz said.

'No, he wouldn't.'

'No.'

Shona sighed. 'Oh, all right. But don't ask him for any more things.'

'He will give us things anyway,' said Liz. 'He likes giving people things. So do I.'

'Me too,' said Roddy. 'People I like, that is.'

'Goodness, yes,' Liz agreed. 'You have to like them. I wouldn't give that Amanda Shand anything unless it was a kick in the teeth.'

'That is a very unchristian way to be, Liz, I am thinking,' Tom said.

Liz took thought and then said solemnly: 'Love thine enemies, Christ said, but I don't think there could have been people like Amanda Shand in *His* time.'

As soon as lunch was over, Roddy went away. The children waved good-bye to the car very politely but as soon as it was out of the gate they forgot all about Roddy, a forenoon of whose life they had commandeered for their own fell ends.

'Dad,' said Liz, 'come into Reachfar and see what we've done!' Jock was about to go with them when I said: 'Look here, if what you are doing in there is top secret from Mum and George and Tom and me, why isn't it top secret from Dad?'

Liz gave me that look that indicated my mental backwardness. 'Mum can't keep secrets from anybody,' she said, 'and George and Tom can't keep secrets from *you* but Dad can keep secrets from everybody,' and they gathered round Jock and dragged him away.

I was growing more and more interested in the activity in the shrubbery but the children were right in their estimate of their father for, when I asked him what was going on, he merely smiled and said: 'Secret and don't pry, Janet. It is to be a big surprise and it will all be clear in the end but kids always know if someone is not really surprised but merely acting.'

'Life with them is one long surprise,' I said.

The next morning, after the children had gone out, Jock said: 'You said yesterday that life with the kids was one long surprise. Well, they surprised *me* this morning. I didn't know that my other grandfather was a sea-faring man.'

'You didn't?'

Suddenly, a gulf of years seemed to yawn between him and me, a gulf much wider than the ten years that separated his birth from mine, but years have no reality except in relation to the experience they contain. I think it was only now that I recognised that my brother had no memory of our mother, although I had always known, as a fact, that she had died when he was only two days old. Although he had been brought up at Reachfar and I in the Lowlands of Scotland from my eleventh year onwards, so that we had never seen a great deal of one another, there was a close bond between us which had led me to the belief that he must know as much of our common ancestry as I did.

'Dad never mentioned Granda Reid to you?' I asked.

'No.'

When I considered it, this was natural enough. Jock and I were of different casts of mind. He had been a silent, contemplative little boy, like his own son Duncan while George and Tom were telling me daily that Liz reminded them more and more of myself at her age, not in looks except for her long pigtails but in her generally active enquiring attitude and when she said to her brothers: 'Look here, you two –' I could hear an echo of my own voice addressing Tom and George in just this way long ago. And I could see that Jock, as a father, had a different attitude and response towards Liz from his attitude and response to the boys which made it seem likely that my father had had a different attitude and response towards myself and Jock. I could remember my father in only my way but I discovered now that the father that Jock remembered was a different man who had spoken to him in a different way, about different things and had never spoken to him, as it chanced, about his maternal grandfather at all.

'Yes,' I said now. 'Granda Reid had his own ship, a little trading coaster, I believe, operating from Aberdeen round the Moray Firth.'

'And his wife was dead and he was lost at sea, leaving Mother as a baby as you told the children last night?'

'Yes.'

'And she was brought up by this old minister, Granda Gordon, as she called him?'

'Yes.'

'Surely,' said George. 'Where there is no vision, the people perish!'

'That was Granda Gordon's great saying,' Tom confirmed.

Jock laughed. 'The kids came into our room reciting that this morning.'

Shona and Sandy Tom were still upstairs, George and Tom now went out into the garden but my brother sat on the table while I began to prepare the soup for lunch.

'I feel like one of the kids,' he said, 'caught between reality and a dream. What was she like, Mother?'

'In looks, the sort of tall thin kind, like me,' I said, 'but much more delicate in every way and much more beautiful. She had big soft eyes – ' I hesitated ' – like Shona's.'

I hesitated because I had begun to wonder if, through some mystery of heredity, Jock had been drawn to Shona because her eyes resembled those of the dead mother he could not remember.

'The thing that always comes uppermost when I remember her,' I went on, 'is her gentleness but there was nothing wishy-washy in her. In the gentlest of ways, really, she controlled Reachfar, Granny and all.'

'Then she certainly wasn't wishy-washy as you call it.'

'I think you are more like her than I am, Jock. She was a quiet contemplative person. She might easily have turned into a scholar – a don, had they had women dons in those days – if she had had the education. She was only thirty-five when she died and, if you remember, when I was thirty-five, I was still a flibbertygibbet. She was the exact opposite. She had a quiet brooding sort of wisdom.'

'I suppose this urge towards writing that you have came

143

from her,' Jock said. 'I haven't got that at all. I am interested in research, criticism, all the analytical side of literature but I have no creative spark of my own.'

'What little urge and what almost non-existent capability I have, I am not sure where they came from. How can one know? But Dad was a creative sort of person, I think, although it never found any expression except in things like building walls and gardening.'

'How stupid can one get?' Jock asked suddenly. 'That is a side of Dad I had forgotten. When he came home from Cairnton to Jemima Cottage, when you went to university and I went down there from Reachfar to live with him and Jean, how he set about that garden! It was all overgrown, shoulder high in nettles and docks.'

'Old Aunt Betsy couldn't look after it,' I said, 'and it lay empty for a bit after she died too.'

'Dad expected me to help him and, lord, how I hated it but, somehow, I could never tell him point-blank that I hated grubbing about in the earth and would rather read a book or play football. I felt it would have shocked him that his own son – ' he paused for a second and continued: 'There was something in him that made one afraid of hurting him in any way, a tenderness in the way that the skin of a baby is tender. I had more scoldings from him over that garden than I ever had over anything else. He couldn't understand that I had no instinct for it, as he had himself and he never thought of explaining why one should do this or that and when I did something stupid, he would look at me as if I were half-witted and then ask me if I were still finding my school work quite straightforward, as if he were reassuring himself that I was not a complete idiot.'

I had many memories of my father in the garden at Cairnton, where he and I had spent many hours together but this was a new picture of my father in a garden. I had had the 'instinct for it' that Jock had mentioned and my father and I had been able to work side by side, with no words of instruction from him to me. We could do naturally what George and Tom called 'working to one another's hand'.

'There were hideous struggles with cement – Heavens, how I hated the stuff! – when he was building the terracings,' Jock went on, 'and when we had done a bit and had taken the wooden shuttering off, out would come his favourite phrase: "That's a job that will last for all time".'

144

'Yes,' I said, remembering, 'he did quite often say that.'

'But I was only seven years old when all this started,' Jock reminded me, 'and at that time "all time" didn't mean much to me and I didn't see any need for all this hard labour and there was no fun in it. Then there was another horrible struggle with cuttings of yew for the hedges and holes to dig for the apple trees and – '

'Jemima Cottage must be quite a place,' I interrupted.

Jock frowned. 'You know what it is like, don't you? You've been there – '

'Never beyond the living-room since Jean was there and not even that since about 1943 – sometime during the war, anyway.'

'Good Heavens!' Jock seemed to feel, as I had felt earlier about our maternal grandfather, that this garden so well-known to him must also be known to me. 'It is certainly quite a garden,' he went on. 'I stand in relation to gardens as I stand in relation to the plays of Shakespeare. I cannot make them but I can appreciate them when they are made. The garden at Jemima Cottage is the garden of a great stately home, but in miniature. It has its stream, complete with rustic bridge. My left thumbnail turned black and came off eventually because of that bridge. It has its vegetables, its lawn, its herbaceous border, its orchard, its rockery – that cost me the nail on my left big toe. It even has its topiary work round the rose garden.'

'Don't draw the long bow,' I said as Shona came in with Sandy Tom.

'Shona, is there or is there not a topiary round the rose garden at Jemima Cottage?' Jock appealed.

'Yes, there is,' she said, as she put the cot down on the sofa. 'It is my favourite bit of the whole garden.' She looked at me, smiling her gentle smile as her eyes misted over with tears. 'I used to go up there during the war when you were both away. I shall never forget the time I arrived and Dad Sandison took me out to show me what he had done. He had clipped two of the bullocks – '

'Bullocks?' I asked.

'Dad's topiary work wasn't your pyramids or twisted sticks of barley sugar,' Jock told me. 'The yews and the privets were clipped into bullocks, horses, hens sitting on nests, cocks flapping their wings and crowing. They still are, come to that. He was a sort of sculptor in yew and privet, Shona, when you think of it,' he ended with wonder.

'Yes, he was.'

'Tell me about the bullocks, Shona.'

The tears brimmed over her lower lids now. 'He had clipped two of his bullocks down, one into a ship and one into an aeroplane. That is Janet's aeroplane, he told me and this is Jock's ship. I can't clip machines as good as I can clip animals,' he said, 'but maybe they will do.' Shona gave a little sob. 'But they weren't just bits of topiary work, Janet. They were prayers, green living growing prayers that you and John would be all right. He was a very very good man, Janet.'

'Yes, I think he was. I am glad that you told me about my aeroplane, Shona.'

'It is still there,' Jock said, 'but my ship grew up into a bullock again after the war. My ship was privet, you see, but your aeroplane is slow-growing yew and although it is bigger than it was, it is still an aeroplane.'

Shona took Sandy Tom out of his cot and carried him out-of-doors to his perambulator which she wheeled along the path to the plot where George and Tom were working.

'I always remember a thing that happened at the end of my second year at university,' Jock said now. 'It was the summer vacation and I had come home with the usual heap of books. One of them was a series of lectures by Sir Arthur Quiller-Couch collected under the title *The Art of Writing*. Wait a minute. I have still got it.' He went away to his study and came back with the book. 'Dad was always poking about among my books – you remember how he did?'

This was another aspect of my father that I did not know. He had always read a good deal but when I was a child he did most of his reading in bed, for he was too busy during the day and when I went to university, I too came home with books but my father lived at Jemima Cottage and I spent my vacations at Reachfar. But my brother had known my father when he was a farm-manager retired on a pension provided by a generous employer so that he was a man whose time was his own and he spent it in helping Tom and George at Reachfar, cultivating his garden and also, seemingly, poking about among my brother's books.

'He got going on this one Sunday afternoon,' Jock said, tapping the volume in his hand. 'You remember the respect he had for learning and for learned men?'

'They spoke to him with the voice of God,' I said.

'That was it. Well, he came upon this passage – ' Jock took a few seconds to find the page ' – yes, here we are. Old Q. was lecturing at Cambridge and he was trying to impress on the young men the tremendous experience that was being offered to them in a Cambridge education. The general drift is that the future of English literature was in the hands of young men with their opportunities. Dad came to this bit: " – we may prate of democracy, but actually a poor child in England has little more hope than had the son of an Athenian slave to be emancipated into that intellectual freedom of which great writings are born." ' Jock closed the book. 'Dad read that out to me and then he looked at me in that indescribable way he had, a look so lost and at the same time so vulnerable, a look you seldom see except in children and then – I can remember his exact words – he said: "I am not sure that I understand the gentleman right. You and Janet are poor children but surely the university can give you intellectual freedom just as well as it can give it to these wealthy young men at Cambridge?" ' Jock's voice was a little unsteady and he wet his lower lip before he went on: 'It was one of those moments when one suddenly makes a great mental stride forward. I realised that, already, at the end of my second year at university, I had been emancipated in a way that Dad had never had a chance to be. I had the intellectual freedom to see old Quiller-Couch as a man, a highly intelligent, very learned man, but not an oracle, as Dad saw him. Dad saw him as speaking for all time, to use his own phrase, so I pointed out that the old buffer had spoken these words in 1913, that things had progressed a bit since then and that Dad himself *had* got the thing a bit wrong – that Q. didn't mean that poor children couldn't be emancipated but that in 1913 they didn't get the chance to be. And then I said: "You wouldn't call Janet a slave of any sort, would you?" And that made him laugh.' Jock himself now laughed. 'I ought to confess to you that whenever I was in trouble with Dad, I used to turn his mind towards you, just as you will see Liz switching Shona on to Sandy Tom.'

'It is absurd,' I said after a moment, 'that I have never thought of this before, but I haven't. You and I altered Dad, Jock. But for us, he would have been more like Tom and George, less involved in the future, with less necessity to try to see ahead. He would have been happier, probably. It was his

147

concern for you and me, always, that brought that bewildered vulnerable look into his eyes.'

'That is true perhaps but –' Jock paused as Liz, Duncan and Gee came chattering into the back hall and crashed into the downstairs lavatory to wash their hands for elevenses ' – I know for certain that, bewilderment, vulnerability and all, he would rather have had us than not.'

'I have always thought of myself as having been conditioned by Dad, Reachfar and all the past but I had never thought till now of Dad having been in any way conditioned by us, by his future, if you like.'

'In this house, as you may have noticed, we are conditioned almost entirely by the future, if conditioning is what you call it,' and as the three came in, he said: 'Don't say it. We know you are hungry.'

' 'smatter of fact,' said Liz, 'we're not really. We've had a half-pound block of chocolate each –'

' – with nuts in it –'

' – and raisins.'

'Roddy left them in Reachfar for us, for a surprise and we didn't find them until just a little ago so it really was a surprise. But we could do with a drink of milk. Chocolate is thirsty stuff.'

'By the half-pound, very thirsty,' I said, pouring milk.

When they had gone out again, Jock, who had nothing else to do this forenoon for once, offered to prepare the vegetables for me and I said: 'All right, as long as you don't cut yourself. It seems to be generally agreed that you are not to be trusted with a tool of any sort.'

He laughed. 'People exaggerate. Like everybody else, I can do the things I like to do and I like to work in water and clean vegetables although I don't like to grow them.'

'Grandfather Reid lives on in you all right,' I said. 'Remember how Achcraggan was divided into two factions, the one that lived by the sea and the one that lived by the land?'

'That wasn't in my time,' Jock said and again the gap of years opened between us. 'The fishing stopped at Achcraggan at about the time I was born, just after the '14-'18 war.'

'So it did.'

'And all the fisher people went away except a few that were too old. There were factions, were there?'

'You bet there were and they fought like anything. My

148

equivalent of Liz's Amanda Shand was a fisher girl called Jean Stewart. The only people who didn't belong to either faction were the doctor, the minister and the dominie. Oh and Jock Skinner, the dealer and his wife. Jock cheated and stole from landsmen and fishers alike.'

'I miss the sea,' my brother said quietly, after a pause, 'living inland here.'

'Why don't you apply for a school on the coast then?'

'Too far from the best academy in the country,' he told me. 'Here, we are in a first-class position for the kids later on. The academy is only four miles down the road with a young and very good man in charge. And then here we are in reach of Granda and Granny too.'

He made me think of my father who spent six long years in exile in Cairnton largely for my sake, because there was a good school in the town.

'I didn't know you had such a deep affinity with the sea, Jock,' I said.

'I never go into town without going down to the front to have a look at it. Have you any feeling for the sea?'

'Not like yours I think but I am a good sailor and I enjoy sea-travel. I would never fly if it weren't for the time factor.'

There was a burst of song from the shrubbery and I saw the three children perched in a row on their high branch. 'When you think of all the complexities in us that come out of the past,' I said, 'it is a miracle that we get through life at all. And those three out there are going to be a generation more complex than we were.'

'I know,' Jock threw a scraped potato with an angry splash into the pan of water. 'This is a thing that makes me sick. There is a growing body of fuddy-duddy opinion in this country that says the modern child is impossible, that children were never like this before, that they have lost all moral standards and all that sort of rubbish but none of these people ever think of just that one thing, that these children have come into a world that is one generation more complex.'

'Liz had a point when she said that there probably weren't people like Amanda Shand in the time of Christ,' I put in.

'Exactly and *what* a generation went before the present young one, with its concentration camps and gas chambers. These old stuffed shirts that write to the newspapers take the attitude that the children don't know anything about what went on

149

during the war and that they can't possibly be conscious of the human guilt of it all.' He stopped working and looked at me across the table, his blue eyes blazing with passion, so that I was struck dead still with my hands in a bowl of flour. 'During the war,' he said in a cold quiet voice, 'I was at the sinking of the *Bismarck*. It was a monstrous affair. Every ship the Navy could muster was round her and we were pumping everything we had into her. It was a debauch of destruction, all of us round this magnificent ship, a triumph of men's brains and ingenuity, killing her, like vultures tearing at her, only vultures have the decency to wait until their prey is dead.' His voice had deepened to a painful grating and he now drew a sharp breath and went on more quietly: 'I try never to think about it, not only because it is painful but because if that memory comes to the forefront of my mind in the children's presence, Liz or one of them is sure to say: What's the matter, Daddy? Have you got a sore place?' He picked up another potato and began to scrape it. 'And those stupid bastards write to the newspapers saying that children are just being born full of sin these days, that it was the Germans who had the concentration camps and not us and all that bloody crap. It was the human *race* of our generation that had the concentration camps and the guilt of them is part of the inheritance of those kids out there. Sorry, Janet, I didn't mean to get the bit between my teeth like this.'

'No man is an island – ' I quoted.

'Exactly,' Jock agreed and in his turn he quoted: ' – because I am involved in mankind and therefore never send to know for whom the bell tolls. It tolls for thee.' He brightened. 'Good old Donne!'

'I wish I could still be here when your school opens, Jock,' I said after a moment. 'I should love to sit in on a class.'

'Mid-September? Won't you still be here?'

I shook my head. 'No. I must be back by then. Not that Twice isn't doing very well without me. He is.' I paused for a moment before I said: 'Sometimes I think it is possible to be too fortunate, Jock. There are so many wanderers in the world, exiles, people with no homes at all and I feel that I have two homes.' I looked round the big kitchen. 'You and Shona have found the secret of living and this is a life-giving place. I am grateful, Jock, on my own behalf and on behalf of Tom and George too.'

'I am glad you find it like this. I wish that George and Tom would come here for good but I don't try to persuade them. They have run their own lives so far with conspicuous success and I am not going to bully them now, even if it might be for their good.'

'No. Let them alone,' I agreed. 'They have always had a knack for knowing their own good and quite a bit about the good of other people too.'

Chapter IX

'O joy! that in our embers
 Is something that doth live,
 That nature yet remembers
 What was so fugitive!
The thought of our past years in me doth breed
 Perpetual benediction:'

WHEN lunch was over, Jock and the children did the washing-up while Shona fed Sandy Tom upstairs and George, Tom and I sat smoking in the kitchen, while we listened to the conversation that came from the scullery.

'Leave that broom alone Fly,' came the voice of Liz. 'Dad, there was another letter from Roddy's trollop this morning. Aunt Janet put his croft address on it and gave it back to the postman.'

'I think we should drop the word trollop. The young woman's name is Miss Lane.'

'Roddy always just called her his trollop,' said Duncan.

'Miss Lane had a pain, went to the loo and back again,' chanted Liz and when all three had repeated this masterpiece several times Liz continued: 'Why did Aunt Janet know about our sailor great-grandfather and you didn't, Dad?'

'Aunt Janet is ten years older than I am,' Jock said, taking the easy way out.

'Ten *years*?' Liz squeaked. 'Older than you and I are put together?'

'Yes.'

'She must be about a hundred,' came the voice of Gee, giving an opinion which, I noticed, my brother neither confirmed nor denied.

'If I knew about them,' Liz pursued, 'I suppose I have got as many ancestors as the Queen. Great-grandfathers are ancestors, aren't they?'

'Yes,' said Jock.

'If you've got them, Liz Sandison,' said Duncan, 'Gee and I have them too.'

152

'Yes, have!' came the supporting voice.

'Of course,' said Jock.

'How can we find out about them, to draw a family tree like the Queen's tree in the Coronation Book?' Liz asked.

'I am afraid it would be nearly impossible,' Jock told her. 'The Queen's ancestors, you see, were all kings and people who played an important part in history but yours were Highland crofters and –'

'Ancient Mariners,' came the voice of Duncan followed by the sound of a sharp slap.

'Was not!' said Liz indignantly. 'Great-grandfather didn't have skinny hands and glittering eyes.'

There was a swish, probably of a wet dish towel and a yelp from Liz, followed by my brother's unmoved voice: 'You bought that one, Liz and there is no use crying. Get on with your work. Maybe Great-granda didn't have skinny hands but you might call him an ancient mariner all the same. And then, on the other side of your family tree, there was Great-granda Murray and he was a poor fisherman and there was Great-granda Watt, another poor fisherman and I don't suppose anybody kept any records of them or their people.'

'In the name of my Highland forefathers,' said Liz, 'how many ancestors have we got?'

'Your forefathers were not all Highland. The Murrays and Watts were Lowlanders,' said Jock.

'And we have the same number of ancestors as your old Queen,' said Duncan, 'on account of it all started with Adam and Eve anyway.'

'Yes and the serpent,' Gee added.

'Nothing of the sort. It started with Darwin and evolution,' said Liz in superior tones.

'Aw, nit-head,' said Duncan, 'don't you see that Adam was just the first man that ever evoluted?'

'Yes, the very first,' said Gee and added scornfully: 'You and your old Queen!'

'The thing about ancestors,' came Jock's voice in equable tones, 'is that no matter who they were, you should be grateful to them, because, but for them, you would not be here at all.'

Shona had told me that, when the household was running in its normal groove, Jock and the children often did jobs together, such as the washing-up but this was the first time I had seen it – or heard it, rather – happening, because Jock had been away from home so much. It was interesting to me to become aware of the difference in attitude of the children to Shona and to my brother.

Shona attended entirely to their physical and social well-being, saw that they were clean, corrected their manners and she was deeply involved with them emotionally. Whenever they were in the room with her, they gravitated towards her, leaning against her or insinuating themselves into the crook of her arm or Gee climbing on to her lap but Shona did not bother with them intellectually. She would listen with interest to their 'news' of whom they had seen in the village if they went to the shop but I could not imagine Shona discussing their ancestry with them. She was not intellectual or contemplative. She was a force of physical life and her unspoken attitude was: 'I have brought you into life. Have you eaten your dinner? Are your ears clean? All right, get on with this life I have given you and come to me for help if you are hungry or hurt yourselves.' Through this attitude which was communicated without words, she gave them a great security, a security that made Liz tell me with conviction that Gee would have no more sores and she no more bleeding arms 'now that Mum is home again'. Shona did not live by the intellect and as if they were instinctively aware of this, the children did not ask her about such things as their ancestors or try to impress her with their knowledge of Adam, Eve or Darwin.

Between my brother and the three, there was less overt emotional involvement. They did not hug him or sit upon his knee but I became aware now, as I listened to the talk from the scullery, that whenever they were alone with him, they were skirmishing to win intellectual approval. With Shona, they were a group of children with their mother, content inside a warm secure relationship; with Jock, they were young persons, declaring their individuality in strident voices which led to slaps with dish-towels and a much less peaceful tenor than when they chatted within the ambience of Shona and yet the slaps and the stridency took place within the authority of Jock which had its own security for them.

'I like to think about ancestors going back and back – ' came the voice of Liz.

' – and back and back – '

' – and back and back – '

'Back to the Army again, Sergeant!' my brother bellowed

154

with a clash of saucepan lids and they all began to sing at the pitch of their voices: 'Back to the army again.'

'The four o' them is booggers for the singing and the poetry,' said Tom, as the third verse crashed about our ears with its percussion accompaniment of saucepan lids and Shona, carrying Sandy Tom came in and yelled through the scullery doorway: 'For pity's sake, you lot, stop that noise! Somebody has been ringing the front door-bell for the last five minutes.'

She dumped the baby in my lap and went through to the front of the house to return with a tall young woman in riding breeches.

'Janet, this is Miss Forth,' she said. 'Sit down, Miss Forth. I'll make a cup of tea.'

'No thank you, Mrs Sandison. I am here on business,' Miss Forth said as Jock and the children emerged from the scullery. She handed an envelope to Liz who at once ripped it open.

'It's a poem! Listen!' and her brothers read aloud along with her: 'My dear Liz and Dunk and Gee, Miss Forth has something for you from me which I hope you will like with love from Roddee.'

They read the verse a second time and then: 'What is the something, Miss Forth?' Liz asked.

'Come out and see.'

As they trooped through the house in the wake of the young woman, Shona said: 'Oh, John!' in a voice so stricken that, momentarily, I thought she was ill again but then they too went out to the front, so George, Tom, Sandy Tom and I followed. On the driveway there was a Land Rover, hitched to it was a small horse-box and looking over the tailboard of this was the hairy face of a little Shetland pony.

'Oh, Janet,' Shona said, despairing, almost in tears, 'that boy shouldn't have done this! They cost the earth!' The near-despair gave way to anger. 'Liz Sandison, come here this minute!' All three children came. 'Did you go – go *saying* things to Roddy about ponies? Did you – '

'Mum, she didn't,' said Duncan.

'No, didn't,' came the echo.

Liz bit her lip. 'But, Mum, Roddy *knew* we were saving up for a pony. You told him yourself! One day at lunch we told him we – '

Miss Forth, George and Tom were leading the pony down the little ramp on to the gravel.

'My, what a bonnie wee lass!' said George.

'Man, look at the little barrel of a chest that's on her!' said Tom.

'George, Tom,' Shona commanded, 'leave that pony alone! Miss Forth, I am sorry. You will have to take it back. I can't have Roddy – Mr Maclean doing this. I just can't. I – '

'Aw, Mum!' the three voices yelled and all three burst into tears.

'Where would you be refusing the boy's present,' George asked indignantly, 'and hurting his feelings?'

'And us with the glebe and that fine wee old stable round at the back for her?' Tom demanded.

They were standing on either side of the pony, each with a hand on the much-loved long-lacked horse hide.

'She is absolutely safe, Mrs Sandison,' Miss Forth said. 'My little sister has been riding her almost since she was born.'

The children had moved over to the side of their allies, George and Tom, the three tearful faces staring across the battle-ground of the gravel drive at their father and mother.

'It's not that, Miss Forth,' Shona said. 'It is just too much. That boy – John, why don't you *say* something instead of just standing there?' she asked exasperatedly.

My brother, obviously, could think of nothing to say because, equally obviously, he was on the side of the children although he did not want to admit this in cold words. He wanted them to have the pony, just as my father had wanted Jock and me to have everything that he could get for us and Jock had fewer social scruples than Shona had.

'Roddy can well afford the pony, Shona,' I said. 'He is quite a wealthy young man. And I think you should let him show his gratitude. Coming here helped him over a very difficult time.'

Shona looked from me to the pony who clinched matters by turning her head and taking a friendly nibble at Duncan's red-gold hair.

'Well, if you think – ' Shona hesitated and was lost.

Liz clasped her arms round the pony's neck, laid her cheek against the wiry mane and sang: 'Hey ding a ding a ding, you are the loveliest thing!'

'Shall I stay for a little and show them – ' Miss Forth was beginning.

'Not at all,' said George. 'Tom and I will see to all that.'

'Go you into the house and get a droppie tea,' Tom said and to the little mare: 'Come, lassie.'

'Her saddle and tack are on the front seat,' Miss Forth called.

'Very good,' George said. 'We will see to it and thank you.'

'Yes, Miss Forth, thank you very much.'

'Yes, thank you, Miss Forth.'

'Very much, Miss Forth.'

When Miss Forth had had her tea and had gone away, all five returned to the house. 'She is in the glebe having some grass for tea,' Liz announced. 'We have all had a ride but not George and Tom, of course. When she comes in to go to bed, we are going to christen her.'

'What is she to be called?' I asked.

Once again they gave me that look that indicated that I was mentally retarded.

'Betsy, of course,' said Liz.

'Yes, Betsy.'

'Betsy, *acourse*!'

'And a very fine name too,' George said.

'One couldna think o' better,' Tom confirmed.

When the pony had been formally baptised in the back garden, in the presence of us all, we came back into the house and Shona, feeling that all control had been taken away from her and that she must assert herself in some way, said: 'Now, you three, there will be no rides on that pony tomorrow until you have written a proper letter to Roddy thanking him for being so generous.'

'Okay, Mum. We'll do him a real extra special one.'

'An enormous one.'

'A gigantic one.'

'All right. Have supper and get off upstairs,' but before they had finished eating, the front door-bell rang again. Shona's face took on a haunted look as she said: 'You go, John. It will be somebody for you anyhow — I hope,' she added with a threatening look at the three at the table.

My brother came back, pushed open the door of the kitchen and pushed in ahead of him a stockily-built middle-aged man who looked round at us all, fixed his glance on me, blinked and said:

'Good lord! Am I seeing things?'

'That is our *Aunt Janet*,' Liz said into the silence, stressing the name. 'She came all the way from St Jago.'

'Alasdair! Alasdair the Doctor!' I said in the same moment.

The three children rose from the table and gathered round him, attaching themselves to various parts of his person. He was obviously a familiar and favourite visitor.

'Uncle Alasdair, we've got a new brother!'

'And a pony called Betsy!'

'And a dog called Fly!'

'And an Aunt Janet,' he told them.

'Which way are you going, Alasdair?' Jock asked. 'North or south?'

'North. I've been down to Edinburgh on a course.'

'You'll stay?' Shona said. 'You can't go on north at this time of night. Fat Mary will you make up the bed in – '

'It's made,' said Fat Mary. 'It's aye made, that bed.'

Alasdair was almost exactly the same age as myself and he and I had gone to school for the first time at Achcraggan on the same day, where we formed a quarrelsome friendship which lasted for the five years we spent there. His presence brought back to me much of these five years but before we could talk I had to go upstairs with the children for 'Reachfar'.

'Once upon a time, long long ago at Reachfar, Channatt had a friend called Alasdair – ' I began.

'Same name as Uncle Alasdair downstairs?' Liz enquired.

'Yes.'

'Was he Channatt's favourite man?'

'No, not really.'

'Uncle Alasdair is Aunt Sheila's favourite man. Go on then.'

I went on to tell the story of Armistice Day of 1918. ' – and Alasdair climbed on to the roof of the Plough Inn and tied the Lion Rampant flag to the chimney and the war was over,' I ended.

'Not the war Dad was at?' Liz asked.

'No. A war a much longer time ago.'

'A war in history?' Gee asked.

'Long ago in history, like ancestors?' Duncan asked.

'Yes. Now you must all go to sleep. You will see Uncle Alasdair in the morning.'

Liz hopped across the floor and into her own bed. 'Uncle Alasdair used to be my favourite man too,' she said, 'but not any more. At the moment, I am badly smitten with Roddy.'

'That's fine,' I told her. 'It is pleasant to have a change.'

When I went downstairs, I told Alasdair that he had lost his position as Liz's favourite man and he laughed and turned to Shona. 'How is my favourite girl?' he asked.

'You will see her tomorrow,' Shona said. 'They are all coming out to tea.'

We spent a long evening gossiping about Achcraggan and its people, both past and present, for Alasdair had stepped into his father's place as doctor in the village. It seemed to me that one phrase recurred all too frequently. 'He died the year before last', or 'she died just shortly after the war', and the gap of years between my present self and the self of my childhood seemed to lengthen by a century each time one of these phrases was dropped.

The next morning, all the men-folk went out with Alasdair and the children to see the pony and I said to Shona: 'Does Alasdair call often?'

'Two or three times a year, maybe. He has a married sister living in town but she only has a small flat with no spare room. He has a partner with him in the practice, you know. There is no doctor at Ardgruanach now. They are both based at Achcraggan. It makes it easier for time off and things.'

'Liz said that Alasdair was Sheila's favourite man.'

Shona laughed. 'Sheila herself called him that. I think he is, too, in a way. Alasdair is a born bachelor, you see and he doesn't bother her. He often takes her to the theatre and so on when he is down for weekends.'

When the pony had been inspected, Shona put the children into the playroom to write their letter to Roddy and while I prepared the lunch, Alasdair sat by the stove and talked to me. It was like living in two different dimensions to talk to this grizzled ruddy-faced man, so like his father as I remembered him and to know at the same time that he had once been the cheeky little red-haired boy who sat beside me in the Baby Class.

'Remember that day of snow and bright sun when we searched for Violet Boyd?' he asked.

'Yes. Oh, Alasdair, it seems so long, long ago!'

'And yet like yesterday.'

'That is true.'

'We were only a little older than Liz is now but one remembers every detail. You had a blue knitted hood and gloves and

159

blue ribbons on the ends of your pigtails and I can still hear the creak of the old barn door at Skinner's place as we shoved it open.'

'And you said: Don't look!' I said.

Alasdair smiled at me. 'It makes one wonder a bit about child psychology. How old were we? Nine? According to the book, two children of nine finding a suicide hanging from the rafter of a disused barn would suffer a trauma that would mark them for life. I never even had a nightmare about it. Did you?'

'No.'

'We must have been a tough pair. Nevertheless, the affair made a mark on me. It was the first time I ever felt real guilt and I was sorry that I had ever laughed at the Miss Boyds or had taken part in jokes about them.'

I was making a cake for tea that afternoon and now I paused with the wooden spoon among the sugar and fat. 'That affair made a permanent mark on me too,' I said, 'but not of a traumatic kind, I think. It was the next day, when all of us of the Top Class who had been searching all the day before were sleeping it off. Your father – ' I said, my voice low as I mentioned Doctor Mackay who was one of the many who had died over the years ' – your father came round all our homes to see that we were all right. He arrived at Reachfar. But, before that, I had found Miss Violet wandering about the moor one day with withered bits of heather stuck in her hair and we had sent for your father. When he came, Miss Violet took one of the sprigs of heather from her hair and put it in his buttonhole and he said something but I didn't hear what. That other morning, after we found her dead, I asked him what he had said when she gave him the heather. It was a line or two from *Hamlet*, the Mad Scene, when Ophelia says: There's a daisy – I would give you some violets, but they withered all when my father died. – I didn't get a trauma as you call it over poor Miss Violet but your father inoculated me with Shakespeare, Alasdair. I have never got over it and I shall always be grateful to him.' I paused and added: 'Your father was a very good compassionate man, Alasdair.'

'Yes, and he was a first-class doctor too.'

'I am glad that you are still in the practice. So much seems to have changed up there at Achcraggan, it is good to know that the doctor's name is still Mackay.'

He gave a short sigh. 'I came back there after the war because of Father and Mother,' he said. 'The rest of the family are strewn the length and breadth of the earth. I was a bit bored in Achcraggan at first, saw it as a backwater and all that but I know now that doctoring has just as much variety there as anywhere, maybe more.'

'What about that awful old stepmother of mine?'

He shook his head sadly. 'She is not on our list at the moment. She is with Gibson at Fortavoch just now but she will soon be fighting with him again and coming back to us.'

'For pity's sake!'

'There is no point in worrying about her, Janet. There is nothing that anybody can do for her in any way. But I'll keep an eye on George and Tom.'

When the children had had their mid-forenoon bread and cheese – they were now referring to it as their 'half-yoking' – they asked me to come to the playroom to check their spelling in their letter to Roddy. They had promised their mother that they would write a real extra-special enormous gigantic letter and it was all of these things in a way that I had not expected. It was written with coloured pencils, no two successive words in the same hand or in the same colour, on the back of a poster in area about two feet by four, which advertised a long-past fete in aid of the Wolf Cub and Brownie funds. 'Dear Roddy,' it said, 'Thank you enormously for Betsy. She was the biggest most wonderful surprise. Miss Forth brought her in the horse box and clouds and clouds of glory. We will love her for ever and ever and use our acting money to buy winter feed. We are sorry you have gone away and so is everybody. We hope that you will come back soon. Aunt Sheila's favourite man is here and she is coming to tea today. Granda and Granny are coming too. Aunt Janet is making a cake and some shortbread. Thank you very much for the chocolate you left in the Secret Place. Thank you again a million times, billion million trillion times for Betsy. There is no more news. Love from Elizabeth, Duncan, George, X Alexander Thomas (his mark).'

'Is it all right?' Liz asked.

'Splendid.'

'We are not allowed to go into the study. Will you ask Dad for one of his biggest envelopes? And come back and tell us the address? For in the name of all my forefathers I am not going to be able to spell that Drumnadrochit place.'

'Me neither.'

'Nor me forbye and besides.'

Having taken sixpence each from their banks, they set off for the village post office with their letter while I wondered what had possessed them to refer to Alasdair not as 'Uncle Alasdair' but as 'Aunt Sheila's favourite man'.

I remembered my earlier conversation with Alasdair, when he had brought back the memory of my blue woollen hood and gloves and I remembered now my warm tweed coat, my hand-knitted knee-length socks and my sturdy, highly-polished, black going-to-school boots. Liz was the chief composer of the letter and I now seemed to turn into myself at her age of eight, walking along the country road towards Achcraggan, with my leather school-bag hitched on my shoulders, my steel-shod heels ringing on the frosty tarmacadam. It was a brilliant morning, the sun bright on the snow-clad hills across the firth, the sea glittering steel-blue and as I came along, a flock of sandpipers, feeding at the edge of the ebbing tide, rose in rapid wheeling flight and went swerving away, their silver underbellies glittering in the sun so that they looked a blown drift of sparkling leaves for a moment, until they changed course and suddenly settled among the stones at the water's edge a hundred yards ahead, becoming completely invisible as their wings folded and their brownish upper bodies merged into the sea-washed stones.

The water of the firth, enclosed by its hills, made me think of the pool that was my own mind, enclosed in my skull, a pool that contained all the people and things that I knew as the water of the firth contained the swans, the gulls and the ships of the Navy. But in the waters of the firth, I knew that there lurked, although you could not see them, the haddock, the flounders, the mackerel and the shoals of silver herring and this was like my mind too for, sometimes, thoughts rose out of it that I had not known were there. And over this pool that was my mind there were thoughts that came and went, thoughts that were clear for a second, glittering like the sandpipers when the light caught their underbellies and then these thoughts would disappear, as the sandpipers disappeared from sight when they settled among the brownish camouflaging stones.

These ladies called the Miss Boyds who had come to live in Achcraggan caused some of these momentarily perceived thoughts, thoughts related to grown-up things like men, old maids and marriage. The Miss Boyds were old maids because they were not married but, although they wanted to be married, men like Tom and George did not want to marry them. But – But when I tried to carry this thought a stage further, it would elude me, like the sandpipers eluding my sight in their rapid flight, to be lost on the cluttered shore at the edge of the pool.

And Liz, now, as she walked to the post office with her brothers, would have a mind very much like what mine had been at her age, a mind with a bright surface over the unexplored depths below which was invaded, now and then, by fleeting flashing adumbrations of knowledge arising out of observation but not yet assimilated and co-ordinated. It was the shimmer of light on the swerving flight of the sandpipers that had decided, although subconsciously, her choice of 'Aunt Sheila's favourite man' when telling Roddy of Alasdair and she also, probably, had an instinctive knowledge that this was the 'news' in her letter which would most interest Roddy.

In the end, the grandparents and Sheila stayed to supper with us, Sheila and Alasdair going out for a walk afterwards in the long summer light while the others went into the garden and Shona and I sat in the kitchen.

'I am glad Alasdair happened to come,' Shona said. 'It has been something of interest for you among all this welter of cooking and kids.'

Shona was always harking back to the unamusing nature of my holiday as she saw it and I was finding it more and more impossible even to begin to make her understand what the children meant to me. She was so naturally and completely a mother, I think, that her imagination could not encompass what had happened to me, as a childless woman, coming into this household. Also, apart from this failure in communication, there was a difference of tradition and history between Shona and me, a difference that reached back through the generations behind us and of which Shona had never thought, I was sure, because she did not think in these terms. She was a Lowlander by race while I was Highland and she was of the sea and the city while I was of landward peasant blood and I, the Highland peasant, had inborn in me a sense of the family, the clan or tribe rooted in the earth, a sense that had never been part of the culture out of which Shona was bred. She saw her children quite simply as her children, to be loved and cared for and corrected while I, from time to time, was overawed by them, seeing them as part of the future of my race.

163

'I wouldn't have missed the welter of kids for anything,' I said now.

'Roddy shouldn't have given them that pony, Janet,' she said, wrinkling her broad brow, her eyes darkening. She was genuinely worried about the pony. 'He can't possibly afford it, a young man like that. Besides it's so – so extravagant. I've never *heard* of anybody visiting for a few days and giving a present like that!'

I remembered, the day that Miss Lane arrived, how Shona's mother had said she had 'never heard' of a young woman running after a young man like that and I also remembered an older fainter echo of this phrase, in the voice of a long-ago friend of mine called Muriel Thornton. Whenever anyone expressed an opinion that was new to Muriel's static mind, she always said: 'I have never *heard* anyone say a thing like that'. When Muriel used this phrase, I always wanted to say snappishly: 'Well, you have heard it now!' but I did not ever say this because, instinctively and without logical reasoning, I knew that Muriel had not heard of the thing even now. The words might have fallen upon her ears but she had not accepted them with her understanding and had no intention of so accepting them, ever.

In a similar way, Shona's mother had no intention of understanding that Miss Lane might 'run after' Roddy. She preferred to shut her mind to both Roddy and Miss Lane because they were not the sort of people to whom she was accustomed and Shona, now, was in a quandary, because the pony had been accepted by Jock and her children and she did not want, like her mother, to accept Roddy who had presented it, because the gift was outlandishly extravagant in her sight and to accept the gift and not the giver seemed to her dishonourable.

'Look, Shona,' I said a little impatiently, 'that pony means no more to Roddy financially than a box of sweets for the children would mean to you and me. He makes a lot of money by his writing and his father was a very wealthy man.'

'He can't make much money by writing,' Shona said, frowning over this doubtful profession. 'And anyway, people just *don't* go giving people ponies!'

'But they do. Roddy has just done it.'

'But he shouldn't have! After all, we hardly know him. He is practically a stranger. Goodness, in a way I wish he had never come here at all. I have never been so embarrassed.'

164

I began to feel sorry for Roddy who did everything in the grand manner and who, now, out of his generosity and because he himself had always had a pony in his childhood, had done his own cause more harm than good, had estranged rather than familiarised himself in this pocket of society, by making himself flamboyant and outlandish in the eyes of Shona and her family.

'Besides,' she continued, evading the main problem in her mind, 'it isn't good for these kids to have everything fall into their laps. You read such awful things about children that get out of hand and some of the things Sheila can tell you are simply terrifying.' She was probably much more sensible about the children than I was, looking towards their future in this practical way instead of thinking of it in vague grandiose terms as I did but, at the same time, I thought she underestimated the children and also herself and Jock.

'Stop worrying your silly head,' I told her. 'I am absolutely certain that with the combination of you and Jock in charge of them, the children will never get out of hand, whatever that means. Those children you read about and that Sheila has to cope with are the victims of their parents. I think a child can get over the gift of a pony or even the loss of a mother, as Jock and I had to do, if the people around them maintain some sort of balance of love and justice.'

Shona looked sympathetic and sad. 'Why,' she said, 'you couldn't have been much older than Liz when your mother died!' and I felt that she had thought of this for the first time.

'I had just had my tenth birthday,' I told her. 'And then there was leaving Reachfar and the advent of Jean into the bargain but I don't think I turned into a juvenile delinquent.' I laughed. 'Apart from my father, George and Tom were there and they would not have held with a juvenile delinquent in the family.'

'It must have been worse for you than it was for John. You were old enough to know what had happened to you. When John first told me he could not remember his mother, I thought it was the saddest thing I had ever heard. But it was worse for you,' she repeated.

'One works things out, if the love of other people is around one and even more important than the love is this thing I can only call balance. You and Jock have a wonderful balance here

165

between love and justice, discipline and freedom. And when in doubt, call in George and Tom.'

'You would have made a splendid mother, Janet. What a pity it is – '

I interrupted her. 'You know, Shona, I honestly don't think so. I am too selfish – '

'Selfish?' she now interrupted me with indignation.

'Too much of an egoist then. I would either have turned my child into a pale depersonalised replica of my own heart's desire or have spoiled it with too much love into juvenile delinquency.'

'What nonsense!'

'It isn't entirely. I think perhaps there is a Providence that decides who shall have children and who not.'

'Sheila would tell you that Providence makes some very queer decisions then.'

'Maybe so,' I said, 'but I am content now with the decision as regards myself.'

'Of course,' Shona was thoughtful, 'out there where you are, you would have had to send them home to school, not see them for months, years at a time, like Roddy's parents with him and his brothers. What a queer way of living!'

'That is what I meant by selfishness. I probably wouldn't have parted with the children to send them home to school. This time, when I came home, I didn't want to come at first, although Twice wanted me to come. In the end, it was my friend Sashie de Marnay, who persuaded me. He told me point-blank that I was smothering Twice, devouring him with my watchfulness over him and that in refusing to make this trip I was worrying Twice for my own selfish ends. And he was right. I was.'

'But that was natural,' Shona protested. 'Away out there, so far from home and Twice is all you have.'

'That brings us full circle. Maybe if I had had children, I would not have smothered Twice so much,' I said. 'One simply doesn't know anything except that some sort of balance has to be maintained and it was when I saw that that I came on this trip, very unwillingly and in a smug spirit of self-sacrifice, I might tell you. And look what has happened. I am having the most wonderful time. When I go back, it will have the quality of a dream, a long summer dream.'

'You are easy to please. Janet, are you really all right away out there in St Jago, so far from home?'

'But St Jago is my home. If Jock had to be four thousand miles away, that would be your home too.'

'No,' she said, shaking her head. 'I would go with him, of course, but I would be homesick. Even with John and the children there, I would be homesick for Granny and Granda and Sheila – even for Aunt Hannah.'

This I did not understand. I had loved my home at Reachfar and its people very much and, although I had spent comparatively short periods there from the age of ten onwards, I had never felt homesick, probably because I seemed to carry Reachfar and its people with me, complete in my mind, wherever I went. But Shona, who lived in a different way, had the need to see what she loved with her physical eyes at frequent intervals and had to make tangible contact with the living flesh of those she loved. She was a strange compound of motherly wisdom and maidenly immaturity, I thought, which was the result of her having stepped straight from being one of the daughters of her secure home circle into the further security of a happy marriage, her own home and her children.

That night, before I fell asleep, I remembered how Gee had said that I must be about a hundred and, in relation to Shona, I felt that I was indeed about a hundred, for I suddenly saw that, in comparison with myself she had no past. Unlike her children, she was not interested in 'ancestors' whom she had never seen and all the ancestors she had ever known – her mother, her father and Aunt Hannah – were still with her. But my past, so much more complex than Shona's, was spread behind me like a great tapestry showing people, places and events in every colour from sombre to gay, a huge experience that made it easier for me than it was for Shona to accept a gift of a pony for the children from a comparative stranger. I had heard of people doing stranger things than Roddy had done in presenting the pony that had caused so much discussion between Shona and her mother on the telephone. For his own sake, however, I was sorry that Roddy had done what he had for it had changed him in the eyes of Shona and her family from 'That poor boy who lost his parents in that terrible way' into an extravagantly wealthy stranger who made gestures of a kind of which they had 'never heard'.

As I dropped off to sleep, falling into that semi-conscious state that is out of what we call the 'real' world, my final

167

thought was that, in this matter of the pony, the true individual personalities of Shona and Roddy were not in play at all. Roddy had acted in accordance with the tradition behind him, a tradition in which children had ponies, a tradition in which, if you were extravagantly grateful, as Roddy had been for the hospitality of Jock and Shona, that gratitude was expressed in the fullest way possible. If Roddy had stopped to think, he might have perceived that, to the people in this circle, a pony as a gift might seem a little florid and flamboyant. And Shona, in her reaction to the gift, was reacting not as herself, who wanted, like most parents, her children to have the best that the world could offer. She was reacting according to her tradition which laid down that expensive presents are not acceptable from comparative strangers. Do we exist in ourselves at all, I wondered, as I hovered at the edge of the abyss of sleep or are we merely a set of reflexes which have been imposed on us by the past?

Chapter X

'Whither is fled the visionary gleam?
Where is it now, the glory and the dream?'

THE following morning, when the grown-up breakfast was over, everybody sat on in the kitchen, for it was pouring with rain out-of-doors. Alasdair, who was to leave shortly, cornered me in the scullery, saying that he wanted to talk to me privately, so I went with him to the study where he rounded upon me and said in an aggressive tone: 'Look here, Janet, just who is this friend Maclean of yours that Sheila was talking about last night?' This aggressiveness took me straight back to my childhood days with Alasdair at Achcraggan School and, shamefully enough, it had precisely the effect on me now at forty-six years old that it had had on me at the age of six and I felt my temper rising at once.

'He is a rather brilliant and successful young poet and writer,' I said as coolly as I could. 'Why?'

'He sounds like a madman to me.'

'Why?' I said again.

'He proposed to Sheila three days after he first laid eyes on her, then he goes careering off into the wilds and starts writing impassioned letters.'

'What is the matter with that? People propose to people all the time.'

'Three days after meeting them?'

'Why waste time?' I asked. 'As my favourite poet has it: "Who ever loved that loved not at first sight?" '

'Poetry!' Alasdair exploded, condensing into the speaking of one word all the differences between minds like mine and minds like his own. 'The girl doesn't know whether she is on her head or her heels. He is worrying her silly. I wish you would write to him and tell him to stop this bloody nonsense.'

'I'll do nothing of the sort. It is not my affair and it isn't yours either, as I see it, unless you are interested in Sheila yourself in that way, in which case it is for you and Roddy to fight it out.'

169

'Don't be stupid!' Alasdair was furious now. 'I am nearly twice Sheila's age. That is the reason why she told me about this. She feels that she can't talk about it to her family. She thinks the man is mad and I don't blame her.'

'Well, I do. I don't see why a pretty girl like Sheila should get all scared because a young man falls for her. He isn't the first, I gather from Shona.'

'But the others made some sense! This one doesn't!'

'Sense?' I almost screeched. 'It is obvious that *you* have never been in love. There *isn't* any sense in the damn' thing.'

'God, you're hopeless. I might as well talk to that table there.'

'Look, Alasdair, if you just calm down and come to your senses, you know perfectly well that this thing is between Roddy and Sheila only. She told you about it because she had to tell somebody to clear her own mind. But I will tell you something. Roddy would not be writing her impassioned letters if a climate for impassioned letters hadn't arisen between them. People don't throw love letters into a vacuum.'

'Climate? Vacuum?' He strode towards the door. 'Oh, hell, don't let's have a row, Janet. We never could make sense of one another and it seems we still can't. Let's forget it. I'll have to be on my way.'

Shortly afterwards, we all went out to the front of the house to see him off to Achcraggan and when the men had gone to the study, the children to the playroom and Shona to do something upstairs, I returned thoughtfully to my cooking.

Had anyone told me a week ago that Roddy Maclean had proposed marriage to any young woman, my reaction would have been one of disbelief and derision for Roddy, as I had known him, had been what is called 'not the marrying sort' but when Alasdair had told me of his proposal to Sheila, I had been less astonished than I had expected and I found, now, that this was because of that phrase: 'Aunt Sheila's favourite man is here – ' that Liz had put into her letter. From the moment I had read that phrase, my attitude to Roddy had changed because, in an unformulated inarticulate way, I had begun to think that his feeling for Sheila must be deeper than I had believed since Liz, as children can do, had picked the vibration of it out of the air.

Also, I came further towards the conviction that, this time, Roddy was emotionally and not only sexually engaged because what Alasdair had told me seemed to demonstrate that, for once, Roddy had lost his head. From Sheila's point of view, he was behaving like a man gone mad and this was not characteristic of Roddy when playing the sex game that had been his favourite pastime. He had been wont to play it with all his wits about him, making move after move to attain his desired end which was a short brisk affaire to be dropped as soon as it began to pall, like his affaire with Deborah Lane. It was ironic that, now, at the mercy of a deeper drive, he had exposed himself to Sheila with the passionate honesty that he brought to his writing and had succeeded only in shaking the earth under a girl who had been brought up in the most conventional of small-town ways. Had Roddy intended to seduce Sheila, he would have out-conventioned convention in his approach, but Roddy in love had plunged like a bull at a gate, in the way that he plunged into all the realities of his life.

Sheila, it was probable, saw courtship and marriage in terms of her sister and my brother, a long drawn out, cautious, firmly founded affaire, interrupted and lengthened in their case by the war it was true, but even had the war not intervened, it would have been a long process of my brother qualifying at the university, finding a job and then perhaps a year of going for quiet walks while he and Shona saved enough money to equip their home. This, with a few renegade exceptions such as myself, was how things were done in families like ours and in saying 'families like ours', I imply that most people of our class who married, married into the class to which they belonged. Marriages 'above' or 'below' one's own class, in the north of Scotland even in 1956, were suspect, as Shona had indicated when she told me of a school friend of hers who had married a Belgian count, met during the war. Shona was patently astonished, although she did not say so in words, that Madame la Comtesse was still with Monsieur le Comte in a château in Belgium with their three children and seemingly very happy, for Madame had not only married 'above herself' but had married a foreigner to boot.

In this milieu of ours, Roddy was a foreigner in more than one way, I now realised and in the same moment I became aware of how far I had grown away from the class stratifications of my own country. This north of Scotland was the most 'backward' area of Britain and had not, as yet, succumbed to the levelling process which had gained such momentum during the years of the war and, unlikely as it seems on the surface, the strongholds of class distinction were the provincial cities, like Sheila's home town rather than the country villages like Achcraggan. Around Achcraggan, even when I was a child, there had been the Big House of Poyntdale and various other big houses, whose people dined together and sometimes entertained the doctor, the dominie and the minister and then there had been the mass of farmers, their workers and the crofters, to which last class my family belonged. In Achcraggan itself, there had been the shopkeepers and the craftsmen of various kinds such as joiners and masons and then there were the people of the Fisher Town who were of a separate race, with their different physical features, different customs and a dialect of their own. But it was a simple hierarchy and bound together by mutual interdependence, for the village of Achcraggan depended upon the farms and crofts round about and on the fisher people to buy from its shops and employ its craftsmen, while the big houses and their work people were interdependent and the same doctor, dominie and minister served all. The children of the big houses attended Achcraggan School before leaving for the preparatory schools for Eton or Fettes. Achcraggan was welded together basically by the dependence of its people on the wayward elements of land and sea which, frequently, through the medium of a failed harvest or a violent storm, cut across all barriers.

Sheila's background, however, was less broadly and securely based than this. No harvest thrives or fails on city streets and they are never lashed into fury by a north-easterly gale but people have a need to be held together in some way and the way of the provincial city is to be bound by the security of class. Just as, in Achcraggan, any stranger appearing in the district was a foreigner and suspect until identified with some family, in the provincial northern city anyone from beyond the class barrier was a foreigner and suspect and Roddy was not only from beyond the class barrier in upbringing and education. He had also been born in St Jago and he was foreign in yet another way – he was a writer, a member of a class that is suspect and foreign to all other classes throughout Great Britain.

Added to all these disadvantages, there was the person of Roddy himself. He was very handsome and handsome is still suspected in many quarters of being 'as handsome does' whatever the sinister meaning of the phrase may be, his parents had been killed in an earthquake which was tragic but at the same time outlandish, he was fairly well off through writing books which was almost indecent and he had proposed marriage to Sheila three days after meeting her like *in* a book, as my grandmother would have put it and as, I had no doubt, Granny Murray would put it too and now, to top off this crazy structure of a personality, he had presented the children with a pony 'that cost the earth'. There were at least three telephone calls per day between Shona, her mother and her sister during which the extravagance of the pony was discussed and rediscussed.

It was all very absurd and amusing and, as I had told Alasdair, there was nothing to be done about it. When Sheila had sorted matters out in her mind, I had no doubt that, if she wanted Roddy, she would have him, foreigner, writer or no but the sorting out would take a little time.

'Aunt Janet,' said Liz at elevenses, 'is Uncle Alasdair your favourite man?'

'Certainly not. Uncle Twice is my favourite man.'

She clapped the dramatic hand to her forehead. 'Of course! Just fancy me forgetting that!'

'Can people have more than one favourite man?' Gee asked.

'Not at the same time, I am thinking,' said Tom.

'You can have a favourite and a next most favourite, like,' George explained. 'And then there are folk that keep changing their favourites all the time.'

'Aunt Janet, who is your next most favourite man?' Liz enquired.

It occurred to me that Liz and the devil were good friends, as the people of Achcraggan used to say. My earlier life had been strewn with 'favourite men' and broken engagements, follies on which Tom and George loved to dwell and I could see them now preparing to enlighten Liz about my past.

'Married people don't have more than one favourite,' said Shona, coming down firmly on the side of convention and saving the day for me.

'Roddy has a favourite and a next most one and a next most one, I should think,' said Liz.

'And a next next next most one –'

' – and a next –'

'Stop that,' said Jock and silence descended momentarily until Liz said: 'I wish Roddy would come back.' She looked at the rain-streaked window. 'Since he went away, brightness has fallen from the air.'

'He was a very good wet weather type,' Duncan opined.

'Yes,' Gee concurred.

'Why?' I asked.

'Stories,' said Gee, solemn in his appreciation as he looked round at us, 'hidyus horrible stories about the Goblins and Ghosts of Dead Man's Gulch.' He shuddered with remembered pleasure.

'Better than the yarn about the ferret in Miss Tulloch's shop?' Tom asked.

The three pairs of eyes looked at him. 'Not the same thing at all,' Liz said after a moment. 'The ferret is not really a *story* – not like Dead Man's Gulch is a story.'

'Not exactly,' said Duncan.

'Not *really*,' said Gee.

There was a short silence during which the children looked almost frightened and then it seemed as if masks had dropped over the three faces. 'Come on, you two,' Liz said. 'Let's go back through there and get on with it,' and they returned to the playroom across the hall.

George and Tom, who never liked to be in the house in the daytime except for meals, retired to the woodshed which was their wet-day equivalent at the schoolhouse of the barn or the granary at Reachfar, Shona went back upstairs and my brother said thoughtfully: 'That was one of the moments when I wished they had the words for it.'

'Meaning?'

'The words to tell the difference that they feel about your Reachfar stories and Roddy's goblin ones. They were face to face with their fantasy for a moment there but there were no words. They had to retire to the activity of the playroom, to the solid things they can get a grip on.'

After lunch, when I was by myself again, baking in the kitchen, I found myself thinking of that moment when the three young faces had become masked and expressionless. This 'fantasy', as my brother called it, which stopped the children in their stride and robbed them of coherent speech was, I was beginning to feel sure, the sudden vision of life itself in all its immensity, eternal in time in a limitless cosmos, which suddenly presented itself to them, a flash of glory, breaking for a second the grey mist at the edge of consciousness. I believed that Sandy Tom lay spiritually enfolded in this glorious dreaming light, just as certainly as he lay physically enfolded, warm and well-fed, among the blankets of his perambulator in the front hall. He still had about his mind, I believed, the clouds of glory that he had brought with him from the spiritual home whence his new-born spirit came and the world, with its doing and knowing, its getting and spending, had not yet precipitated those rainbow clouds down into the well of subconsciousness. But for Liz, Duncan and Gee, the world had already dissipated the clouds of glory, sinking the visionary gleam into their subconscious minds and hedging their conscious minds about with the grey mists of the materially unknown, except for moments such as had come at elevenses time, when their minds attempted to define their 'fantasy' of Reachfar and they discovered that it was beyond definition, because it partook of that spiritual glory with which they had entered the world. Reachfar and these children had the mutuality, the balance, the reciprocity, the coherence which characterises the great forces of nature, that functional relation by which the vision of Reachfar held in their minds made of Reachfar the stuff that dreams are made on so that, being dream stuff, it could raise from the subconscious stuff of its own kind, something of the glory and the dream which, as infants, they had brought into the world with them and which was now nearly lost to their consciousness. I remembered how, once, during my own childhood, I had had a momentary vision of the glorious dreaming immensity of life. I could not have been five years old, because it was before I went to school and I must have been more than three because my hair was long enough to be dressed in two shoulder length pigtails.

On Reachfar, there were two places which were reckoned to be dangerous for children, one of them being a disused quarry with a high precipice of rock, the other being the deep well in the moor above the house. With the idea of making me afraid of these places, so that I would not go near them, George and Tom peopled the old quarry with a dreadful old man called Rory, who had black whiskers and who spent all his time waiting for disobedient children to come near his precipice so that he might either throw them over or throw rocks down on top of them and kill them. In the well, George and Tom said, there was another dreadful character called Sandy, who had red whiskers and he spent all his time sitting at the bottom of his well waiting for disobedient children to come so that he might reach up with his skinny old hand, pull them in and drown them. George and Tom would have done better, in my case, had they peopled these places with old women rather than old men, for it happened that there were some terrifying, witch-like old women around Achcraggan but most of the old men of the district were noble-looking and benevolent. Also, I liked old men with beards. They made me think of my kind patriarchal grandfather. And so, naturally, I made up my mind to visit the red-whiskered Sandy of the well and, when I was a little older, I would visit the black-whiskered Rory of the quarry which was about four miles away.

It was a November day of hoar-frost and clear blue sky when I went to the well with my dog, Fly. It was within clear sight of the kitchen window so Fly and I went into the dark thicket of firs which was my Thinking Place and, already trembling with the secret thrill of the forbidden together with the fear of the possibility that Sandy's skinny hand would reach up to seize me, I lay down on my stomach and began to crawl out of the thicket into the rough foot-high heather that surrounded the well. Sandy would not get me, I knew, because Fly would not let him. If that grasping skinny hand came up, she would have it in her sharp teeth in a flash. Flat and invisible to the kitchen window, the two of us inched along through the hoar-frosted heather. It was Fly who had taught me to move like this for, when she was rounding up sheep, she could go down like this at one place and come up in quite another where the sheep did not expect her. Soon we were at the five-strand barbed wire fence that made the well safe for the animals and we inched ourselves in under the lowest strand, then very slowly and warily, I peered over the edge of the deep black hole, while Fly had already taken a good grip on the tweed of my pleated skirt. At first I could see nothing at all, but no grasping hand came up and I went on looking down between the mossy stones of the well walls. Then I could see a dark disc, like a black looking-glass that yet held an unearthly light which seemed to become brighter as I looked until I could see reflected in it the white hoar-frosted heather that overhung the well mouth and next I could see my own face with the pigtails on either side, heather and face very still, as if frozen in time. Then, as I looked something began to move across the water mirror, a long arrow shape, like a V lying on its side,

176

visible in its entirety for a second and then dying out of sight as the tails of the V became too far apart to be contained in the mirror. I experienced a second of glorious mystery, of faraway, inexplicable shadowy things, of eternity and infinity, but I drew back from the edge of the well, not only because Fly was tugging me back with all her might but because what I had seen and felt was too glorious to be borne for more than a second. Having wriggled back beyond the fence, I rolled over on to my back among the frosty heather and stared up into the limitless blue of the sky where a long arrow-shaped skein of wild geese was losing height, as they honked their way down to their resting-place in Poyntdale Bay. . . .

Having finished my baking, I went through to Jock's study to find something to read and, noticing the volume of Wordsworth's poems, I took it from the shelf. Jock was writing at his desk and he looked up and said: 'Why don't you take a leaf out of Shona's book and have a lie-down on your bed? This sort of weather is not fit for much else. I'll bring you a cup of tea in an hour or so.'

'Thanks Jock. I think I will.'

When I came out of the study, however, the three children were in the front hall.

'Are you finished baking?' Liz asked. 'Can we come into the kitchen? I am sick of the sight of the playroom and those two.' She jerked a scornful thumb at her brothers.

'And we are pretty sick of you too,' said Duncan.

'Yes, sick as sick.'

'Now then,' I said, 'let's not let a bit of rain get the upper hand,' and I turned back through to the kitchen.

'What's the book?' Liz enquired and read aloud: 'Poetical Works of William Wordsworth, never heard of him.'

'Haven't you? I thought you had. He is the clouds of glory man.'

'Is he?' They sat down in a row on the hearth-rug. 'Will you read some? The clouds of glory bit?'

I turned up the *Ode on Intimations of Immortality*. 'It is quite a long poem,' I said, 'and not easy to understand,' thinking that *We are seven* might be more suitable.

'Does it sing?' Duncan asked.

'Oh yes, it sings.'

'Read it,' said Liz, so I began:

177

'The child is father of the man;
    And I could wish my days to be
    Bound each to each by natural piety.'

'Stop!' said Liz. 'We *never* interrupt when anybody is read-ing to us but you have never read to us before and is this a holy-oly sort of poem? Piety and all that? We don't like holy-oly stuff — all that be-good-sweet-maid-and-let-who-will-be-clever sort of pious poultice.'

This was the voice of my brother speaking, I knew.

'I don't think this poem is the pious poultice sort,' I said. 'I think you are mistaken about the word piety as this poet uses it. Its true meaning is to have a dutiful attitude towards life and good relationships with your family and friends. You three should be bound to Mum and Dad and Sandy Tom by natural piety, this poet means and I think you are.'

'And we have piety for you too and for Aunt Sheila?' Liz asked.

'And Granny and Granda?' asked Duncan.

'And Tom and George?' asked little Gee.

'It would be pleasant if you had,' I told them, 'if you felt that we were all a little more important to you and a little closer to you than just any other odd person that you happen to know. That is natural piety. There is nothing holy-oly about it.'

'If that is what it is, I am stuffed to the gills with natural piety,' said Liz, 'except the bits of me that's stuffed with the opposite thing, like what I feel about that Amanda Shand. Okay. Start at the beginning again. There will be no more interruptions.'

As instructed, I began at the beginning again and went on:

'There was a time when meadow, grove and stream,
    The earth and every common sight,
        To me did seem
    Apparelled in celestial light,
    The glory and the fresnness of a dream.'

Whatever my brother had or had not done for the children, with his 'treating them as if they were a university faculty' as Shona expressed it, he had taught them to listen and although I was sure that the meaning of a poem that was obscure enough to have caused some critical disagreement as to its purport was not penetrating to them, they were catching the music of the words, their bodies swaying a little with the rhythm and coming to rest with a soft sigh of satisfaction at the end of each stanza.

Now that I had begun to read a poem which had always been a favourite of mine although I had not read it for some time, I found that I had much of it by heart and did not need to keep my eyes constantly on the printed page. For much of the time, I was looking at the children but they, although their wide eyes looked straight at me, were not seeing me. They were lost in the music of the words and the six eyes held a far-off visionary look that went through and beyond me to some dreaming infinity. When I came to the end, they seemed to come back from some remote place and Liz said: 'It sings all right. Aunt Janet, will you do the clouds of glory bit again, just that tiny bit?'

> 'Not in entire forgetfulnes,
> And not in utter nakedness,
> But trailing clouds of glory do we come
> From God, who is our home:' I read.

'I like that. It makes me sad and happy all at once,' Liz said with conviction and, this time, it was not my brother's voice that spoke but her own.

I went on, at their request, to read some more of Wordsworth to them but the Ode was the thing and, in the end, I had to read the entire poem again, they suddenly speaking with me the 'clouds of glory bit'. I was reading the last stanza when Jock came through from the study and George and Tom came in through the other door.

> 'The clouds that gather round the setting sun
> Do take a sober colouring from an eye
> That hath kept watch o'er man's mortality:'

I paused but Jock, George and Tom stood still in the door-ways and I read on to the last falling cadence:

> 'Another race hath been and other palms are won.
> Thanks to the human heart by which we live,
> Thanks to its tenderness, its joys, and fears,
> To me the meanest flower that blows can give
> Thoughts that do often lie too deep for tears.'

The children came out of their tranced silence, sighed and then Liz said: 'Dad, Aunt Janet is a splendid poetry reader, far better than you.'

'But then Aunt Janet is more of a poet than I am,' Jock said.

'Och, aye, she has always been a great one for the poetry,' Tom said and began to recite: 'From Reachfar and looking east – '

Liz sprang up and stamped her foot. 'Stop that! That is a Channatt poem!'

'Yes!' The boys were on their feet too.

'Yes. Channatt's!'

Jock stopped in mid-floor with the kettle in his hand. 'Don't you like the Channatt poems any more?' he asked.

The sudden rage seemed to die out of the children, leaving them at a loss and there was a little silence until Liz found the incoherent words: 'No. I mean yes. We still like them but they are private.'

'Secret,' said Duncan.

'Yes,' Gee concurred with an emphasising nod of his head before all three trooped out and across the hall to the playroom with a curious air of making a new departure.

'A person wouldna know where one is at with them,' Tom said. 'Time was when they couldna get enough o' Janet's bitties o' poetry.'

'What I am thinking,' George said quietly, 'is that they kind of know that their Aunt Janet is Channatt as they call her, but they are not wanting to know it, especially Liz. They would rather think of the wee lass running among the heather than an old wifie that is going grey in the hair,' and he gave me his kind teasing smile.

I took the kettle from Jock's hand and went to the scullery to fill it but he followed me and, as the water rushed from the tap, he said quietly: 'George is right. That is what I tried to say in the garden that night. That you may once have been Channatt is, for the kids – in fact for all of us – a thought that lies too deep for tears.'

We made the tea and when the children came back, their mood had changed in their rainbow fashion and they announced that, rain or not, they were going to put on their mackintoshes and Wellington boots and walk down to the village with Fly to fetch Sandy Tom's goats' milk which was now sent to the shop each day by some country network of the goat-owner's

180

neighbour giving it to the mail-car which delivered his news-papers.

'All right,' Jock said. 'It will save me getting the car out.'

We had prepared a tea tray for Shona, but before we could take it up she came down with Sandy Tom, who was having one of his short wide-awake spells, came to me and entertained George and Tom by taking one of their fingers in each hand and giving them a hearty shake. He next subjected his own hands to a long inspection, as if he had newly discovered these attachments and then, with a bored sigh, he stuffed most of one of them into his mouth and lapsed into sleep, just as the telephone rang.

As Jock answered it, I was thinking that if this was to be one more long discussion between Shona and her mother about the pony, I would have to retire upstairs to contain my temper but a sudden tenseness spread from my brother across the room, causing us all to stare at him as he turned round. 'It is Aunt Hannah, Shona,' he said then. 'She has had a stroke. They have taken her to Roseville.' Shona took the receiver. 'Sheila?' Shona began to cry as she listened. 'Yes. All right. We'll be in as soon as we can.' She put down the re-ceiver, mopping her eyes and looked at Sandy Tom on my knee. 'I suppose we had better take the baby with us, John?'

'Where would you be taking the bairn to a house o' sickness?' George demanded.

'You will have plenty to do, nursing the old leddy without the bairn as well,' Tom said.

'I think you should leave Sandy Tom at home, Shona,' my brother told her. 'I won't stay in town. I shall just drop you and come back. There is nothing I can do at Roseville and the four of us will manage here very well.'

'All right. I'll go up and put a few things in a bag.'

Sandy Tom and I went upstairs with her and I laid him in his cot. 'Don't worry about him, Shona.'

'I am not worried about *him*. It's you. What a farce of a holiday this has been.'

'Oh, rubbish. I'll get your sponge-bag.' I went to the bath-room and came back. 'About Aunt Hannah – is it severe?'

'Pretty bad but she is conscious.' Shona gave a little sob. 'Sheila always promised her that she would never let her go to hospital. She has a horror of hospitals.'

'Most of them have, that generation,' I said. 'Dad had it.

181

In fact, I have more than a little of it myself. You go and do what you can, Shona and don't worry about us. We'll manage splendidly.' They were ready to go when the children came back from the village with the bottle of milk.

'Aunt Hannah is sick,' Jock told them, 'and Mum and I are going to town. I'll be back soon but Mum may stay for a day or two to help to look after Aunt Hannah.'

After a startled moment, the children rose to it. 'Mum, tell her that we hope she will soon be better,' Liz said formally.

'Yes.'

'Yes, better soon.'

'I'll tell her,' Shona said. 'And you three will help Aunt Janet and not be a nuisance.'

They nodded their heads and Shona got into the car but as it went out of the gate, the six eyes looked up at me and Liz asked: 'Why was Mum crying? Is Aunt Hannah going – going to die?'

'We will hope not,' said George firmly. 'Mum has gone to nurse her and try to make her better. Tom, rain or not, I am needing a little Oven Garden for my supper. We will be getting some vegetables.' He looked at the children. 'Since you have your big boots on, would you be giving us a hand?' and all five of them went tramping through the rain round to the back garden, while I hastily decided that Fly would have to have her scraps of meat and bones roasted this evening, that I might derive the residue from them to make gravy. The long mortal life of Aunt Hannah might be winding down to its end but the immortal generations tramped on and, like a mortal army, they marched largely on their stomachs.

The children, Tom and George came in with their load of vegetables and, while I bathed and fed Sandy Tom, they prepared them in the scullery, except for Gee, who came through to the hearth-rug with his basket of green peas and his bowl.

'You like that job, Gee?' I asked over Sandy Tom's bottle as I watched the neat little fingers picking the peas out of the pods one by one.

'Yes but I am not very quick.'

'You don't have to be quick. Your peas don't go in until the garden is nearly cooked.'

'Look! One, two – eleven in this one! Just fancy!'

'Yes. Fancy!'

From the scullery came the chatter of the other two, punctuated by the slower, deeper voices of Tom and George. The rain streamed down the windows but the fire was bright and from the oven came the savoury smell of the roasting scraps of meat and bones and the fact that Aunt Hannah might be nearing the end of her life only a few miles away made all the glowing life of this kitchen, with its cooking smell, its lively voices, the popping of Gee's pea-pods and the contented sucking snuffles of the baby richer and fuller. And now they all arrived at the kitchen table, George carrying the bowl of brightly coloured vegetables and Tom the big casserole.

'Did you do the onions?' I asked.

'Dang it, do we need them things? They are fine to eat but the skinning of them always puts me to crying,' Tom protested.

'You always have to pay in some ways for your fun,' said Liz. 'An onion is worth a weep. I'll do one and Dunk will do one,' and she fetched two onions from the scullery.

Sandy Tom finished his milk, sent a fine belch over my shoulder which everybody applauded and just as I laid him in the cot, the telephone rang. Suddenly, the kitchen was silent and even the oven seemed to stop sending out its smell, the fire to grow dim. I picked up the receiver from the window-sill, my back to the room as I looked out into the heavy rain.

'Who? Oh, Roddy?'

'It's Roddy!' said the pleased voice of Liz behind me and I smelled the oven smell again as Roddy began to speak. 'Janet, I am in Inverness. Janet, may I come back to the schoolhouse, do you think?'

'If you want to, Roddy but — '

'Look here, who is this man that's staying? Liz said in her letter — '

'As old as I am and no longer here,' I said.

'Oh. But I'd like to come back anyway, Janet. It's grim up at the croft.'

'All right, Roddy, come but Shona is in town. Aunt Hannah has had a stroke and you won't see much of — of anybody.'

'I don't care. I'll come straight on now. See you later.'

'Roddy is coming back,' I announced and the children burst into song. 'He says it is grim up at his croft.'

'And so it will be,' Tom said, 'up on yon hill in this weather.'

'It was foolishness him going up to that place in the first place,' George said. 'What would he be doing up at a wild place like that all on his own? It would be different if he had the right kind o' company.'

'When will he get here?' Liz asked.

'Not until after you are in bed. You will see him in the morning.'

'Aw, poop!' 'Poop for two!' 'Poop for three!' 'And another poop for Sandy Tom!' Liz ended.

My brother came back about nine o'clock, came into the kitchen and merely shook his head in reply to our questioning glances. George poured out a little whisky for each of us and now Jock said: 'It is pathetic, terribly pathetic. She was always so cross-grained and thrawn and aggressive and now she is lying there, completely docile, all the fight gone out of her.' His voice trembled a little and his hand trembled too as he raised his glass to his lips.

'Old Hannah is not one to be sad about, Jock, lad,' George said. 'She has had a good long run and she has enjoyed herself on the whole, fighting with everybody. There is sadness in a young person going but not in the going of an old person. That is the way I see it, whatever.'

'And me too, forbye and besides,' said Tom.

'The kids behaved themselves?' Jock asked me.

'Yes. They went to bed in high fettle, to make the morning come sooner, Liz explained. Roddy is coming back. He is somewhere between Inverness and here right now. It seems that he found the croft a bit depressing all on his own.'

'And he will be a bittie nearer to Sheila down here,' said George.

'Aye, that is in it right enough,' Tom agreed and my brother smiled silently.

George and Tom went up to bed about ten o'clock but Jock and I sat on by the fire until Roddy arrived about eleven.

'It's all right my coming back, Jock?' he asked, standing in the doorway, a vivid dominating presence with drops of rain sparkling on his rough, dark gypsy hair.

'I am glad you are back, Roddy, to be here with your car if I have to be in town, apart from anything else. You know about Aunt Hannah?'

'Yes. Janet told me. Sheila will be very upset. She is devoted to that old woman.'

'Yes. She has put in for fourteen days leave to nurse her but I don't think it is going to take that long,' Jock said. 'I'll get you a dram, Roddy. Have you had a meal?'

'Yes, thanks. Aunt Hannah is as bad as that?'

'I am afraid so.'

'Actually,' I said, 'the sooner she goes the better. She can't get well again. And George and Tom are right. She has had a good long run. It is the rest of you, especially Sheila, that I am sad for. You are all going to miss her but the gap will close.'

When I went upstairs, I went first to my room to look at Sandy Tom and then into the other room to see the other three. The two boys were lying on their sides, Duncan's longer body tucked round Gee's as always and Liz, as always, was lying spread-eagled on her back, one foot projecting from under the covers, the pigtails spread from end to end of her pillow on either side of her face.

'She looks as if she were airborne,' said Roddy's voice behind me, as Jock, too, came into the room.

I picked up the bedclothes, pushed the foot in and tucked the blankets back under the mattress and when we all came out on to the landing, Roddy said: 'That first night that Janet and I arrived and those three kids fought in the kitchen and you walloped them and they all howled, I thought you were demented, saddling yourself with such a madhouse. I just want to tell you I take it all back. You are a bloody lucky man. Good night.'

He went along the landing to his room, Jock raised his eyebrows at me and we all shut our doors and went to bed.

Chapter XI

'We will grieve not, rather find
Strength in what remains behind;
In the primal sympathy
Which having been must ever be;
In the soothing thoughts that spring
Out of human suffering;
In the faith that looks through death,
In years that bring the philosophic mind.'

THE next morning, the sun was shining, a fact which Liz imputed entirely to the return of Roddy, before she and her brothers disappeared into the shrubbery, but the rest of us were aware of the shadow on the horizon when Shona telephoned to say that Aunt Hannah had come through the night but there was, of course, no improvement in her condition.

'Should I go in and see if there is anything I can do to help?' Roddy asked.

'No, Roddy,' I told him. 'Jock is going in. Will you help me down the steps with the pram?' I wheeled Sandy Tom along to the plot where George and Tom were at work and said: 'Here you are, you two. He is asleep but keep an eye on him for me and put his hood up if the wind rises.'

'We will be seeing to him,' Tom said.

When I came back to the kitchen, Roddy was glooming by the window and I decided on the principle of: 'If it did not do any good, it would not do any harm,' to speak my mind.

'Roddy,' I said, 'this is none of my business, perhaps but in my opinion, you have lost your head a bit in this Sheila affair.'

He turned to face me, his eyebrows raised. 'You put it mildly,' he said. 'Since the start of what you call this Sheila affair, I haven't had any head to lose.'

'You have scared the girl out of her wits.'

'Scared her?' He glowered at me.

I told him how Sheila had told Alasdair and how Alasdair had told me of his precipitate wooing and went on: 'Conventional provincial people like Sheila – I don't mean these words in your clique's derogatory sense either – conventional and provincial are not bad things to be, in my opinion, but people like Sheila don't understand young men who propose marriage after three days' acquaintance, Roddy. You know this as well as I do, if you could only gather your wits and think. Ordinary people are inclined to think that quick into marriage may mean quick out. And a thick layer of tradition and custom has wrapped itself round people's minds since the days of Romeo and Juliet and Aberdeen was never Venice anyway and Sheila is no hot-blooded Italian maid. She is a cool-headed chip of good native granite.'

' Go on,' he said, fixing his dark eyes on me, giving me all his attention.

'I am no spaewife, Roddy, who can see into Sheila's heart and mind. She may have no feeling for you at all – '

'But she has,' he interrupted me positively. 'She has never said anything but one simply knows.'

'Then, as my grandmother used to say, patience is a virtue that is well worth the cultivating, so I think you should busy yourself with the cultivation of what is, for you a, most difficult plant to grow.'

'You might be surprised,' he told me. 'One doesn't write novels in a flash of inspiration. They need a lot of patience and I can be patient with anything that matters to me. You seem to know what you are talking about. Go on.'

I described to him the long-drawn-out courtship of Shona and Jock, the conventional white-silk wedding at the height or depth, rather, of the postwar shortages of food and clothing, the measured solidity of it all.

'And all this aside,' I continued, 'there is yourself and your profession, Roddy. There is a hangover of Puritan suspicion in the provinces about people who live by the arts. You know how much even your own parents disliked your being a writer at first. You know how you had to cheat them in order to be a writer at all. You have to give Sheila and her parents time to get used to an idea so peculiar as having a chiel among them takin' notes.'

Roddy smiled wryly. 'I am beginning to see what you mean. And then Deb didn't help, crashing into the middle of every-thing.'

'No. That certainly didn't do any good.'

'So what do I do?'

'If I were you, I would just hang about and try to be as undramatic as you can. Don't bother them just now while Aunt Hannah is ill anyway.'

'But how long are Shona and Jock going to be bothered with me hanging about here? I've felt all along that time is of the essence.'

'I shouldn't worry about that,' I said. 'You outraged Shona's sense of fitness a bit by giving the children that pony. She felt it was overgenerous and if you stay here for a bit she may feel that she is repaying you a bit. And, though Heaven knows why, I have been batting for you like mad, trying to convince Shona that you aren't off your head and that it was valuable for you to come here after the earthquake and everything and –'

'And it has been valuable,' he interrupted me. 'Dad and Mother are mixed up in this thing of Sheila and me, Janet. So is this household of your brother's. It was seeing how Mother and Dad were after they decided to retire and then seeing this family here and Sheila's family in town – it all piled up and made me know that something like this was what I wanted, that the London carry-on with Deb and the rest was of no real value.' He grinned ruefully. 'I am a provincial family man at heart, it seems.' He became very serious again. 'It goes back even further than all that, back to that time at your father's funeral, as I told you before. Seeing Sheila for the first time that day we went to the hospital and saw the baby was just a culmination of a long process. Even Jock saying that Sandy Tom was a mystery was part of it.'

'I know. There seems to be no point where things start and –' I thought of Aunt Hannah ' – I am not sure that there is any point where they finish either. But anyhow, I know that you are welcome to stay here for as long as you like and if you want to write, Heaven knows there are plenty of quiet empty rooms. The point is, as I see it, that you have got to let people get used to you and stop rushing your fences, that is if you are sure that Sheila's way of life is what you want. You are going to have to adopt her way in the main, you know, not she yours.'

'I am quite sure about what I want,' he told me.

My brother came through, had a cup of coffee and then left for town, just as the children came in for their bread and cheese.

'Roddy,' Liz said, 'did you know that Aunt Janet was a tremendous poetry reader?'

'No, I didn't but I have always thought she was a bit of a witch and tremendous poetry reading is witchcraft.'

'Don't talk nonsense, Roddy,' I said.

'I have heard tell,' Tom said, 'that there was a witch among Aunt Janet's ancestors.'

'Then the witch was *our* ancestor too!' said Duncan.

'Yes, ours!' said Gee.

'Was she a good witch or a wicked one?' Liz asked.

'Och, a very good one on the whole,' George replied.

Liz looked at me thoughtfully. 'The kind that makes wishes come true?' she pursued.

'Well, now – ' George hesitated, 'yes, I suppose she was that kind. At any rate, if this ancestor witch didna want what one wished to come true, it never came true, as I mind on it.'

'That is quite so,' Tom corroborated.

'I suppose that explains it,' Liz said, still looking thoughtfully at me.

'Explains what?' I asked.

She shook her head. 'Nothing' and the two echoes came: 'Nothing' and 'No, nothing'.

They began to eat and went on eating in silence until I said: 'How is Betsy this morning?'

'Very well, thank you. She sends her regards.'

'That is very civil of her.'

'She needs a good grooming,' George told them.

'And we have the old brushes from Reachfar out in the sheddie there,' said Tom, 'and when you are all done of eating for the moment, we will just go out and see to her.'

I was alone in the kitchen with the perambulator outside the window when the telephone rang and my brother's voice said: 'The old lady is gone, Janet.'

'Jock, I am sorry,' I said, looking out at Sandy Tom in the depths of his morning sleep at the other end of life's rainbow span from Aunt Hannah whose sleep was of a sounder kind. 'Jock,' I said, after a moment, 'do you want me to tell the children or shall I leave it till you come home?'

'I won't be back till after the funeral now. I have all the arrangements to make. Tell George and Tom and they will see to the kids.'

I was appalled, momentarily, at the magnitude of the

demand that Jock and I had made down the days of our lives on George and Tom, the demand that we were still making. They had shepherded me through the dark days after my mother's death and they had shepherded Jock through the death of my father and I had no doubt that, once again, they would be the shepherds who could best ease this thing into the minds of Liz, Duncan and Gee.

'All right, Jock,' I said.

'The funeral will be the day after tomorrow,' he went on. 'Maybe you could find Shona's black suit and hat and my dark suit and black tie and stuff and send them in with Roddy?'

'Of course. How are Granny and Granda?'

'Not too bad. Sheila is the one. She was devoted to Aunt Hannah. She went completely to bits but she is asleep now. The doctor gave her a sedative.'

'Poor Sheila. Not so tough in spite of being a nurse.'

'No. Far from tough this morning.'

I went out and wheeled Sandy Tom round to the glebe where, supervised by Tom and George, the children were grooming Betsy's shaggy coat and as I came towards the group over the grass, the two old men looked at me, a question in their eyes. I merely nodded my head, whereupon they both took off their tweed caps and looked up at the sky for a moment before covering their heads again. The little gesture was as impressive as the tolling of a passing bell.

After watching the grooming for a little, I wheeled the perambulator back to its place in the lee of the scullery wall, went into the house and found Roddy.

'Aunt Hannah is dead, Roddy,' I told him. 'Jock asks if you would go in the day after tomorrow with some clothes for him and Shona and perhaps you will be good enough to take George and Tom in to attend the funeral?'

'Of course. Sheila will be terribly cut up.'

'She is. I had no idea she was so fond of the old lady.'

'She loved her very much,' he said.

George and Tom told the children about the death before they all came in for lunch and, during the meal, they were very silent, saying nothing of this thing that was in their minds. Afterwards, they did the washing-up with Roddy, speaking in quiet voices of everyday things and then they went out to the shrubbery and were not seen until tea-time. After tea, they went out again and did not return until it was time for supper, after which they bid Tom, George and Roddy a quiet good night and went up to have their baths and go to bed.

When I went into their room for 'Reachfar', after Sandy Tom was asleep, they were all three in the boys' bed, Liz under the covers with her brothers and not merely under the eiderdown at the foot of the bed as usual and their big eyes were very solemn as I sat down on the bed's edge.

'Aunt Janet,' Liz said in a hushed voice, 'Long ago, at Reachfar, Channatt's mother died, didn't she?'

'And there was a funeral?'

'And they buried her deep down in a grave?'

'Yes,' I said and I thought that if Jock and I made demands on Tom and George, there were others to make demands on him and me. 'Will you tell about it, please?' Liz asked.

I took a deep breath. 'Once upon a time, long long ago at Reachfar,' I began, 'Channatt came down to breakfast early one morning and her father told her that, during the night, her mother had died. Channatt's mother had loved Reachfar and the thing there that she loved most of all was the wild flowers that grew in the moor. Always, when the violets and the harebells came out, Channatt used to pick a bunch to bring to her mother but, this morning, when she died, it was very early spring and not anywhere on the moor was there any flower to pick, although Channatt searched and searched. To find some flowers seemed to be the only thing she could do, you see. All day, for two days, she searched about and on the third day was her mother's funeral but that forenoon, she suddenly remembered that the earliest flowers to bloom at Reachfar were the celandines in the old quarry, at the bottom of the rock, where they were sheltered from the cold and wind. Channatt went there and found three bright golden celandines and some little round buds and she tied them into a bunch. Then she brought them home and laid them on top of her mother's coffin.'

The six bright eyes watched me, waiting, I knew although I did not know how I knew, to hear of the deepdown grave, for this was the finality that the young minds could not encompass, this last disposal of the corruptible body. I had not attended my mother's funeral but I had attended that of my grandparents, who died within twenty-four hours of one another many years later and, thinking of this, I continued: 'The coffin was put on one of the farm carts which was drawn by Betsy and Dick to the churchyard and there was the grave, a great deep hole in the ground and the coffin was carried forward and laid down beside it. The minister prayed and all the people sang a hymn and then the coffin was lowered away, away down out of sight and Channatt saw the big heap of earth that would cover it up. And after that, Channatt and her people came home to Reachfar.' I paused and looked from the face of Liz to the face of Duncan and then on to the face of little Gee. 'Now, this is the bit of the story that is very hard to tell and I am not sure that I can make you understand at all. The springtime went on and then the summer came and all the flowers that Channatt's mother had loved came into bloom on the moor and all over Reachfar, the dog roses, the wild orchis, the double buttercups, the white gowans and the yellow corn daisies. And Channatt used to pick the flowers and take them home although her mother was not there to give them to any more. But when Channatt put the flowers in water and set them on the window-sill, her mother *was* there for, although people could not see her sitting by the fire doing her sewing, Channatt could see her inside her mind. Channatt could always see her, afterwards, for ever and ever.'

'Amen,' said Gee softly.

'I can see Aunt Hannah in my mind,' Duncan said quietly after a moment, as he stared at the wall. 'She says: "Stop kicking that chair-leg, boy", and then she gives you threepence.'

'She was *always* saying to stop doing something and then giving you threepence,' Liz said.

'Yes, all the time,' said Gee.

'That was the bit about Aunt Hannah that mattered,' I said. 'What gets buried in the grave can't tell anybody to stop doing anything or give them threepence.'

I got up from the bed and began to tidy odds and ends about the room while I wondered whether they would settle down to sleep. After a few moments, Liz got out of the boys' bed, crossed the floor quickly and quietly and settled into her own bed while her brothers tucked themselves down on their sides, close together.

'I suppose the stop doing things and giving you threepence bit of Aunt Hannah will go to Heaven,' Liz said thoughtfully. 'I suppose she will tell God and all the Heavenly Host to stop doing things and then give them threepence for ever and ever.'

'I suppose so,' I said.

'She is very kind really,' Liz said, sliding further down under her covers. 'You have to be told not to do some things and it is always nice to get threepence. Yes. Aunt Hannah is all right.'

'Yes, quite all right,' said Duncan.

'Yes, really,' said Gee.

'Good night,' I said.

They murmured their replies and in less than fifteen minutes, they were all asleep.

During the next day, they did not mention Aunt Hannah but were very helpful to me in the house between spells with Betsy and spells in the shrubbery with Fly and, on the morning of the funeral, which was to take place at noon, they did their breakfast washing-up and disappeared into the shrubbery again.

'I have packed the case with Shona's and Jock's things,' I said to Roddy. 'Will you put it in your car while the children are outside?'

'Sure,' he said and went upstairs.

When he came back to the kitchen, George and Tom came down already dressed in their dark suits and black ties.

'I think we should just have our breakfast and be off,' Tom said. 'The less the bairns see of us in these clothes, the better.'

'We will see how things go,' George said non-committally.

It was nearly nine-thirty before the grown-up breakfast was over, the children had been in the shrubbery since before eight but it seemed to me that George was loitering deliberately, although both Roddy and Tom were anxious to be away and when the three taps came on the kitchen door, I became certain that George had been waiting for this. Liz came in, followed by the others and she was carrying a very battered-looking inexpertly-made wreath of the white Granny roses from the shrubbery which she laid in my lap.

'We made this to go on Aunt Hannah's coffin,' she said, 'but it is not very good.'

'It is very hard to make wreaths.'

'Awful hard.'

I looked at the piece of white card on which was written: 'With love to Aunt Hannah from Elizabeth, Duncan, George, X Alexander Thomas (his mark)' and tied an end of rough string out of sight on the wire frame which had obviously been made by George.

'It is beautiful and very well made,' I told them, close to tears.

George stood up and held out his hand for the flowers. 'And now we will be off,' he said. 'Tom and I will see that they go on Aunt Hannah's coffin. We mustn't be late.'

Silently, the children watched the car drive away but they showed no disposition to go back to the shrubbery or round to Betsy in the glebe so I said: 'I tell you what. Let's take Sandy Tom down to the village in his pram to fetch his milk.'

This, said on the spur of the moment, proved to be an inspiration for Sandy Tom had never been beyond the garden since he came home except on the Sunday when he was christened and it had not occurred to any of us that the people in the village were all interested to have a closer look at the new baby from the schoolhouse. It was only about half a mile to the village but we spent the entire forenoon there, in the course of which I had three cups of tea in three different houses.

Down the years, I had forgotten something of the tenor of life in a Scottish village and this particular one had retained more of the old character than many, I was sure. It was in the centre of a shallow basin of grain-producing land and on the way to it we passed the church, the manse, the parish hall and what had once been a smithy but was now more of a garage and welding-shop, surrounded by cars, tractors and agricultural machinery. Then we came to the cluster of old grey houses, flanked by the newer County Council homes and, here, what had once been an inn was the village shop, a prosperous place that sent four large travelling shops roving over the wide farming hinterland each day.

The shop-keeper and his wife paid their respects to Sandy Tom, presented him with a useful pair of rubber pants from their varied stock and gave the other three a bag of sweets to celebrate their brother and entertained me to a cup of tea. We then left, having tucked the goat's milk into the perambulator, to come home, but it was a lengthy process. All the housewives who had seen us pass to the shop were now at their garden gates with their children round them to greet us and everybody had to gaze upon Sandy Tom and decide at great length whether he resembled his mother or his father and one old man, leaning on his Dutch hoe, talked the women down with the announcement that: 'the bairnie is nae like the ane or the ither o' them but like his gran'uncle Tam, the fine auld chap' and I saw no point in telling him that Tom was Tom Forbes and not Tom Sandison. Then I had a cup of tea with the old man and his wife and another with the garage-owner's wife while Liz, Duncan and Gee were allowed to put on masks and watch the two welders at work in their noisy inferno in the old smithy. We reached home just in time to feed Sandy Tom at two o'clock and only a short time before George, Tom and Roddy.

The three men changed into their everyday clothes before lunch and during the meal the children told of their forenoon in the village, seeming to have forgotten all about Aunt Hannah until, doing the washing-up in the scullery with Roddy, Liz said: 'Now that the funeral is over Roddy, will Dad and Mum be back soon? Did they say?'

'This evening,' he told her. 'Are you longing for them?'

'Not exactly but we have never had such a time of them being away as this time since you came to stay. It seems to me you are an earthquake-ish sort of person.'

'Me?' Roddy protested.

'Yes, just earthquake-ish,' Duncan said.

'Yes,' Gee confirmed.

We had not spoken in their presence of the earthquake that had killed Roddy's parents but, possibly, they had overheard the word and had connected it, in their mysterious way, with Roddy.

'You have them in St Jago, don't you?' Liz asked.

I prepared to go through to the scullery to intervene as Roddy said: 'Yes. But if I am earthquake-ish, Aunt Janet and Uncle Twice must be earthquake-ish too. They live in St Jago much more of the time than I do.'

'They are *not*!' said Liz indignantly. 'They are Reachfar people and Reachfar people *aren't* earthquake-ish.'

'No, they're not!'

'Just *not*!'

'And these old dishes are done. We are going out,' said Liz and all three marched in single file, their spines indignantly upright, through the kitchen, across the back hall and out of the door and into the shrubbery while Roddy appeared in the scullery doorway drying a saucepan.

'There you are, you see,' I said. 'You are earthquake-ish. How was Sheila?'

'I wish I knew how these kids think. I didn't see her. The doctor kept her in bed but Shona says she is all right now, just tired. Mrs Murray invited me in for tea tomorrow.'

'Good,' I said, 'and as George and Tom would say: "Just ca' canny".'

When he had completed his task in the scullery, he went away upstairs and George and Tom being in the garden, I began, inevitably, to bake for, in spite of keeping the kitchen cupboard locked when I remembered, the food simply melted away but while I took pleasure in laying out the materials and utensils on the big table, I was struck by the awareness that this short, strange and unexpected interlude in my life was nearing its end. I had only a few days more before I would have to go back to St Jago.

The island, all my friends there and even Twice had taken on a dream-like aspect and my actuality was centred here, in the kitchen of this Victorian barrack of a house, preparing food, sterilising baby bottles and ready all the time at the back of my mind for emergency, from the big assaults like birth and death, through sudden illness like food poisoning to the almost daily outbreak of violent clawing disagreement between Liz and her brothers. As they forged their way ahead, propelled by the life force that was in them, it seemed that they must always be in violent disagreement with someone so that, if they were not calling down on their heads my wrath or the wrath of another adult, they were quarrelling among themselves. For most of the time, they were 'at outs', as they called it, with someone and now, as I stood at the kitchen table, I could see them in a row on their high branch, welded solidly together, probably because they were at outs with Roddy. They were chanting something and, curious to know what is was, I went out and bent over the perambulator in Sandy Tom's corner by the wall where they could not see me but I could hear the young voices, solemn and measured in tone, floating down:

'Drake he's in his hammock till the great Armadas come,
(Capten, art tha sleepin, there below?)
Slung atween the round-shot, listenin' for the drum,
An' dreamin' arl the time o' Plymouth Hoe.
Call him on the deep sea, call him up the Sound,
Call him when ye sail to meet the foe;

Where the old trade's plyin' an' the old flag flyin'
They shall find him ware an' wakin' as they found
    him long ago.'
'Amen,' came the voice of Gee.
'That was her most favourite one of all,' Duncan said.
'Yes. She always gave us fourpence for that one,' Liz agreed
and only now did I realise that what I had heard was the end
of their requiem for Aunt Hannah.
'Look here, you two,' came the now brisk voice of Liz after
a moment, 'what we need for the ceremony is proper feathers
for our hats. Mum's got these great huge ostrich feathers in a
box upstairs. You two have got to ask for them. It's no use me
asking, the lord knows, but she might lend them to you two.'
'We'll see,' said Duncan in George's canny voice.
'We'll see,' Gee repeated.
'You'll see nothing about it!' shouted Liz. 'You'll do as you
are told!'
There was a sudden scuffle, a sound of twigs breaking,
then a scrabbling noise, followed by loud laughter from the
boys who came wriggling out from under a laurel, did not
even notice me by the house wall but went running and laughing along the path to Tom and George. I followed them while
infuritated yells came from Liz in the shrubbery.
'Please will you come and get Liz?' Duncan said to George.
'She is hanging up in Reachfar – '
' – by the belt of her trousers,' Gee yelled and, overcome with
mirth, they hugged one another, laughing more loudly than
ever while the fury from the shrubbery rent the Heavens.
And so the balance of alliance shifted again. Liz was at outs
with her brothers and also with Tom and George who had
seen her in all her indignity, suspended by her leather belt from
a branch and she helped me and positively ogled Roddy for
the remainder of the afternoon. When we had had our afternoon
tea, she began to clear the table in a businesslike way, pointedly
ignoring George, Tom and her brothers and when she began
to wash up in the scullery, Roddy went through and said: 'I'll
dry, shall I, Liz?'
'Yes,' we heard her say with dignity. 'It is kind of you to
offer.' Then the dignity changed to a sort of patronage as
she went on: 'I think you have more natural piety than when
you first came here, Roddy.'
'Natural piety?'

'Yes. You never used to help with the dishes when you first came.'

'But what has piety got to do with the dishes?'

'I think you are mistaken about the meaning of the word piety as I am using it,' came the voice of Liz. 'It is nothing to do with holy-oly, you know. It really means having good relationships with your parents and your family. In a family, your relationship with your mother is better if you give a hand with the dish-washing, so it *has* got to do with piety, don't you see?'

'Yes, I see.'

'You live by yourself all the time down in London, don't you?'

'Yes,' lied Roddy.

'So of course you have never had a chance to learn about natural piety but if you stay with us for a bit longer you will find out. I have tremendous piety about all my family except when I am at outs with some of them, no names, no pack drill but I can't raise any piety at all about Cousin Cissie.'

'No? Why not?'

'She is about a million years old to start with and she tells you stories about mice that talk and wear clothes and cook and things, mice that have names like people, you know.'

'You don't like that sort of story?'

'I can't be doing with lies. You know as well as I do that mice can't eat a morsel without going to the loo. If they get in a cupboard, they leave a ghastly mess of little black things. How would they get along in pink frilly pants? And I bet Cousin Cissie would run a mile from any mouse that got up *her* pants.'

'I bet she would,' Roddy agreed. 'I don't like mice stories either. But you like goblin stories, do you?'

'Oh, yes. Goblin stories are true. People have goblins in their minds but not mice.'

'I see. And I am terribly glad that you think my natural piety is improving.'

'Oh, yes, it is,' Liz said. 'Definitely.'

Shona and Jock came back just before the children went up to bed and their coming, for some reason beyond my comprehension, signified the end of the quarrel between Liz and her brothers, Tom and George and the three went up to bed and had 'Reachfar' as if the difference of the afternoon had never

198

taken place. Naturally, however, George and Tom told of Liz having been hung up by her belt and Shona said: 'How they don't break their necks in that shrubbery, I don't know.'

'No, nor break their necks,' said George.

'Not at all,' Tom added. 'Janet was for ever climbing when she was a bairn. She lived half her days in the trees like a monkey.'

Roddy laughed. 'That daughter of yours is the end, Jock. She told me this afternoon that my natural piety had improved a great deal since I have been here.'

'Cheeky little brat,' said Shona, 'you should have given her a good slap and, anyway, what did she mean?'

I laughed now because this was so typical of Shona's attitude to her young. It was disrespectful in them to make any comment on the character of their elders so you slapped them first and only later enquired as to what the comment might have meant.

'I didn't know either but she explained to me,' Roddy said. 'She said that natural piety is having good relationships with your family and I gather it is naturally pious to do a bit of dish-washing because this improves your relations with your mother.'

'John,' said Shona, 'you will have to speak very severely to Liz.'

'What about?'

'That is for you to know, not me but she definitely needs a good dressing-down,' Shona replied firmly if somewhat obscurely.

Shona's attitude amused Roddy and he went on to say: 'Yesterday, Shona, Liz told me that she did wish God wasn't so muddling. He keeps on being different all the time, she said. On one Sunday, he has his only one begotten son called Jesus and the next Sunday they tell you that all the people in the world are God's children. God must be in an awful muddle about family allowances, she says and maybe that is why they collect money at Sunday School for the hungry children of Asia.'

'Honestly,' Shona said, her eyes wide, 'you simply don't know what to do about them. They go to Sunday School. We can't bring them up as heathens, after all, can we? But it gives them such queer ideas.'

'Janet went, not to Sunday School, but to church itself from when she was about three,' said Tom, as if invoking some final authority, 'and it never did her any harm.'

'And the Lord said unto Choshua – ' I began in the accent of our old minister at Achcraggan, whereupon Tom broke in with mimicry more true to life than mine: 'See, I haff kiven into thine hand Cherico and the Keeng thereoff and the mighty men off falour!' so that a summary history of this great character of my childhood, the Reverend Roderick Mackenzie, had to be given to Roddy.

'But,' I said then, 'you have seen him for yourself, Roddy. He was the minister who impresssed you so much at my father's funeral,' and with this it had to be explained to the others that, by a strange chance, Roddy had visited Achcraggan on the day that my father was buried.

'I have aye been thinking, lad,' George said, 'since the day you came here that I have seen you somewhere before. You were up at the top o' the path behind the Seamuir gravestone.'

'Yes,' Roddy said.

'You should have made yourself known to us, lad.'

'But I didn't know then that you were Janet's people, George,' Roddy told him. 'I don't know then that Janet came from Achcraggan.'

'Then what brought you to Achcraggan?'

'I don't know. I was staying in Inverness and just took a but run to Achcraggan that day.'

'What a strange thing,' said Tom. 'A *fine* sort of thing, when ye think on it.'

In talking of these homely things, the things that families talk about, ranging up and down their generations, the evening passed and towards bedtime I said: 'You know, I have only a few days of this holiday left.'

'There is little good in speaking about that,' George said.

'No good o' the world,' said Tom and, very shortly, they went away upstairs.

'But I have to speak about this,' I said to Jock and Shona. 'The children have had such an upheaval all this summer. They are conscious of it.'

Roddy told them how he had been accused of 'earthquake-ishness' that afternoon.

'Your leaving is going to be worse than Aunt Hannah, Janet,' Jock said. 'I have been thinking about this. There is a finality about death that some instinct helps them to accept but it is hard for children to part with somebody they have grown fond of. Your going will seem to them like a freakish whim. I think you should go at night, after they have gone to bed and without telling them you are going. You simply won't be there in the morning. It will give you the character of a dream right away and that is what you have to be for them, a dream for Gee anyway, maybe more of a memory for Liz and Dunk. You will turn into something like their conception of Reachfar or Liz's half-memory of driving Twice's car – that is if they don't actually see you driving away from here. What do you think, Shona?'

'You know more about it than I do, John,' she said and turned to me, 'but, for myself, I would gladly do without the tears and the questions after you drive away. If they don't see you go, they will quarrel themselves out of their disappointment over your disappearance among themselves in the shrubbery.'

'That settles it then,' I said. 'Roddy can take me to the night train at Aberdeen.'

'And is it all right if I stay on for a bit?' Roddy asked bashfully, a very ill-fitting and unusual mood in him.

'Surely. Stay as long as you like,' Jock said. 'The longer you stay, the longer George and Tom will stay. You will help to keep their minds off Jean and Jemima Cottage.'

'We are just awful about Jean,' Shona said. 'I feel it is so wrong to be like this about somebody but what can one do? I do feel it is better for Tom and George to be here but it is dreadful her being all alone.'

'Isn't there some theory,' Roddy asked, 'about seeking the happiness of the greater number?'

'Spoken like a true member of the clan, Roddy,' said my brother, laughing but at the carelessly spoken phrase a dark proud flush mounted over Roddy's forehead.

The next forenoon, while we worked together in the kitchen, Shona asked me again how Roddy had come to be in Achcraggan on the day of my father's funeral and I told her of his sudden fit of disgust with his life in London, his getting drunk and then boarding the train for Inverness to explore the country that had given birth to his ancestors.

'But what a thing to do,' Shona said, 'making a journey like that in the middle of winter on the spur of the moment.'

Poor Roddy, I thought, you are like the peacock that Tom

201

and George brought home to Reachfar and put down in the barnyard among the homely cross-bred hens. As I had done over the pony, I began to 'bat' for Roddy with all my might.

'Have you never decided to go to town to see your family on the spur of the moment?' I asked rather sharply.

'But that's different!'

'Not really. Roddy lives on a more world-wide scale, that's all. Or he used to. I think he wants to narrow his orbit now.'

'And he just took a bus in Inverness by chance and landed in Achcraggan?'

'Yes. He had been exploring around, doing a different tour by bus every day, you see. It is quite an ordinary thing to do. I used to do it all the time when I first went down to London.'

'It is still very funny,' said Shona thoughtfully and I felt that this was going to turn into another King Charles' Head like the pony. 'I must ring up and find out how Sheila is,' she said then.

I once knew an old woman who frequently used the phrase: 'That makes all the difference' and, very often, she used it in a context where it seemed to me to be meaningless but, now, as Shona spoke into the telephone by the window, I began to think that this phrase had meaning in any and every context, that there is nothing that can happen without 'making a difference'.

Roddy's visit to Achcraggan was, in Shona's mind, quite different in character and significance from his gift of the pony, it was becoming clear. The fact that Roddy, in a chance way of which Shona would normally have disapproved, had been present at my father's funeral, this sad event in the annals of our family, made the difference that she approved his fortuitous arrival in Achcraggan on that day because she approved of the result to which it had led. And the fact that Roddy had been present at the funeral made a difference to her mental image of him. It seemed to make him more respectable, less exotic, to bring him almost within the boundaries of the family and that he had been deeply impressed by the simple ceremony conducted by the aged minister seemed to bring Roddy within the bounds of humanity as Shona knew it. Before, he had seemed to her more like a creature from another planet except when she actively remembered the tragic death of his parents.

As she spoke to her sister on the telephone, her talk was all of this coincidental visit by Roddy to Achcraggan and I could hear her changed attitude being transmitted to Sheila while I imagined that I could feel Sheila's attitude making a subtle alteration also. They talked together for a long time, going over and over the same ground until, at last, Shona said: 'And we will be expecting you all for tea on Tuesday. Yes. Janet is going on the night train on Tuesday. No. He is not going. He wants to stay on for a bit and it will be nice to have him. Poor fellow, I think his parents' death was more of a shock than he admits. And he is very handsome, really and *he* is not to be blamed if women run after him. And he is sweet with the children. Liz just dotes on him. But *wasn't* it funny that he was at Achcraggan that day? In a queer way, it is as if it were *meant*.'

The last phrase had in it an acceptance that, after all, Roddy in all his outlandishness had been sent among us of this close-knit family by an act of fate and that there was no need for further scruple about him.

When the family gathered for elevenses, Duncan and Gee crowded their mother into a corner and pulled her head down while they whispered to her.

'For the ceremony?' she asked then.

'Yes, Mum, it is a very special ceremony.'

'Top special.'

'Very well. You can have the feathers but you must take great care of them and put them back in the box the moment the ceremony is over. They belonged to your Grandmother Sandison who died long ago and I think she must have inherited them from your sailor great-grandfather so you must promise not to spoil them.'

'Promise, Mum.'

'Yes, promise.'

'Promise for four, Mum,' said Liz and then announced: 'The ceremony is on Tuesday everybody at three o'clock in the afternoon and everybody is to be properly dressed.'

'Ball dress and decorations?' Jock asked.

'It is not a ball, Dad. It is a ceremony. People have to be dressed for a solemn ceremony –'

' – like a wedding –'

' – or a christening.'

'And me with my tile hat not here with me,' said Tom.

'And damn a sporran or anything,' said George.

'Stop your capers, you two,' Liz told them severely in a

phrase which she had copied from myself. 'Mum, will you wear your flowery hat?'

'Yes,' said Shona.

'And tell Granny and Aunt Sheila to wear theirs?'

'Yes. But where is this ceremony to be held?'

'In Reachfar, of course!'

'Of course!'

'Acourse!'

'But we can't get in there in flowery hats and high heels!' Shona protested.

'You can. Roddy has a plan for getting you all in.'

Shona sighed. 'All right. I suppose we'll manage.'

When the children had gone out again, Shona asked Roddy what the ceremony was about but he could only say: 'I don't know, Shona, honestly. They have asked me to help with a few odds and ends but they are as close as clams.'

Shona sighed again. 'Since we have all been invited, I don't suppose it will be really dangerous anyway,' she said in her accepting way.

Chapter XII

'Thanks to the human heart by which we live,
Thanks to its tenderness, its joys, and fears,
To me the meanest flower that blows can give
Thoughts that do often lie too deep for tears.'

LIT by warm sunlight, the last days of my holiday ran swiftly down. The children spent all their time in the shrubbery now and were unusually silent when they came in for meals but, out of this silence of theirs, there was born a strange tense excitement such as surrounds something elemental like the rising of the sun or the day when, borne on the wind, the first sweet breath of spring can be recognised. It was an excitement quite unlike that which had held the house on the night that Sandy Tom was born for, now, there was no anxiety that anything could go wrong, only the bright certainty of hope that is beyond disappointment, like the hope that comes at sunrise or the less frequent dawn of spring.

'Dad,' Liz said on the Monday, 'will you come to the playroom after tea and help us with our parts?'

'All right,' Jock said at once and when he had gone with them Shona said: 'Goodness, another theatrical nonsense!'

But only a short time passed when Jock came back to the kitchen and said: 'Janet, have you still got my Wordsworth?'

'Yes. It is on the table by my bed.'

'Don't move. I'll get it,' he said and went away again.

He stayed in the playroom with them until it was well past their customary bedtime but when they were at last upstairs and we had had 'Reachfar', he was waiting for me on the landing when I left them and came with me to my bedroom.

'They know you are leaving tomorrow,' he said.

'Who told them?'

'Nobody. They took it out of the air. They are not admitting even to themselves that you are going or that they know you are going but this business tomorrow is in your honour.'

'Oh, dear. I wish I had a smarter hat.'

'You won't need a hat. I have been told to tell you that you are not to wear one.'

'But why?'

'You'll find out. I wouldn't tell for the world. But I want you to know that the idea for the performance is entirely their own. I helped them to find words for their idea and to incorporate four lines they chose from Wordsworth's *Ode*, that's all.'

'Oh, the clouds of glory bit as they call it?'

'No – ' he opened the volume which he had replaced on my bedside table ' – this:

> The homely Nurse doth all she can
> To make her Foster-child, her Inmate Man,
> Forget the glories he hath known,
> And that imperial palace whence he came.'

He looked up at me, closing the book. 'You would have made a good teacher, Janet,' and after a pause, 'of English literature, at least. You have made the kids love that poem so that they have their own understanding of it. Would you like me to type a copy of their script to take away with you?'

'Yes please, Jock.'

That evening, as we sat in the kitchen, I could not believe that this was my last night in this house, in this company and none of us wanted to think of parting so we talked more than usual about the children and their plans for the next day.

'Are all children as creative as this lot of yours, Jock?' Roddy asked at one point.

'Ninety-nine per cent are, if they are allowed to be,' my brother said, 'but creativity is a queer plant. It can be treated too carefully. You can kill it with kindness, by trying to encourage it too much but you can also starve it to death by being afraid the children will hurt themselves and in a million other ways.'

'When I was a kid, we never went in for acting.'

'The acting is purely a money-making concern,' Shona said. 'Liz found out when she was three that Granda gave her pennies for reciting nursery rhymes and they have been acting ever since.'

'The acting is the least of it,' Jock said. 'Most kids like to dress up and perform for adults. The most creative thing about the three upstairs is their attempt to translate what is really a dream in their minds into the world of physical fact. This is what every artist tries to do – to pick a dream out of the air and pin it down in words or paint or some other medium. That is what you try to do, isn't it, Roddy?'

'I suppose so.'

'And if the process is perfectly carried through, the dream turns out to be more real and true than what we usually call reality?'

'Yes,' Roddy said.

'Well, this is what the kids try to do in the shrubbery out there. They have a dream of our old family home at Reachfar and they are trying to realise it in physical terms.' He looked away from us into the fire, a shyness showing in his face but pride as well. 'Having heard their script for tomorrow,' he said, 'I find that they have hit upon an elemental truth about their Aunt Janet.' He smiled at me, then visibly changed direction in his mind, broke away from thought of his own children upstairs into thought of children in general. 'All kids have a liking for grand ceremonial and solemn ritual too,' he said.

'Not only kids,' I broke in, 'or maybe I am still a kid but I found the film of the Coronation terribly moving and my stomach always gives a heave when I think of the Trooping the Colour.'

'I bet the guardsmen's stomachs give a different sort of heave at the thought,' Roddy said.

'In point of fact, I know about that too,' I told him. 'When I was in the Air Force, I was marker for one of those picked squads that paraded during War Weapons Weeks and things. I know what it is like to hold formation on a January day with sleet blowing in your teeth or on a July day with your shirt sticking to your back but I still get that inner heave when I see the Trooping on a film news reel.'

'What I like,' Tom said, 'is to hear Liz imitating the Provost when the man got the freedom of the burgh.'

'And me too,' George agreed.

Shona tried unsuccessfully to look stern as she said: 'You two are not to encourage her with that. I will not have the children mimicking their elders.'

'They will do it anyway, Shona,' Jock said and he turned to Roddy again. 'That is another uncanny thing. Children often display very good taste. This ceremony in the local burgh was pure corn from start to finish, with the Provost in moth-eaten rabbit fur handing a freedom casket to a native son who became

207

a millionaire by very dubious means after the war and presented the burgh with a public park to be called after himself. Liz asked me on the way home what was inside the tin box that the man in the funny hat gave him and that just about summed up the whole thing.'

When we went upstairs, I went in to look at the children as usual and they were lying as they always lay, the boys neatly tucked together, their bedclothes undisturbed and Liz spread-eagled on her back, her arms, even in sleep, seeming to be reaching out towards tomorrow, one foot out, ready to spring on to the floor and into action. During the day when, most of the time, all three moved and spoke in unison, I saw them as a group and around them was an aura of all the children who attended Jock's school and beyond this there was an aura of all the children in the world – the younger generation. But when they were in bed like this, Liz was on her own, the time would come when Duncan and Gee would be on their own too and I had an awareness of them not as units of a generation but as individuals, standing within and yet apart from their time, in all their dignity and also in all their fundamental loneliness.

After lunch the following day, all three disappeared, not even emerging from the shrubbery to welcome their grandparents and aunt. Sheila was looking very beautiful in a 'flowery' hat of copper-coloured silk petals and Roddy was stricken into a vibrant silence that was more strident and noticeable than any noise until the inevitable ₋ubject of his presence at my father's funeral was raised and marvelled over at great length.

'And you didn't even know that Janet belonged to Ach-craggan?' Granny asked when he had told the whole story again.

'No,' Roddy said, his eyes on Sheila.

'What a very queer thing. You would have liked Granda Sandison if you had known him. He was a man that everybody liked. It was nice that you were there that day,' the old lady said with a gratified sigh.

Granda, standing apart with George and Tom, was more interested in what was to happen in the garden. More than the others of his generation, he seemed to live by the children. Although he was younger than Tom and George, he did not bestride the generations as they did and he did not find as close a unity with his daughters, my brother and Roddy as his wife did. When he was with Tom and George, he seemed to

be the oldest man of three old men but when he was in the
presence of the children, he seemed to take on vitality from
them, to throw off his years and become again as young as they
were. When Jock came to tell us that it was time to go into the
shrubbery, Granda was first out of the door. 'Not that way,
Granda,' Jock said, picking up Sandy Tom in his carrying cot.
'We are going out through the front and in over the wall from
the glebe.'

'Jock,' I said, 'are you sure that I don't wear a hat? Sheila
has brought me out a really flowery one.'

'No. No hat.'

In the glebe, a kitchen chair stood by the wall forming a stile
over to another chair inside the shrubbery and with much gaiety
and laughter, stout Granny was helped over in her best rather
tight dress by George and Tom, who led her away along a
narrow, newly-cut path into the overgrown jungle while Fat
Mary, dressed from top to toe in royal blue sprang spryly over.
When we had all climbed in, Jock told me to stay by the wall
until he came back for me and went away along the path with
Sandy Tom in his cot and when he was out of sight, I found
myself trembling, a little afraid, as if I were standing on the
edge of an unknown world but soon Jock came back and said in
a comforting everyday voice: 'Right. Come along.' We went
through between the tangled shrubs and overhanging trees, to
come out into a clear grassy place behind the little pre-
fabricated garage that Roddy had erected. Its doors stood
wide open and in front of them the family sat in a formal
row on kitchen chairs in front of which stood a single chair to
which my brother led me before he went away round to the back
of the wooden building to stand outside the window at its
far end. I now looked into the garage and my sight blurred as
my heart seemed to stop beating. At one side of it stood an
old table which used to occupy a corner of the kitchen at Reachfar, the table that had held my 'bitties drawer' when I was a
child. On it there sat Liz's little porcelain bank with its gilt
trimmings and painted blue flowers. In the middle of the floor
was the old wooden stool on which I had sat, between George
and Tom, at the Reachfar fire throughout all the evenings of
my childhood. Against the left-hand wall, opposite to the table,
there was a little discarded fire-grate with a canopy above it of
bent corrugated iron and a chimney of bent pipe going out
through the wooden wall. In the grate was a neatly laid heap

of paper and twigs. And now I noticed that the concrete floor was almost covered by a hearthrug that George, Tom and I had made from rags nearly forty years ago. On it, in brown rags, there was the picture of a house, with black smoke trailing from its chimney across a blue sky and on the green rag grass in front of the house was picked out, in yellow rags, the word: 'Reachfar'. The rug was so placed that this word lay like a barrier across the entrance to the little garage.

My reason told me what had happened. The rug and all these odds and ends had come here to Jock and Shona with the other furniture when Reachfar had been sold but reason was far away in this moment. It was no more than a flat picture of a furniture pantechnicon rolling along a moorland road in some remote distance between Ross-shire and Aberdeenshire. I was inside a dream.

On the rag rug beside the stool lay Sandy Tom, asleep in his cot which had a tall white ostrich plume standing upright in the corner by his pillow and behind him stood the three children, Liz in the middle, dressed in long robes which were old velvet curtains and on their heads they wore old velvet berets, each decorated with a great, white trailing ostrich plume.

Liz began to speak. 'Ladies and gentlemen, we are gathered here today to perform a most solemn ceremony, to confer an honour upon Aunt Janet who came to visit us from beyond the seas to the great and undying benefit of this kingdom in that – ' she turned to Duncan who now went on: looking down at the baby while he spoke ' – she took care of our dearly beloved youngest knight of this kingdom in time of need and in that – ' Duncan now turned to Gee ' – she helped to make my deep and grave sore get well again and in that – ' once again it was the turn of Liz ' – she has given us good and true tidings of the past history of our kingdom.' She paused, took a deep breath and quoted slowly and solemnly:

> 'The homely Nurse doth all she can
> To make her Foster-child, her Inmate Man,
> Forget the glories he hath known,
> And that imperial palace whence he came.'

Again she paused and continued: 'But by virtue of what has been told to us by Aunt Janet, we shall remember for ever and ever whence we came.' She now turned grandly to Duncan and said: 'Good my Lord Duncan, light the sacred fire,' and then to Gee: 'Pray you my Lord George, place the crown in my hands.' The little heap of twigs began to crackle while, from the 'bitties drawer', Gee took a small daisy chain and laid it on Liz's out-stretched hands. 'Good, my lords, I charge you lead her to the throne.'

Duncan and Gee came to me, took a hand each, led me across the yellow-lettered barrier of the word 'Reachfar' to the stool, turned me round to face the family, sat me down and, from behind, Liz placed the daisy chain on my head, while the boys fetched a long velvet curtain which was draped round my shoulders and tied under my chin by its cord.

'We hereby confer upon Aunt Janet our highest honour, the Most Memorable Order of Reachfar,' said Liz.

The two boys then picked up Sandy Tom's cot and placed it in front of my feet while Liz fetched the little porcelain bank and laid it on the baby's stomach and, it now being about his time for waking up, he opened his eyes at the disturbance and squinted over the edge of his coverlet at this strange object in front of him. The three children behind us were now speaking in unison: 'And so on this day, in the presence of those who belong in this sacred place, we give to Aunt Janet, by the hand of the youngest knight of our kingdom, Lord Alexander Thomas, this Bluebell Bank which is the sacred symbol of the freedom of Reachfar, to be hers to hold for ever and ever, amen.'

I felt Liz prod me between the shoulder-blades and I bent down and picked up the little porcelain bank from the cot. There was a little silence when even the birds in the shrubs were still. I saw the tears standing in the eyes of Shona, Granny and Granda and I saw that Roddy and Sheila were holding hands tensely, as if each were afraid the other would disappear into the dream that the children had created before my brother came round and closed the doors, shutting himself and me inside the 'kingdom' with the children, leaving the rest of the family outside.

'Was it all right, Dad?' Liz asked.

'Yes. It went very well.'

'It was simply splendid,' I said, 'and thank you all very much,' and I sprang up, pushed the doors open and charged out, while my long robe pulled 'the throne' over with a clatter behind me. I could hear the rest of the family making their way out to the glebe by the path and the improvised stile but I took off my robe and, clutching my Bluebell Bank, I made my way, stooped down and sometimes almost crawling, along a little path beaten out by the children. Soon, I came to another little clearing and here was the dead tree trunk over which the white Granny rose climbed, so I sat down on the grass and opened the little gilt-bound porcelain casket. It contained a folded sheet of paper on which was written: 'It is hereby certified that Aunt Janet, as a freewoman of Reachfar, has the right to anywhere in this kingdom without let or hindrance. Signed: Elizabeth, Duncan, George, X Alexander Thomas (his mark).'

With tears in my eyes, I folded the paper and put it back in the little casket. 'This Bluebell Bank which is the sacred symbol,' they had said. My mind boggled as I tried to comprehend the mystery of the web of thought and association that had led Liz and her brothers to present me with this little box.

When I was a child, I had, for a long time, a confusion in my mind about a ridge of stony earth which divided one of the Reachfar fields from the moor. It was a rabbit warren which, in summer, was covered with blue harebells which tinkled out a faery tune on the breeze while the young rabbits played in their dozens round the mouths of the burrows. With the flowers among the stones, it made me think of the branch of the Bank of Scotland in Achcraggan, which had a rockery in front, up through which steps led to the door. It had been explained to me that, if I saved my pennies and gave them to my father to put into Mr Foster's bank, Mr Foster being the bank agent, the pennies would 'get more' and for a long time I thought that Mr Foster, in this mysterious place of his which I was never allowed to enter, had a breeding place for pennies in his rockery. I thought that he placed two suitable pennies, a Queen Victoria one and a George the Fifth one, for instance, in a hole in his rockery where they proceeded to produce farthing babies, just as the rabbits in the Bluebell Bank produced young rabbits. It was strange, yet at the same time natural that, although I had mentioned Channatt's Bluebell Bank only once or twice to the children, they had associated it immediately with this little porcelain box decorated with painted harebells that Granda had given to Liz. It was strange and at the same time natural, mysteriously paradoxical, that my childish confusion about the Bluebell Bank with the rabbits and Mr Foster's bank with the pennies had come full circle and on into a new dimension where the children saw this little porcelain box as the only feature of Reachfar as they knew it that could be given to me to carry away with me.

The ceremony had made a profound impression on me and, only now, sitting alone among the scent of the Granny roses, was I beginning to return to my normal self, beginning to come out of the dream and look about me. At the foot of the dead tree I now noticed a round wooden washtub which was sunk to its rim in the ground and full of water, making a little pond. It was easy to understand the fascination that this overgrown place had for the children for it had, in miniature, something of the character of the Reachfar I had known as a child. In here, where I sat, the house, although only a few yards away, was out of sight, so that this place was a private world within the secure boundaries of the home world.

On the other side of this little clearing, the ground rose in a hillock which was crowned with the thicket of fir trees and to the side of this grew the big sycamore in whose branches the children had sat to recite their requiem for Aunt Hannah. It was when I looked up at their branch that I noticed the white board nailed to one of the fir trees on the hillock. Painted on it, in blue, were the words, upside-down: 'Produce of South Africa' but underneath this, in large black letters, were the words: 'Thinking Place'. I now saw the significance of the sunken wooden washtub. My Thinking Place at Reachfar had been in the dense thicket of fir trees above the well.

I rose to my feet urgently and found my way out to the gravel of the garden path, feeling that if I stayed alone in the shrubbery any longer, I would be borne away to become a changeling, borne out of the world and time as I knew them into that strange other dimension that the children had created out of the memories I had given to them.

'Tea,' my brother said, meeting me at the back door. 'Where were you?'

'In there,' I said, nodding at the shrubbery and then looking down at the little box in my hands. 'Say what you like, a moment ago I heard the horns of elf-land blowing and not too faintly either.' He reached out and took the daisy chain from my head. I opened the box and as he dropped it in, he said: 'I am not surprised. I thought my own feet were leaving the ground for a bit this afternoon, in spite of having rehearsed them last night. At the rehearsal, you see, only their minds

213

were engaged, remembering their words and gestures but, this afternoon, they were in the thing heart and soul. Come and have some tea.'

Sitting at the big table, it was difficult to believe that these three ordinary children were the almost mythic figures of the shrubbery, as Liz plied her wiles on her grandfather and the two boys gallantly passed scones and cake to their grandmother. The adults were all a little silent for a variety of reasons. Sheila and Roddy, side by side, seemed to be enclosed in a separate world; Granda and Granny smiling over the grandchildren; George and Tom, I knew, were thinking of my departure and my brother, like myself, was I think still slightly overcome by the experience in the shrubbery while Shona was fully occupied with the feeding of Sandy Tom.

Inevitably, into the silence, came the voice of Liz as she looked over a lump of cake and the width of the table at Sheila and Roddy. 'You two can get married any day now, I should think, now that you've got a house,' she said. 'I thought you would get married when you had the Drumnadrochit house but I hadn't connected up. That place would be too far from a school for the children but you are all right now.'

Sheila and Roddy seemed to cringe together in the face of this open attack, while mischievous grins spread over the faces of Tom and George and Granny gave a pleased little flutter.

'What are you talking about?' Jock asked sternly, coming out of his silence and into action. 'What house?'

'Aunt Hannah's house, of course. You are to get the ship in the bottle, Dad – '

' – and Mum is to get the best tea-service – ' said Gee.

' – and Aunt Sheila is to get the house and all the rest,' Duncan announced in conclusion.

'People always get married when they get a house,' Liz continued. 'The Porters down in the village had to wait for a whole year for a council house before they could get married.' She turned to her aunt. 'So aren't you the lucky one?' she asked and then she slewed round in the chair to look at her mother. 'Mum, are the Porters going to have a little Porter? Mrs Porter is getting very fat around the middle.'

'Liz,' Shona said sternly, 'will you hold your tongue? We are sick of the sound of your voice.'

'Sorry, Mum,' Liz sighed. 'But sometimes there is such a muchness that I have to talk or bust.'

'All right.' Shona spoke less sternly. 'But you and the boys will take your cake out into the garden and mind your own business.'

'Okaydoke,' said Liz agreeably and to her brothers: 'Come on. Let's leave 'em to it,' and all three went out of doors.

Shona, outraged, glared at us all over the baby's bottle and then said: 'Honestly, John, you have got to do something about Liz. I don't know how she got to be the way she is.'

'Ach the bairn is fine,' George said as Sheila and Roddy rose and pushed back their chairs as if they hoped that none of us were noticing their withdrawal.

'And anyway, how does Liz know the terms of Aunt Hannah's will about Sheila getting the house and everything?' Shona asked indignantly when the door had closed. 'Honestly, you can keep nothing from her and nothing is sacred and the boys are just as bad but it is mostly Liz's fault. What will Roddy *think*? Properly brought up as he was, he will wonder what on earth kind of zoo we've got here. You will just have to have Liz in the study, John, and give her a proper dressing-down'.

'Oh, nonsense, Shona,' I said. 'Liz has done more good than harm, I should think. Sheila and Roddy have got themselves to the point where they don't know whether they are going or coming and they are all the better for a good prod and a bringing down to earth.' I turned to Granny. 'Roddy is not a bad fellow, you know, although he has sown a wild oat or two.'

'And Sheila is the sort of lass for him,' Tom said, 'and not yon painted trollop that came here yon Sunday.'

'Sheila and Roddy will please themselves no matter what you are all saying,' said George, 'so you might as well save your breath.'

'Just fancy,' said Granny, 'him arriving in Achcraggan like that and attending Granda Sandison's funeral!' and while Jock and I washed up and Tom, George and Granda went out to the garden, Granny and Shona, all over again, recounted to one another in strophe and antistrophe this remarkable happening which, in a fateful way in their eyes, opened the door of the family to Roddy. It was decided that Granda, Granny and Sheila would stay for supper for the very good reason that Sheila did not reappear to drive her parents home but this did not interfere with Shona's iron routine that sent the children upstairs at half-past six. In a subtle way and without argument, they had lengthened their day by half-an-hour, as Liz had predicted they would, since Sandy Tom came into the family but by seven o'clock they were in bed and I went into their room for 'Reachfar'. The two boys were sitting against the pillows at the top of the bed, Liz under the eiderdown at the bottom, their pink cheeks shiningly clean, their eyes dark and wide at the end of their long exciting day.

'Aunt Janet,' Liz said, 'tonight will you just tell about Reachfar itself?'

'And the Thinking Place and the Old Quarry?'

'And all Channatt's other places?'

'All right,' I said and began: 'Once upon a time, long long ago at Reachfar, Channatt went out early one morning to have what she called a proper look round, which meant that she was going to visit all her special places on Reachfar. She went through the little gate at the west end of the house, across the field and came first to the Strip of Herbage – ' It took a long time to make this memory tour for, in the course of many evenings, I had mentioned many places and I did not want, now, to miss a single one. At last, I came to the end. 'And now Channatt came back to the top of the Strip of Herbage, where she had first started, but now she turned to her right instead of to her left and this brought her to the Bluebell Bank or to where the Bluebell Bank should be but it didn't seem to be there any more.'

'But it *was* still there!' said Gee urgently.

'Yes, yes, it *was* still there!' said Duncan.

'Yes. There is still a Bluebell Bank at Reachfar,' Liz said positively, 'although we gave you a symbol one today. If you gave a symbol Thinking Place or a symbol Old Quarry, they would be too big to pack, especially for an aeroplane journey. You understand about symbols, do you?' she asked but before I could reply she explained: 'Symbols are representations of other things.'

'I see,' I said.

'So at Reachfar, the Bluebell Bank was still there,' she said.

'Yes,' I agreed. 'The Bluebell Bank was still there but Channatt could hardly see it because it was the blue-grey light of evening now. But when Channatt stood quite still she could hear it, because the bluebells were making a little tinkling noise that came and went on the wind.'

All three sighed in unison before Liz hopped in a businesslike way over to her own bed and slid down under the covers as if into an envelope.

'Good night, Aunt Janet,' she said then.

'Good night,' said Duncan.

'Good night,' said Gee.

'Good night,' I replied and managed to get out of the room before I began to cry.

I went to my own room, changed and put the last few things into my suitcase, the Bluebell Bank wrapped in a woollen sweater, before I went down to supper.

I was glad that Sheila and Roddy had told the family of their decision to get married, for this caused a screen of banter to be set up by Tom and George, behind which I could be sad by myself and, as soon as the meal was over, I went alone out to the garden and into the shrubbery which, only today, I had been given the right to enter. I found now that it was criss-crossed by little paths and tunnels that the children had made through the tangled bushes and, as I wandered about in it, my hair pulled from its pins by straying branches of dog roses, I felt again the thrill of the beautiful unknown, the thrill I used to know at three or four years old when Fly and I began to explore in depth the Home Moor, which seemed to us to be limitless. But now I recognised something that I had not recognised as a child. In addition to the thrill of the unknown, there was the deep known certainty that this joyous, growing adventurous world was something of which I, out of some mysterious bounty, had been given the freedom.

I passed the little wooden building where the ceremony had taken place but its doors were now shut and padlocked for the night. I passed the bee-hive which gave forth a drowsy hum into the dying light, like an echo of the day that had gone and I came back to the open space where the Granny roses grew and stood beside the washtub, looking down into the water. I saw my own face reflected there, the only thing in that dark looking-glass and, in the silence, I was suddenly invaded by a sense of isolation, a cold apartness. All my feeling of involvement with the children, my family, the rest of the world, the generations dropped away and, for a moment, I was aware of my own separate identity, of the core of aloneness in us all which can never reach out to involvement with the family, the rest of the world or the generations. Cold panic clutched at me as I felt again about me the disintegration, the disruption,

217

the disorderly chaos that had followed the earthquake, as I discovered that to face the total separateness of the self's identity is, paradoxically, to become an anonymous cipher suspended in a meaningless void. To be alone like this, detached, unrelated to the rest of human kind would be to die, as the acacia tree whose roots had been torn from their element the earth would die.

Breathlessly and hastily, I made my way out to the garden path and hurried towards the house, pausing only when I was within earshot of the kitchen voices, as my identity as a member of my family, the world and the generations flowed back, to pin up my hair and pick the twigs and leaves from the sleeves of my sweater. And now I became aware of the voices of Sheila and Roddy, coming from Sandy Tom's little sheltered corner on the other side of the scullery which jutted out from the main building.

'And it will be all right if I come up to see them fairly often?' Sheila asked. 'They are going to miss me around the house, you know.'

'Up from where?' Roddy asked.

'London. We'll have to live in London, won't we?'

'For Heavens sweet sake why?'

'I thought because of your writing. I mean, writers mostly live in London and that was why with Aunt Hannah and everything I – '

'London!' Roddy exploded, 'I can write anywhere! My lord, the reasons you can find for making things difficult! We'll live *with* the parents if you like!'

'No,' said Sheila in calm contrast to his vehemence, 'at Aunt Hannah's, for the moment, anyway but we'll have to have some painting done.'

Smiling, I let myself into the house quietly through the back door. It had been arranged that Roddy would take me to the train but, an hour later, it was Jock and Shona who drove me to the city station. George and Tom put my suitcase into the car and then, as they tried to smile at me, I said: 'All right, you two, look after these bairns of mine till I get back.'

'We will see to them, Janet,' Tom said.

'Aye, Janet, they will be all right,' said George.

I jumped in beside my brother and slammed the door shut. 'Hurry,' I said. 'Get us out of sight!'

About thirty-six hours later, I stepped out of the aircraft on to the hot tarmac of St Jago Bay airport and looked away across the cobalt and silver sea to the northeast horizon under the vast tropical sky. Not a bird moved in the heavy humid air of that great emptiness but, for me, it was not empty. It was criss-crossed with gossamer threads that were hung with dew-drops on which shone a wavering rainbow light. It held the glory and the freshness of a dream.

Epilogue

'There was a time when meadow, grove and stream
The earth and every common sight,
    To me did seem
    Apparelled in celestial light,
The glory and the freshness of a dream.'

In the Customs Building, Twice was waiting for me and I
seemed to be seeing him for the first time, as if time itself
had slipped back to the day when I first glimpsed his blue eyes
at Slater's Works in Ballydendran. The eyes were even more
blue now in contrast with the tropical tan of his skin and I
stared at him, unmoving, while I marvelled at how vague and
dim had been my memory of him compared with this vital
reality and, as I had felt eleven years ago when I first saw
him, I felt again now that the world had turned topsy-turvy as,
for the second time, I fell in love.

'Twice!' I said, stammering as I spoke his name.

'Darling, you look ten years younger!'

'Don't be stupid!'

'Sashie is outside. Let's go to the Peak and have a drink. You
had a good time?'

'Marvellous.' As we exchanged the banal phrases, a couplet
from the *Ode* which I had read so many times to the children
echoed at the back of my mind:

'And custom lie upon thee with a weight,
    Heavy as frost, and deep almost as life!'

and, speaking in conformity with custom's weight, I went on:
'The entire trip was splendid from start to finish.'

'And George and Tom are really well?'

'Fighting fit. And the children are great fun. I have got lots
of photographs, including some of your namesake, Sandy Tom,'
I knew exactly now what Liz meant when she spoke of 'such a
muchness I have to talk or bust' and incoherently I went on
talking: 'Jock is a wonderful but rather comic father. He refers
to the children as the Hungry Generation –'

220

A SELECTION OF FINE READING AVAILABLE IN CORGI BOOKS

Novels

War

☐ 552 08975 3 THE YOUNG BRITISH POETS   ed. *Jeremy Robson* 30p
☐ 552 08974 5 BRUCE TEGNER METHOD OF SELF DEFENCE
                                                    Bruce Tegner 40p
☐ 552 98479 5 MADEMOISELLE 1+1 (illustrated)
                        Marcel Veronese and Jean-Claude Peretz 105p
☐ 552 08943 5 MEMOIRS OF THE CHEVALIER D'EON
                                           trans. Antonia White 50p
☐ 552 08928 1 TELL ME, DOCTOR   *Dr. Michael Winstanley* 35p

Western

☐ 552 08907 9 SUDDEN: TROUBLESHOOTER   *Frederick H. Christian* 25p
☐ 552 08971 0 NO. 68 TO ARMS! TO ARMS IN DIXIE   *J. T. Edson* 25p
☐ 552 08972 9 NO. 69 THE SOUTH WILL RISE AGAIN   *J. T. Edson* 25p
☐ 552 08131 0 NO. 5 THE BLOODY BORDER   *J. T. Edson* 25p
☐ 552 08896 X HOW THE WEST WAS WON   *Louis L'Amour* 30p
☐ 552 08939 7 TUCKER   *Louis L'Amour* 25p
☐ 552 08922 2 NO. 13 LAW OF THE JUNGLE   *Louis Masterson* 25p
☐ 552 08923 0 NO. 14 NO TEARS FOR MORGAN KANE
                                              Louis Masterson 25p
☐ 552 08940 0 THE PIONEERS   *Jack Schaefer* 25p
☐ 552 08906 0 SUDDEN: MARSHAL OF LAWLESS   *Oliver Strange* 25p

Crime

☐ 552 08970 2 KILL THE TOFF   *John Creasey* 25p
☐ 552 08968 0 ACCUSE THE TOFF   *John Creasey* 25p
☐ 552 08977 X UNDERSTRIKE   *John Gardner* 25p
☐ 522 08640 1 RED FILE FOR CALLAN   *James Mitchell* 25p
☐ 552 08839 0 TOUCHFEATHER TOO   *Jimmy Sangster* 25p
☐ 552 08894 3 DUCA AND THE MILAN MURDERS *Giorgio Scerbanenco* 30p
☐ 552 08884 6 MY GUN IS QUICK   *Mickey Spillane* 25p
☐ 552 08938 9 SHEM'S DEMISE   *Michael Underwood* 25p